Deadly Sec

CW00429896

Riveting... rewardin
from start to finish... a complex, multi-layered novel that
demands the reader's undivided attention to keep up with
the fast pace... a gritty read that leaves you reeling... very
impressive.
DUNDEE COURIER

Loosely based on the Willie McRae killing, a fast-
moving novel... keeps you involved right to the end... a
very good read.
SCOTS INDEPENDENT

This former press officer's debut mystery is a page-
turner.
EVENING TELEGRAPH

Scott cleverly weaves together this nuclear-charged
thriller across the Highlands.
SCOTTISH FIELD

Entertaining conspiracy fiction with the Brits as the
baddies.
DAVID CLEGG, DAILY RECORD

Real page turner... keeps up the tension throughout
...beautiful descriptions of Scottish landscapes and the
nuclear waste theme is very relevant.
LESLEY RIDDOCH

Scotched Nation

Andrew Scott is the author of sixteen books, most under his full name of Andrew Murray Scott, including biographies of Alex Trocchi and Graham of Claverhouse. A former freelance journalist and media lecturer, he worked as press officer for senior parliamentarians in Scotland for ten years, returning in 2016 to full-time writing. His first novel, *Tumulus*, won the Dundee International Book Prize in 1999. *Scotched Nation* is his sixth published novel, the second in the Willie Morton Scottish mystery thriller series.

Website: https://andrewmurrayscott.scot
Twitter @andymurrayscott
Facebook/Andrew Murray Scott

Also by Andrew Scott / Andrew Murray Scott

Novels

Tumulus
Estuary Blue
The Mushroom Club
The Big J
Deadly Secrecy

Non-fiction Books

Alexander Trocchi: The Making of the Monster
Bonnie Dundee: John Graham of Claverhouse
Britain's Secret War: Tartan Terrorism and the Anglo-
American State (with Iain Macleay)
Modern Dundee: Life in the City since WWII
The Invisible Insurrection: A Trocchi Reader (editor)
Discovering Dundee: The Story of a City
The Wee Book of Dundee
Dundee's Literary Lives Vols 1&2
Letters of John Graham, Viscount Dundee (editor)

Poetry

Dancing Underwater

Further information can be obtained from
https://andrewmurrayscott.scot

Scotched Nation

Andrew Scott

Twa Corbies Publishing

First published in 2019 by Twa Corbies Publishing

Copyright ©Andrew Scott, 2019

Twa Corbies Publishing:
twacorbiespublishing@gmail.com

The moral right of the author has been asserted
in accordance with the Copyright, Designs & Patents
Act 1988.

British Library Cataloguing-in-Publication Data
A catalogue record for this book is available on Request
from the British Library.

Typeset in Perpetua.

EBook version ISBN 978 0 9933840 6 6.

ISBN: 978 0 9933840 5 9

Scotched Nation

Andrew Scott

CHAPTER ONE

Somewhere in the vast freezing night, a frightened dog barked. Somewhere beyond Arcturus. It was that kind of night. Lit up in the heavens by vast heaving shoals of cold stone stars, a single ugly sound could be magnified and broadcast to every living soul across the universe. In the humming, deserted press room of the *Scottish Standard*, Willie Morton glanced down at his work, clicked his mouse and rearranged and improved sentences on a blue screen. He could feel the adipose softening on his waistline. Feel it? He could almost hear it! He wasn't, by nature, a sub-editor but, as a freelance, knew he ought to be grateful for the occasional shift, even subbing. Even a shift that began at 11 p.m. and crawled through the Edinburgh morning till 6 a.m.

He glanced up at the digital clock on the far wall above the photocopiers. Only another four hours. The tele-printer spewed out occasional messages, gibberish for the most part. In each computer, each smartphone, each tablet, secret databases updated silently. Facebook and Twitter and Instagram liked, tweeted and circulated gossip and nonsense, emojis, fact and fiction in their own micro-worlds and, best of all, the coffee percolator perked. He couldn't exist without that, stuff the rest of it! Business as usual. A slow news night. The pubs were long since empty, shuttered and barred, and those punters out and about were drinking themselves silly in the dim interiors of nightclubs and likely to remain there for an hour or two.

In the charge room at St Leonard's Police Station, a mile or so away, the desk sergeant, Ron Wilkie, an experienced officer with only a year to retirement, glanced with disapproval at the computer screen and the list of usual suspects. 'A' Division of the City of Edinburgh Police was busy. Only one guest room vacant. Saturday night. He sighed, and tried to ignore the howling of the drunks from the basement corridor emanating up the stairwell.

Elsewhere, under the stars, the streets of the Scottish capital were quiet. Under sour-lemon streetlights, at Leith docks, away from the red glow of traffic lights and the neon of closed-up Italian restaurants, a prostitute blew temporary life into the cigarette cupped in her palm. Trade was slow on Salamander Street. Behind closed doors, convivial noise and warmth, and pleasurable and entirely legal licensed sin continued unabated. Another hour or so, maybe two and the streets would suddenly sprawl into life as clubs and discos emptied.

On Leith Walk, cars flickered past each other slowly at a safe distance, stopping at measured intervals for red lights. Pedestrians were few, almost invisible, slim shadows at street corners, caught for a second or two on CCTV. One walked quickly, erratically across the wide road and found a car that had been parked earlier in Picardy Place, hemmed in by other vehicles. The figure could be seen more clearly under the streetlight, if anybody could be bothered glancing at the monitors in the control room deep inside Edinburgh City Chambers in the High Street. A youngish man, tall and smartly dressed in evening suit, white shirt, bow tie, fair, wavy hair that shone in the light. He stood looking at the cars to the front and rear of his. He seemed excessively irritated and kicked at the tyre of the car in front. Then he fumbled with his keys, got into the black VW Passat and the lights came on. Letting in the reverse, the car backed. There was an audible crunch as it went over the bumper of the car behind. Damn and blast! The driver overreacted and shot into first, engine roaring. He turned and barged out, scraping the bumper of the car in front. The car lurched into the middle of the road and continued slowly, on the wrong side.

Three whiskies was all he'd had. And that Glayva for the toast, or perhaps a couple – and the brandy after dinner. Large ones though. Forgot that. Damn. He took the corner rather wide and heard a hoot of anger from an oncoming vehicle, but as it was already past him, there was no problem. With his left hand he patted the thick hair at his temple. Too late he saw the jeep double-parked. Collided with its bull bars. No-one saw. Quiet side street. He pulled away, was pulling away, when he became aware of the blue light. Damn it! He'd have to stop.

'Been drinking have we, sir?' the policeman asked, a young working-class rozzer, with an unpleasantly over-familiar tone.

'Just the one dram, occif-fficer.'

'Step out the car, please, sir.'

'For goodness sake! I can't. I won't. I've got to get home, do you see.'

'Step out!'

The policeman leaned in and grabbed his arm. 'Switch off, sir.' Then he whipped out the keys in his gloved hand.

So he had to do as he was ordered. Suddenly, he realised that the bloody oiks were taking him to the police station.

'My car!' he exclaimed. 'What happens to it?'

'We'll arrange for it to taken to…'

'You don't understand!' he shrieked. 'I work for… I'm on official business. Damn it – I work for the Government! Let me go.'

'Why… so do we, sir' the older cop said, smiling in the shadows. They were enjoying this, he knew dimly.

'Papers,' he managed to gasp. 'Very important papers… inside. They must come with me… they could be stolen.'

'We wouldn't want that, sir, would we?' the younger policeman remarked sarcastically. He went over to the driver's seat and looked in. After a moment, he held up a leather briefcase. 'This it? Valuable, you say? Alright, we'll bring it with us.'

The man in the dinner suit was getting angrier. 'Please be careful with it… they're very important. You bloody fools,' he added. 'You've no idea what you're doing.'

'Of course not, sir, but not to worry. Step this way.'

At St Leonard's, Sergeant Wilkie was less than pleased to see another customer. He now had no vacant cells to offer and it was only 2.15 a.m. The clubs were still in full swing. There was always a late rush for premier accommodation. But the man had failed the breath test and was well over the limit. The police doctor was on his way over.

'Put him in sixteen,' he instructed his turnkey. 'The customer there is asleep, there'll be no trouble. Up before the Sheriff in the morning.'

Morton was on his way out, out and home, heading for bed, when he heard the sound of a snigger from the overweight, dishevelled duty editor who, for the last half hour, had been cackling on the phone to a crony.

'I could do with a laugh,' Morton hinted, pausing alongside. The duty night editor, Michael Donnelly, a former tabloid editor, was a middle-aged has-been who Morton especially disliked. His shirt collar was awry and large yellow patches of sweat circled his armpits.

4

'Wilkie, St Len's nick,' Michael told him, gesturing abruptly with the phone.

'Anything I should know?' Morton asked.

'Fuck all,' Michael said, replacing the receiver. Then he seemed to change his mind. 'But what a laugh that guy is. He sees it all down there, you know. Seems they picked up a drunk driver around 2 a.m. Bow-tied, monkey suit. Claimed to be a Government official,' he grimaced. 'Westminster, that is, not Holyrood. On official business. Way over the limit. Lot of airs and graces and how-dare-yous. Called them all bloody fools as well.'

Donnelly sniggered and wiped his nose on his shirtsleeve. 'Invitation to a posh dinner in his pocket, but nothing else apparently. No wallet, no nothing. Shoved him in a cell. But… but an hour later, there's this call.'

He leaned back in his chair and lit a cigarette, unofficial perks of the night-shift. Morton winced but Donnelly ignored Morton's obvious distaste. Morton was a bloody freelance, not a staffer.

'Yeah. Wilkie gets this call,' he said, exhaling luxuriously. 'From the Home Office no less. Two-thirty in the bloody morning! Has to let the guy go *in the national interest*. Of course, Wilkie couldn't take a decision like that – passes it upstairs. Ten minutes later, his boss is on the line, none too pleased. Had just got to bed after a late night Rotary do. Upshot is, chummy walks.' Donnelly belched and goggled up at Morton. 'Can you believe it? No court appearance tomorrow, no records, no nothing. He walks.'

'Yeah? What's this guy's name?' Morton asked, yawning.

'Never gave it. Well, he did, but it was a Mickey Mouser, y'know – fake. They couldn't get a name out of him, but someone must have known it, because he was sprung within the hour. The name they used to spring him was Gallimont, Philip Gallimont, and the address was fake too. According to Wilkie, there is no 24b Charlefont Street. Fun and games, eh?'

'You think they'd have known that,' Morton said. 'Wilkie's been around. Not like him to be fooled by a chancer. Government official though?'

'Is what he said. Home Office.'

Morton frowned. 'No, I meant…'

'Oh, see what you mean. Yeah, some kind of Government flunkey, maybe even a sort-of spook. Card-carrying Tory too probably. The invitation on him was a Tory Party social. At the Royal Windsor Club. Strictly invites only.'

'I know it,' Morton said. 'The London Road?'

'That's the one. Swanky joint.'

'Interesting,' Morton said. 'Anyway, I'm off. Night.'

'Yeah, oh, Wilkie said something…' Donnelly screwed up his beery face in an effort to remember. 'Yeah, Wilkie said, he – that's this guy Gallimont – was very protective about some letters in a briefcase that he had. Wouldn't let anybody touch them. The briefcase was locked and he wouldn't give them the bloody combination.'

Morton grinned. 'State secrets perhaps? The Home Secretary's skimpiest lingerie? *Something* smelly.'

Morton had rarely spoken a truer word. But it was several days before he remembered the incident. Life took over, the daily grind; small cogs turning a mighty big wheel. On the Thursday, he was sauntering idly along a windy, cold Princes Street when he saw Celia in a long blue woollen coat with her clipboard, trying vainly to engage passers-by in conversation. Celia Thornton, the red-haired younger sister of a rugger team mate from his schooldays at George Watson's. He'd always rather fancied her, but had kept his opinions to himself. She was gently humorous, teasingly provocative, but despite her charm, wasn't having much luck with the punters.

'Willie! Hello,' she greeted him brightly. 'I don't suppose you'd…?' She indicated her clipboard.

'Oh no,' Morton said firmly. 'You've done me before.'

She laughed ruefully and Morton saw the raw redness under her nose and the moistness of her blue eyes.

'Got a cold?' he ventured.

'Wouldn't you, if you'd been stood here for three hours?'

'Fair point. What is it today?'

She sighed and then sneezed. 'Oh, I should be home in bed,' she said. 'It's a…' She sneezed again. 'It's a political survey… about attitudes to whether or not… excuse me… whether there should be another independence referendum within ten years.'

'Huh, the usual. How many more people do you need?'

'Loads. Oh dear.'

'You should be in bed.'

'I said that.'

'I know. You need to get warm. I'll walk you.'

'Hmn, well…'

'At least, let me buy you a coffee?'

'Well, okay. I could, I suppose.'

'You know I'm spoken for these days, to use that quaint phrase.' And it was, surprisingly, true.

'I know that, Willie, but it's not you I'm worried about, sweetie, it's me,' she said enigmatically, snapping shut her clipboard and slotting her pen into a plastic loop at the side of it. She sighed. 'Still twenty-three folk to get for this. Needs to be done by close of play today. I'm struggling as usual to find the C2s and the Ds.'

'Too many posh folk in Edinburgh,' Morton joked. 'Too few horny-handed sons of toil.'

Sitting with mugs of Kenya coffee at the Vienna stall in Waverley Station's concourse, they chit-chatted for some time on this and that against the background of noise and clatter. Spoken for – it was a quaint phrase from another age. He was with Emily now, though he still marvelled at how it had come about. She was so sorted, organised, positive and he was none of these things; a man of neuroses, self-doubts and at forty-three, his confidence ebbing away, demoralised and feeling irrelevant most of the time. He sipped his coffee and tried to relax. Celia said something he didn't hear then suddenly Morton remembered that Celia was a Conservative.

'Not for a long time,' she frowned. 'Not too keen on the cult of wee Ruth. Something a bit too…'

'Butch?'

Celia laughed. 'No, that's the *best* thing about her. A bit too latter-day imperialist for me, too gung-ho. Seeing her posing on a tank… They still send me letters, asking for money mainly, but I haven't put as much as a leaflet through a door for years. I can't, you see.'

Morton looked up from his black coffee.

'Working as a market researcher means I can't be politically involved,' she told him. 'In theory at least.' She sipped her latte, frowning. 'I mean, they couldn't very well check up, I suppose.'

'Yeah, but you know some of the local party faces at the grassroots?'

'Oh yes.' She narrowed her eyes and laid her hand on his arm. 'What do you want to know, Willie? Come on, out with it.'

He grinned sheepishly. 'Gallimont, Philip. Mean anything to you?'

Celia looked thoughtful. 'Funny name. Yes, I've heard it before, or seen it on some letterhead somewhere.'

'A local activist?'

She pushed back her hair and her eyes twinkled. There were, he noticed, with alarm, faint tiny cracks around her eyes and her mouth, beneath her foundation cream. He did a swift calculation and her age came out as forty-five, two years older than him. 'Well, maybe, but I don't think so, Willie. It's some other connection, some business perhaps. Anyway, what are you up to now, you sly boots? Is it a story you're working on? Some juicy scandal or something?'

The truth was, Morton didn't know what it was. But he didn't like people who used funny fake names that might turn out to be real. And he resented people using their connections to evade the law. He had a fondness for the line from Robert Burns: 'Ye see yon birkie ca'd 'a lord,' wha struts, an stares, and a' that?' Like many of his fellow Scots, he had a deeply ingrained sense of democracy: all men and women equal. Not that he was political, although each New Year the media announcement of the Honours List sent him into a spasm of disgust. Yes, many good and decent people were honoured for services rendered and amazing achievement but for every one of those there were a dozen crawling Tory apparatchiks, toadying businessmen who had donated to the coffers, creeping sports people and vomit-inducing *celebs*. He knew of several persons who had taken up charity work after retirement simply to – and they had made no secret of it – go all out for a 'gong'. It was disgusting, embarrassing, medieval; the most visual evidence of the

9

corruption and rottenness of the British State. Not that he was political, of course!

Celia phoned him six days later.

'How's the cold?' he asked.

'Eh?' she paused. 'Oh, better. But listen,' she said joyfully, 'I've remembered about Philip Gallimont. Are you still interested?'

He put on the louche, sleazy voice he associated with an actor from the 1970s whose name he could never remember. 'Int-er-es-ted? Oooh! *Ra-ther*!'

'Give over. No, interested in hearing about Philip, I meant.'

'Philip now, is it?' he purred. 'So what do you know about him?' Morton was in the bath. He had the window open and could hear light rain on the glass and the gentle sound of wind in trees.

'Well not a lot really. He looks rather like you.'

'He... *what*?' Morton gagged. 'Philip Gallimont? You've seen him?'

'Yes. I'd forgotten he was at the wedding reception for my friend Serena's younger sister, Natty. At the Fitzherbert Hotel last year. And you know what, Willie, I even *danced* with him. Fancy me forgetting that! He does look rather like you, you know. Didn't really strike me at the time.'

'Should I be flattered? You've never danced with me.'

'You've never asked me. Down, boy!'

'I should tell you, Celia, that at this moment I'm in the bath.' He splashed his hand in the water. 'Can you hear?'

'Oh! Oh dear, am I exciting you?' She broke off into a paroxysm of giggles. 'Are you playing with your rubber duck?'

'Hmn. Let's stick to business, shall we,' Morton said, embarrassedly. 'Anything else about our friend you can tell me?'

'I remember something about a business he was setting up. But the funny thing is, he worked, or was working for, some sort-of Government department which he couldn't tell us about. London-based, I think. He made a big fuss about it. We assumed it was some kind of security thing. Or that he was just showing off, trying to impress, you know.'

'Security thing?' Morton's toes played with the taps. 'You mean he couldn't tell you for *his* security?'

'No, something in the security line. Intelligence, something like that maybe, but I can't really remember. But the business venture was a bit mysterious, some sort of trust, and he was getting lists of supporters or donations or something of the sort.'

'Interesting,' Morton mused. 'Can I maybe get more by speaking to your friend?'

'Serena? No chance. I wouldn't let you within a mile of her. She was rather taken with him at the reception. You're her type, just as he was.'

'And what's her type exactly?'

'You know. Don't be naughty.'

'Spell it out, Celia.'

'Rugger types, but slim-ish with long hair. Blond. Has to be. But sensitive, arty maybe.'

'And that's what Philip Gallimont is like?'

'And so are you. Which is why you won't get Serena's number out of me.'

'Does the word *tease* mean anything to you, Celia?'

'I think I'd prefer to finish this conversation when you've got your clothes on. Goodbye.'

11

CHAPTER TWO

Morton's night shifts at the *Standard* continued for a further week until Hugh Leadbetter returned from Washington. Leadbetter barged in to the press room just as Morton was leaving. It was 8 a.m. and Morton, having fallen asleep in his chair, was late.

Leadbetter, a burly man in a creaking brown leather jacket, chewed the remains of a fat cigar which glowed faintly amidst the hirsute thickness of his black beard. He opened the window to let out any suspicion of smoke and stubbed the cigar out in an ashtray he kept on the windowsill.

'God, Willie, they've still got you doing the subbing? Fucksake, I'll get you a real job. Come on into my office.'

The office of the editor of Scotland's self-proclaimed leading broadsheet was, as usual, cluttered with back issues piled on the floor, a chorus of white polystyrene cups and used pizza boxes in Italian colours. Leadbetter flung himself down into the swivel chair and pushed a stack of folded newspapers off the desk onto the floor.

'Go down to Westminster, Willie,' he commanded, 'and send me a damn fine report on the Statement for the Draft Legislation on more powers for Holyrood. I know… I *know*… but I want you to cover it as a foreigner. Seeing it for the first time as an alien establishment. It's ten years since the number of Scottish MPs was reduced to fifty-nine and maybe soon down tae six if Madam gets her way. Show up its sheer bloody irrelevance, Willie. It's the dog-end of this Parliament, only a few months till a General Election, with opinion polls showing strongly for Nicola.'

'Okay. When is it again?'

Leadbetter gave him a look of mild disfavour. 'Eh? Thursday of course. Get some quotes from Scots down there – not the MPs – except those representing English constituencies, or in the Lords.'

Morton zipped up his jacket. 'Derick Mason not doing a piece then?'

'He's off on his holidays,' Leadbetter grunted. 'Two weeks. Imagine, a London political correspondent takes his holidays just as the legislation is about to be announced.' He shook his head gravely. 'How he got away with it, I don't know. Changed days though, eh? In my younger day there'd be half a dozen there to do the job. Now he's the only one, and he has to combine the brief with Royal Correspondent and all, but he thinks he can wipe his arse with the rules.'

'That's because the rest of us prefer it up here. More going on for a start. But I'll be happy to do the job. Air fares?'

'Na, get the train,' Leadbetter instructed. 'Catch up on some reading, aye? We'll get pictures from the agency. Give me plenty copy. And get the boot right in: is Westminster still relevant, or an out-dated anachronism? You know the type of guff.'

With these few words of encouragement ringing in his ears, Morton booked first-class seats on the Waverley to King's Cross train for Wednesday.

It was true that his work – and Scottish politics – had greatly changed in the last few years, since the Holyrood Parliament had been set up. Even since the failed referendum. From the first, it had sought to maximise its power and expand its responsibilities, even under the Labour Administrations of Donald Dewar and then the Lib Dem – Labour coalitions of Jack McConnell. Alex Salmond, leading

13

the first SNP minority Government in 2007, had speeded up the process of expansion, and back in Government with an overall majority in 2011, had pushed to its limits, holding meetings with foreign premiers, developing foreign policy and other policy in areas where remits remained in Westminster hands. Nicola had ramped up that work further and now few Scottish reporters or broadcasters would work anywhere else. Few politicians in Scotland – certainly none married with families – sought a posting to the green leather benches. To be in London was, increasingly, to be ignored where it mattered for their readers. The numbers of MPs from Scotland (SMPs) had shrunk from seventy-two to fifty-nine and the Prime Minister planned to reduce them still further to fifty-three. The SNP had described the proposals as 'unacceptable' but wanted to abolish SMPs altogether and send six national representatives instead. And with a whopping overall majority at Holyrood, and a massive and growing membership (second largest party in the UK), the SNP were drafting referenda on independence and options on the monarchy, calling for devolution of social security, taxation, energy, defence, immigration and foreign policy. Spoiling for a fight, despite the crushing of their hopes in the referendum only three months ago. Cultural revival in Scotland had led to an ever-diminished sense of Britishness. You rarely saw a Union flag in Scotland now, even on public buildings.

Such was the excitement that Morton had found new opportunities with new lobbying organisations and PR companies which thronged the capital. He was the stringer for a London-based political magazine and, more lucratively, for two German newspapers and a Japanese press agency. Not that he spoke Japanese, or German, if it came to that, but they took as much as he could give them and money appeared in his account on time. And Leadbetter still gave him odd jobs for the *Standard,* though *The Times* and *The Independent* had rebuffed his suggestion of regular columns or diary pieces.

Morton came out of the front entrance on South Bridge. It was a cold, crisp morning with an anaemic sun dodging over the rooftops as he walked the long way home, Chambers Street into Forest Road, along Lauriston Place. It was good to get some fresh air. He'd been lucky – the way things turned out – to get the housing association flat in Keir Street, a stone's throw from the centre of things. His former flat in Shandon Place, Merchiston, was too large and expensive. He had also sold the car, which he didn't need, had drawn in his horns and lowered his outgoings and now was just about solvent. Since property prices had rocketed, the chances of him buying a property on his low income were non-existent, yet he had a small, comfortable flat within easy walking distance of the city centre on a fixed, regulated rent.

When he got into the flat, he felt the warmth of the central heating which had come on at 8 a.m. He stripped and got into his bathrobe. He didn't feel tired so he sat down to watch the breakfast TV bulletins. They had some footage of the previous afternoon's First Minister's Questions. Nicola Sturgeon fully in command of her brief: a walkover again. Two rows behind her, Donald Stevenson, the former leader, smilingly content as Sturgeon defended the cost of the Government's decision to intervene to save Prestwick airport, safeguarding 1,400 jobs. Jim Ferrie, the Independent Socialist MSP, normally her fiercest critic, strongly praising the FM. In his constituency – and he used the word without benefit of the letter *t* – many were employed at the airport.

15

Morton switched channels and came back in time to hear a question discreetly framed by Sir Hector Lloyd-McLay. One of the few remaining Tory gentlemen of the shires, he represented the aging maidens of Milngavie, for whose sake, he sported a red handkerchief in the top pocket of his blue pin-striped suit.

'Ah, Mr Presiding Officer, if I may…?'

Morton killed the TV and went into the kitchen-diner. His overdone politeness. An old sweetie-wife. A former bus driver. Won an election, lost the next one, was appointed on the Tory list to Holyrood and gained a peerage for services rendered… to transport. You couldn't make it up!

It wasn't quite like old times for Morton, being back at Westminster. Two years he'd served there as reporter for the Scottish Radio Group, doing commentaries on Parliament for news bulletins, covering the odd, the silly and the insane and of course it was in London that he'd met Sally. God, he was young then. Twenty-four? A Tory Government. Mrs Thatcher. *Who?* It seemed like centuries though it was only twenty years. But a lot had changed. The Parliamentary Estate had sprawled out from the Palace of Westminster building into four new buildings around Westminster Jubilee Line station, interconnected by tunnels and new entrances and exits.

The two armed policemen on the door at the Cromwell Green Visitors' entrance had snub-nosed black Heckler & Koch machine guns held downwards across their high-vis jackets. He didn't remember that before.

He entered the concrete maze which sprawled downwards to a new entrance porch. The queue moved along surprisingly quickly. Inside the porch, airport-style security staff checked his bag into an X-ray machine and Morton passed them his authorisation letter and his press card and received a Visitor's day pass and lanyard, which he put on.

'Thank you, sir, that's all in order. You're good to go.'

Morton smiled. 'Right. Where do I go?'

The other policeman glanced over at him and Morton imagined his finger tightened imperceptibly on his trigger.

The man pointed. 'Up the ramp and nip in on the right, sir, by St Stephen's Hall. Mind how you go.'

And Morton, walking up the ramp inside New Palace Yard, felt that familiar sense of being at the centre of decadence. While Holyrood was a modern, efficient and exciting place, there was none of the sense of grisly events of broken Crowns and smashed Parliaments, or conspiracies at the highest level, which Westminster had in spades.

He saw the entrance to St Stephen's Hall but realised he didn't need to go in that way and continued to the Colonnade. Once under the arcade roof, he turned right and from there found his way to the stairs and climbed to the second floor and the familiar route to the press hall, the exclusive preserve of the lobby correspondents. There were one or two journalists working but no-one he knew, even professionally.

He saw his old desk by the high window and went over. How small it looked. Two years he'd spent behind it. No point in getting morbid.

'Here for the mothballs?'

Morton turned with a smile and saw Fergus McLaverty of SBC. 'Fergus! Good to see you, man. Aye. I've been sent down by the *Standard* for the further Devolution Statement. But last time I saw you, you were on the box from Washington.'

17

'True. Well, someone had to do it.' McLaverty, a shambling bear of a man, whose thinning fair hair stood up on end in the light like a crest, grinned ruefully and swung his elderly Marantz onto the desk, depositing the soft microphone on top of it.

'So?' Morton queried. 'Fiddled your expenses or what?'

'Cheeky beggar! I was homesick.'

'Aw.'

'Anyway, Willie, the bar's open. Seem to recall you owe me one.'

Morton glanced at his watch. 'Crikey. Suppose it is nearly lunchtime.'

McLaverty grinned. 'It's always lunchtime down here, Willie. You should remember that.'

CHAPTER THREE

He emailed the piece from his laptop in his hotel room on Friday afternoon. He'd enjoyed writing and reworking it to maintain a sufficiently sour and irreverent tone. He knew Hugh would love it. He had bad smells from broken toilets, dry rot, creaking noises, sickly sycophancy, even woodworm in the piece. He closed the laptop. Morton felt the sunshine of the quiet, tree-lined South Kensington Street beckon him with an insistent urge to revisit old haunts of his bachelor days. There was really no reason for him to return to Edinburgh immediately. He had an open ticket and could catch a later train.

He packed his leather holdall, dressed in his dark blue woollen suit and ox-blood Church brogues, a white silk shirt, unbuttoned at the top, and a dark blue overcoat. He checked his appearance in the mirror while clipping his imitation Rolex Oyster onto his wrist and left the room. The Romanian desk clerk, Grigor, didn't demur at retaining the holdall till his return.

He had the best part of the day to himself. He could have a minor adventure, or just window-shop, call on a former colleague at an address in Notting Hill and have an expensive lunch in Soho, or call an old girlfriend who worked in Paddington. But he knew he couldn't call the ex-girlfriend. He was with Emily now and that would be… well, not the sort of thing to do any more. She was probably married now anyway, with three kids; probably didn't even work in Paddington. Life moved on.

19

He hopped onto a bus in Fulham Road, which took him up by the high trees along the side of Hyde Park and round Marble Arch into Oxford Street, in heavy traffic. The conductor called out the names of the big stores for the benefit of tourists as the bus crawled at walking speed. Morton was interested in the faces and sights and sounds.

He got off and walked alongside the bus, then crossed the road and lost himself in Mayfair, walking south. It brought back many memories, strolling in the sunshine in the busy streets. He saw a restaurant, whose magenta frontage was decorated with painted vine leaves and bunches of grapes. It looked okay. In the dim interior, he perceived it was not busy and the waiter in a white apron ushered him to a decent table in the corner near a pillar.

Morton ate a good lunch of crabmeat and prawn brioche and a well-done steak with pepper sauce, washed down with two large glasses of a reasonable Chilean Merlot. In between courses, he fiddled with his mobile phone like the few other customers were doing. He avoided the sweets trolley and had a black coffee. The bill was reasonable.

After lunch at Chez Mijoux, he found himself strolling loose-limbed down Piccadilly and into St James Street. He was feeling affable and free of any overriding concerns, savouring the richness of the pepper sauce, with the acerbic fruitiness of the Merlot tickling his nostrils.

Passing an office building complex, he felt a hand on his sleeve and turned quickly.

One of two men, smartly dressed in suits and understated ties, was addressing him. '… good work you're doing,' the older man said. Morton regarded him. A flabby civil servant, quite senior possibly. 'Up in Scotland. Good show.'

Morton smiled blankly. 'Do I know you?'

The man tugged at his heavy blue jowls. 'Oh come now, Philip,' he said, blandly. 'Only last week… why, we've met several times now. You don't remember? Your CO and mine went to school together.' He mimed the actions of a rower. 'Steady boys, steady.'

Seeing the perplexed look on Morton's face he stopped, looked at his colleague who hovered behind him, clutching a black leather attaché case, which, Morton noted, was fastened to his wrist with a discreet steel chain. 'I don't know what's got into you today, Philip,' he said, shaking his head with a mock-serious expression. His heavy jowls wobbled above the tight collar of the Oxford striped shirt.

The second mention of the name triggered an instantaneous recollection in Morton's memory. Celia, Natasha's Wedding Reception. The man who looked like him. Gallimont, Philip. 'Ah yes,' he said, shrugging. 'I'm sorry. Bit preoccupied you understand.' He took a wild guess. 'Ah… Frobisher, isn't it?'

The man's jowls wobbled in disbelieving mirth as he chortled at his colleague. 'Good grief, Philip – Dardon. Internal Affairs. Just last week, at Chuffy's you told me all about your work up north.'

Seeing the alarm on Morton's face, he quickly amended this. 'On the QT of course, old man, no worries there.'

'I shouldn't have told you, Dardon,' Morton said slowly. 'Chuffy's, was it? Funny, I don't seem to remember. I hope I didn't go into too many details of my work?'

'Whatever you said is gone, old man,' Dardon said, tapping his forehead with his index finger. 'I won't peach.' He smiled and turned to his colleague. 'By the way, old chap, this is Menzies. Don't know if you've met? He's a Scot, too, you know. Not met? Oh, well. And, Philip, goes without saying we'll see each other soon in Chuffy's. Matter of fact, old chap, as it's Friday, I'll likely be heading in that direction very soon. Cheerie-bye.'

At the corner, Morton allowed himself to look back but both men were gone. He retraced his steps to study the office building they had emerged from. He read the small brass plaque on soot-begrimed stone. Department of Trade and Industry, Administration Division. Could be anything at all. It meant nothing to him. Did Gallimont work there? Where was Chuffy's? A bar presumably. Was it a gay bar? Was that it? Were Gallimont and Dardon homosexual acquaintances? It hadn't seemed so. He had an instinct about that. But most of all, Morton wondered, what was 'the good work in Scotland' that Gallimont was doing?

Morton walked reflectively through St James' Square, cut across Regent Street and Haymarket to Leicester Square and went into the Westminster Reference Library at the junction of St Martin's Street and Orange Street. He had used this a lot when he worked in London. He liked the place: its polished wood stairs and bannisters, the mezzanine balconies.

The collection on the ground floor, of legal and official Government publications, was familiar to him but he knew the best place nowadays to find out about UK Government departments was online. Using a library terminal, he visited Gov.UK and read that the DTI Administration Division was responsible to the Home Office for 'investigations and inspections of internal matters related to the Home Office's wide ranging remit'. Whatever that gobbledegook was supposed to mean.

Morton knew Duncan Campbell's investigations on the inner workings of the security services provided almost the only beacon of light into the increasingly sinister world of national surveillance. He'd met his fellow Scot once – one very sharp cookie – and was a long-term admirer of his books and articles in *Time Out, New Statesman* and, more recently, *Computer Weekly*. He had a helpful website too and it was on there that Morton discovered a reference to the DTI Administration Building in St James Street being a suspected cover for Box 500, the 'front office' of MI5, which had previously been in Great Marlborough Street, W1. Because of the transfer of the giant Preston system, the comprehensive national database, from Chelsea to Thames House, several operations had had to be rehoused or moved.

It was a short step from that to speculate that Dardon was involved in security intelligence policing in the UK, possibly involving Scotland. Speculation, and impossible to prove of course, but interesting nonetheless. He recalled, with a shiver, his previous entanglement with secret police spooks over the McBain case eight years before, and he had a mental image of the fearsome Daniel McGinley. But McGinley was dead and it was all years ago anyway.

Oddest of all, perhaps, was the thought that occurred to Morton as he returned his books at the library desk. Holyrood had full authority over its own policing. They had used it to amalgamate eight regional forces into one national police force, which included Special Branch and definitely would involve liaison with security and intelligence services. Presumably, again, the First Minister had oversight over any security and intelligence matter in Scotland, but whether that happened, or to what extent it happened, he was not sure. Was it just a phone call, or did it involve proper scrutiny of the files?

He was not aware exactly how the operations of the security and intelligence services, MI5 and MI6, had been affected by the Scottish Parliament's remit over policing in Scotland. It was a grey area. And it shouldn't be. Devolution was sixteen years down the line. He frowned and standing in the street, made a note in his pocket notebook. He could imagine making a big investigation out of it, a real front pager. Full media follow-ups and lots of brownie points for himself. Yes. He might write something. He vaguely recalled there had been a briefing paper produced by the UK Government in advance of the Referendum. One of their Analysis series and he remembered the furore over that. But that was a political document of course, not an actual neutral study of arrangements and operations strategy.

With Chuffy's he had had rather more luck. It turned out to be Civil Service slang for the British Empire Club in Chandos Place, whose clientele mainly consisted of Government officials and civil servants, a sort of second-rank White's or Boodle's.

Morton walked slowly back across Leicester Square reflecting upon his resemblance to Gallimont. Even his lookalike's drinking buddies had been convinced. The physical resemblance must be equalled by his voice. He must also sound like Gallimont. And sounding right was important to those types. He already knew, from what Dardon had said, that Gallimont was Scottish, and tying in what Celia had told him, probably from Edinburgh. There had been no suspicion whatsoever from Dardon or his colleague that he was *not* Gallimont. Strange, given that Morton had failed to identify Dardon, had exhibited ignorance of any details of their previous meeting, or their mutual acquaintances. So it was much more than merely a passing resemblance. He didn't

24

merely look and sound like Gallimont. To them, he was, without question, Philip Gallimont. And if that was the case… why not be Gallimont once more? Why not play his twin at Chuffy's one more time? He might even get to meet his alter ego – an amusing idea.

Morton easily found the British Empire Club in Chandos Place. It was two minutes' walk away. A four-storey whitewashed building whose front porch was guarded by an extensive red, white and blue canvas canopy descending the stone steps to the pavement. A dim green light emanated from the leaded panes of glass in the revolving door entrance.

As Morton entered the small, wood-panelled lobby, a portly little man in a black drape jacket decorated with gold braid intercepted him discreetly. He smiled regretfully, as Morton hung up his coat.

'I didn't recognise you, Mr Philip.'

Morton frowned and stood still, undecided whether to go or stay. He looked over to the door marked 'Bar and Smoking Room' which was at the other end of the hall but the little man had his elbow and steered him effortlessly to the doorway of his little office.

He coughed discreetly behind his hand. 'I don't…' he coughed again, 'ah… recognise you, sir,' he said, indicating with a discreet flourish, Morton's lack of tie.

All became clear. 'So sorry,' Morton said. 'I was exercising and simply didn't have time to change.'

The porter smiled. 'Apology accepted, sir. Come with me, Mr Philip,' he said, leading Morton into his tiny windowless booth. From a shelf he lifted down a cardboard box and extracted one of a number of dull and rather shiny ties. 'This do, sir?' he inquired.

'Perfectly,' Morton said, wrapping it around his neck. 'Perfectly. Old chap.'

CHAPTER FOUR

Willie Morton had been in a few clubs in his time – the Scottish Arts Club in Rutland Square, Edinburgh, with its small but secluded garden space and The New Club on Princes Street with its view of the Castle – but had not imagined that clubs such as Chuffy's continued to exist outside the pages of PG Wodehouse or the early Bond novels. The elegant, unfussy comfort, reassuringly solid and old-fashioned, seemed familiar though he also noticed the complete absence of younger people or females. He was puzzled by the sign: Bar and Smoking Room. Surely… the Smoking Act… Must be an old sign he decided. He spotted a woman but it was easy to imagine she must be a cleaner or in some similar humble occupation.

To his astonishment, the Bar and Smoking room stank of smoke and people were actually smoking in it. He was confused. It was like stepping back in time. They must have special dispensations, being a private club, Morton thought. But then he recalled the bitter battles in England to try and exempt private clubs. In 2010, he remembered, a Tory MP had introduced an amendment but that had failed at a first reading. Still, he was here as Gallimont. He couldn't query it. There weren't many residents, a few balding heads visible over the backs of wing armchairs. Most reading newspapers or sipping drinks and thinking deep thoughts.

He thought he could smell cooking as he made his way over the deep pile carpet to the far corner where he saw a heavy armchair bathed in a musty light from an obscured screened window. It was partially obscured by a high mahogany bookcase, glass-fronted, containing many sombre leather tomes. On the periphery of the room, he could observe yet remain unobtrusive. Here he was; at the heart of the British Empire, he thought ironically.

Very soon after he had sat down, a soft voice in his ear asked: 'Your usual, Mr Philip?'

Morton hesitated only for a second. 'Ah yes, I think so.'

He cleared his throat and looked around guardedly. His arrival had caused no stir. There were, he counted, around ten elderly or middle-aged men in the Bar and Smoking Room, sitting singly, absorbed in solitary tasks. If Philip Gallimont was his age – well, why on earth would he come *here*?

His reflections were interrupted by the discreet arrival on the small table of a small crystal decanter of whisky and a crystal glass on a small tray, with a glass jug of water. He had to smile. It was a malt whisky. He poured two fingers into the glass and added six drops of water, sniffed it – a Speyside – its pale colour told him so; mild, sweet. Glenfiddich? Or Benromach? So Gallimont liked a Speyside single malt too? Perhaps he wasn't so dodgy after all? And, he laughed to himself triumphantly, the drinks were on his doppelganger!

He looked up and saw a man approaching his table. He felt his stomach churn. Not Dardon, the other one. What was his name?

'I see you made it, Philip. Good show.'

'Um…' Morton rose to shake the other's hand. 'Please.' He indicated the armchair opposite.

The chubby youngish man with an open and ruddy complexion sat and said: 'Fraid old Dardon can't make it, or he might be along later, he told me to tell you that. Anyway,' he grinned, 'as it is quite likely you've forgotten my name…'

'Well, sorry,' said Morton, 'but we weren't properly introduced.'

'Quite so, Philip. I'm Menzies, Gordon. And like you, a Scot, I believe.'

'Really?'

'Yes. Brought up in Moray, but I've been down here for, well, decades, now.'

'You work with Dardon?'

'Good grief, no. He's at the DTI now, I'm still with the Home Office, minor echelons you know, for my sins.'

'Having a drink?'

Menzies nodded. 'Sutter will bring it along in a minute. Actually I don't come here very often. Haven't been, in a week or so. Hasn't changed.' He leaned forward. 'Confidentially, old man, I'd rather be in the pub.'

Morton grinned, 'Know what you mean.'

'The quality of the totty here is distinctly poor.'

Morton laughed. 'We could go to the pub?' he suggested.

'Well, Dardon might not like that.'

'Oh well, in that case… It still comes as a shock to see people smoking here.'

Menzies was unsuspicious. 'Yes. Me too. In fact I only joined a month ago. I understand that there is a smoking shelter on the roof but some of the members are quite elderly,' he laughed, 'as you are well aware. And so to save them the effort, it seems Sutton here will swear, on oath if need be, that you have just come down from said smoking shelter, and of course, if any Environmental Health Officers arrived, there is a system of warning throughout the building. One of the perks and privileges as they say, Not that I smoke myself.'

'Nor me.'

29

'And when are you going back up north?' Menzies asked.

Morton frowned. 'Not sure if I'm supposed to say really.'

'Well you can trust me, of course. It's just that I don't get much opportunity to get home, to see my parents you know. Twice a year if I'm lucky, and here you are bobbing up and down every week or so.'

'How do you know that?' Morton frowned.

Menzies pulled a face. 'Crikey, Dardon said you were a stickler. What does it matter who knows that? Anyway, we've all sighed the oath of allegiance, haven't we? I mean, I presume you did?'

'Of course,' Morton said. 'I forgot.'

'Not that I didn't think it a load of play-acting at the time.'

'Quite.'

Menzies made a rueful face as he put down his beer. 'Actually, I tried to get into your lot myself, because I thought I might be able to get home more often. But I wasn't accepted.'

'What a shame,' Morton said. 'Why do you think they didn't take you on?'

Menzies fingered his beer bottle, his thumb absent-mindedly unpicking the Peroni label. 'They didn't say, but what I think is, it was the school or family connections did me in. They wanted people with no obvious political connections.' He sniffed. 'My people have been Tories and landowners for generations, MPs, local Sheriffs, you know, bigwigs in a small town. I might be wrong, but I think they thought I was...' he searched for a word... 'too obvious for such a subtle task.'

'You could be right.'

'Not that I'm casting aspersions on you, of course.'

Morton smiled. 'Course not.'

'Which school did you go to, Philip?'

And without thinking, Morton said: 'Um, George Watson's.' *Idiot!* 'You?' he inquired, to deflect the conversation.

Menzies nodded, unsuspicious. 'Good school. I was at Gordonstoun, of course. Like my pater and his pater. Anyway, you know, it would have been a great chance to serve my country in a more obvious way than I am doing. Making a difference. Of course what we are doing is pretty useful too, I mean the fund…'

Morton leaned back. 'Of course, the fund. I was forgetting. Getting pretty big now, I hear.'

Menzies gave him an odd glance. 'Eh? Well you should know. Don't you attend the meetings? Or maybe they changed the job description since I applied. In fact, Philip, we were rather surprised to see you today. Then of course, you're probably on a later flight. That was what Dardon said.'

Morton didn't like the idea they'd been talking about him and he realised then there was a meeting he – Gallimont – was meant to be at and from what Menzies had said, suspected it was in Scotland. He wondered if he could find out more. He looked at his watch. 'Yes, I've got to watch my time.'

'You could have got a lift with Lord Airlie, you know. He is driving up. Well, being driven up.'

'Oh, that's a pity. When's he leaving?'

'Already left, I imagine. It's 345 miles to Coldstream.'

'Lucky I'm booked on the plane.' He sniffed. 'Edinburgh, then car.' He tried to visualise where Coldstream was. The Borders, somewhere between Berwick and Kelso. Then he remembered an old stone bridge across the Tweed. He'd been there; had fished the Tweed there. He remembered the

31

main street, a pub, with a leaded bay window, called... the Black something?

'Another?' Menzies asked as the waiter came towards them. Morton murmured assent but was distracted by the arrival of a backbench MP, a former minister who had been forced to resign years ago. A portly sleek figure in a grey suit with shiny red tie askew. He looked well-fed and over-tanned, almost orange, with tufts of white hair on the sides of his head and down his cheeks. Financial scandal. He had spoken to him once, but there was little risk that Cecil Spadeworth would remember him. He wondered if Spadeworth was a member of the group. What *was* the name of the group? How could he find out? Menzies was a bit of a simpleton, overly trusting. But he had to make sure he didn't give the game away.

He picked up his glass and sniffed it. Glenlivet, of course. He nodded over at the MP. 'I suppose he's... one of us?'

Menzies poured his bottled beer into a tall glass. 'Old Spadeworth? Not sure. A supporter of course, that's pretty certain, but whether he's an actual paid-up member, well, who knows?'

Morton smiled. He decided to take a gamble in order to learn more. 'But of course, Gordon, there's a big difference between being a member and what I do.'

'Goodness, yes. You spend the money, we just help to raise it. Must be a good feeling, I mean taking real steps... getting real people in place, vote by vote.'

But as Morton looked up at the waiter's return with his whisky, he noticed Spadeworth was looking over at them. Morton tore his eyes away. He couldn't have been recognised. But the old devil was still looking. 'Don't know him, do you?' Morton was forced to ask Menzies. 'Oh, he's coming over.'

'I don't actually. How odd!'

'If I didn't know otherwise, I'd be inclined to be a bit suspicious of you two bloody Scots sitting there in my club!' Spadeworth boomed.

Morton grinned nervously and saw that Menzies too was a little uneasy.

'Mind if I sit?'

'Of course not. Please do.' Menzies said. 'I've not had the pleasure before. Menzies, Home Office and this is…'

'Oh, I know this old rogue,' he grinned, shaking hands with Morton. 'We've met several times in the passing, at various… events.'

Morton smiled affably. 'Of course, but I meet a few chaps in my line you know.' He was finding the lingo really easy, like putting on an old school uniform. And it was working a treat. Sounding right was half the battle.

'Quite so,' Spadeworth nodded, taking out a cigar case. Morton saw Menzies blanch a little. 'You're the chap that's sticking it to those sweaty socks… oops! Ha ha!' He roared. 'Old habits die hard. I do apologise. I meant the Jocks. Decent good chaps on the whole. Except for those bloody nats, but you're sorting *them* out for us, eh, m'boy?'

'Oh yes,' Morton said. 'We do what we can.' He smiled modestly.

'Yes, I was in at the beginning, y'know. Plenty of chaps issuing warnings even before that confounded ninny Cameron agreed to a referendum but it was clear what needed to be done. So we got to it.' He looked around for approval.

'That's what I heard,' Menzies said. 'Of course things have moved on since then.' He nodded at Morton who lay back, outwardly calm.

'Yes,' Spadeworth sniffed, 'the internet thingy was big news, so we got lots of chaps seconded to work on that. What they call,' he spoke the words with distaste, *social media.* That got things heated up alright. But my input in the early days was ideas about culture, you see. Britishness. Bring back the Blitz Spirit, you know. After all, we had it once, eh? I've always said, scratch the surface of any Jock and you'll find a pretty decent Brit underneath.'

'I wasn't involved in *the early days,*' Morton prompted. And the old fool fell for it. Morton, with a journalist's long experience, knew when to sit back and keep quiet. Spadeworth was proud of his work for, presumably, this organization whatever it was called, so let him boast about it.

Spadeworth puffed out a cloud of cigar smoke. Menzies made an obvious movement to keep clear of it but Morton sat and listened, sipping his malt.

'Oh, others worked hard on culture too. Got to give them credit. But we had direct liaison with the media or key media anyway, direct, don't you see, to programming and commissioning. That's when we started to get them to move forward with new programmes with *Great Britain* or *British* in it. And for a time, nearly everything on the box had Britain in the title: Great British Heroes, Great British master bakers, Great British politicians, poets and engineers, endless programmes on the two world wars, on Churchill, Queen Vic, Great British war poets, Great British railways, Great British walks, Great British sport. None of that happened by accident, you know, though the good old Beeb was jolly helpful. And flags too. We had direct input to the marketing

34

boys, see. Got the old flag on everything from cabbages and potatoes to soap to handbags, to famous people, celebrities. Endorsements, you know. Product placement. Well, it all served. Yes, we did our bit and it helped.'

He stopped, and puffed his cigar, sniffed a bit, looked at Morton. 'But we always knew,' he said expansively, 'at least *I* always knew, that what was needed was more positive action, stronger… no more tinkering around the bloody edges, you know. So the group,' he paused and made a disapproving face, 'the group – GB13, bloody stupid name if you ask me – diversified and then there was the fund, and, well, you know the rest.'

'I do,' Morton smiled. 'But I'm very sorry, I'll have to cut along. That old meeting, you know?'

'Of course, enjoy it, Philip,' Menzies said. 'Give my love to Coldstream. You lucky dog.'

'Watch out for the sweaties,' Spadeworth chortled, waving his cigar like Winston.

CHAPTER FIVE

Morton hailed a taxi and returned to his hotel. He kept the driver waiting while he collected his bag and they were soon heading through the busy streets to King's Cross. When he arrived he saw on the station clock that he had ten minutes to catch the 3:15 p.m. to Edinburgh and saw on the Departures board that its arrival time at Berwick-on-Tweed was 6:45 p.m.

He just made it, settling into a seat as the engines started. Virgin Trains East Coast had just taken over the service, not that that meant much, apart from a new livery and logos. Morton sat back and reflected on his two days in the capital. The pomp and circumstance of the Parliament, the eager well-fed faces of the elected members, the robes, self-serving hyperbole of the Westminster bubble. And then the creaky old British Empire Club – Chuffy's. What a ridiculous name. It was hard to take the place seriously, its old-fashioned paternalistic interior, and equally, its members. But what he had heard there… well, what *had* he learned? That there was an organised group working to frustrate Scottish Independence? That was not news. There were dozens of such groups, perhaps hundreds, and individuals, business people, celebrities, actors, musicians, who had intervened to give opinions, funds and god knows what else in support of such causes. He had suspected, as everyone had, that the sudden rash of overt Britishness on TV and in retail marketing was down to intervention but had assumed it was the work of the Tory Government. So what if it was the work of this group, GB13 instead?

He plugged his laptop into the socket by his seat and logged on to Virgin's much-vaunted WiFi and googled GB13. Well, so much for secrecy! They even had a Wikipedia page! And the group was listed among many similar groups: *Britannia, Stronger Union, Sovereignty, United Britain League, Scotland is British* as a participating organisation in the Referendum. Morton frowned. He hadn't noticed it before. So presumably there would be accounts and financial records open to public scrutiny? It didn't have a website of its own though and most of the references to it on the search page ran the same glossary: 'formed in 2013 by a group of parliamentarians and leading business people concerned with the disintegration of the UK in the face of terrorist and internal political threats…' Morton noted the implied linkage there, of terrorist and *internal* political. That was clever. That would cover the Yes campaign, the SNP, Greens and whoever they deemed a threat. He saw a reference to Lord Ashbury, a Tory peer, as its president. He recalled Ashbury, a figure 'adored by the public and all sides of the House' as the *Daily Telegraph* would have the public believe. He was practically senile, attracting persistent but so far unsubstantiated claims of paedophilia and child abuse in his early career. These had appeared and come to nothing but continued to reappear every few years.

Morton gazed out of the train window as signs for the outer stations on Tube lines flashed before his eyes. They were almost out of the Great Wen. He must look up who had called it that. He planned to run by Hugh Leadbetter what he had learned but he already knew what he would say: "Where's the beef, Willie, where's the beef?" All he really had was an insight into an apparently legal group and only the vaguest hints that anything untoward had occurred. There was "the

37

fund" of course, which Menzies had mentioned so reverently, whatever that was. Was it being used for illegal purposes? Had any of it been acquired via money-laundering or dodgy deals in the Cayman Islands? Even so, Morton thought, the public were immune to that kind of corruption. It was practically endemic in the British political system. Anyway, proving it was an impossibility without hiring specialist accountants and legal experts. Menzies had also said that he – or Philip Gallimont – was the one spending the money. And he had said it was 'vote by vote' – was it being used for bribery? His lookalike was up to his neck in it, whatever *it* was.

Morton checked out Philip Gallimont on internet search engines. There were a few references that turned out to relate to people of similar name living in Florida and Medicine Hat, Ontario, and somewhere remote in Finland but not one in the UK. He tried several variations of spellings of surname and first name – nothing. It was a little unusual. Morton had made a few ego-searches over the years on his own name and there were plenty of other people with the same name as him. In fact, the chances of no-one in the UK having the same name as you was very slight. Unless you course you had a daft name like Xezekial Xzybrodt or something. It made him wonder. The SIS of course had technical experts who could clean up internet records, remove someone… ah, but that would be paranoid, wouldn't it, to think such a thing? He chuckled quietly to himself. Philip Gallimont was probably just a civil servant with Union Jack underpants who thought he was Biggles, flying sorties over dear old Blighty against the fearful Hun.

Morton bought a coffee and flapjack from the customer service trolley as it slowly processed through the overheated and busy train, somewhere south of York. It was a fair bet that Gallimont would be at the meeting in Coldstream. Where in Coldstream he had no idea, but it was a small place and he could probably discover the whereabouts of the meeting. Observe. But it would be too risky to try to attend the meeting himself. He smiled. Two Gallimonts, at the same meeting, would be at least one too many.

The train stopped at York for nearly ten minutes. The person sitting next to him got off, with many others, and an equal number of new passengers got on. He waited until the train was underway again and everyone in their seats; there was no-one now sitting in the airline seat next to his, so he strolled up the train, telling himself it was just to stretch his legs.

When he reached the first class carriages, where he should be sitting, according to his ticket, he took a careful look at the passengers but couldn't see any likely GB13 acolytes. What did he expect to see? Men in solar topees and Union Jack waistcoats?

He returned to his seat and began googling Coldstream. There were two hotels and the Hirsel Holiday Park and House. Ah! The stately home of the former PM Sir Alec Douglas-Home. That would be the venue. He explored the town on an internet map and remembered some of his previous visit: He found the 18th century seven-arch Coldstream Bridge over the Tweed where he had parked and fished the river. Hadn't caught much, tiddler trout, but he remembered having heard a large salmon crashing about. He also remembered having a meal there with Emily and a pint or two at a pub in the High Street and saw now that it was called the Besom. She had had to drive but they hadn't stayed there, they'd gone on to Wooler and climbed a Cheviot, but he couldn't remember which.

When the train finally pulled in to Berwick on Tweed, after miles of grey east coast sand and sea, he found he had little enthusiasm for getting off. It was dark and he thought about his neat little flat and was apprehensive about what he might find, or not find, in Coldstream. Even the name put him off.

Wearily, he dismounted, bag over his shoulder and walked up to the bus station, which was deserted, streetlights shining on the tarmac. He read on the moving display that a Number 67 to Kelso, due in a few minutes, called at Coldstream.

Soon he was riding out into the dark countryside, between hedges and across bridges and a blur of occasional hamlets. It took nearly half an hour. He got off opposite the Co-op in the High Street, a short walk to the Castle Hotel.

It was a white-harled establishment with a low-walled beer garden in front of it on the pavement, presently being used by several smokers and, through the windows, Morton could see a pool table and a bar.

He entered through the front porch and got a room on the first floor. Basic, small but cheap and clean, no view from the window, just darkness. He was at the back of the building and wondered if, in daylight, it would look out to the countryside.

In a rack of leaflets in the lobby he had found a useful map of the Hirsel Estate and various public walks through it. Studying that, he noted that the stately home was in the middle of the park. It was, he learned, a Category A Listed Building, seat of the Earls of Home since 1611. A large, mellow Georgian house, mostly 18th century, encircled on two sides by Leet Water, facing a large artificial lake. There were large rhododendron and azalea gardens, woodlands, a walled garden, craft centre, Museum of Country Life, craft workshops and a tearoom. The public had access to several walks that traversed the woodlands. And he noted there was a separate golf club. That might prove handy if he was discovered wandering about. He could claim to be lost.

But was he really going to be able to infiltrate a meeting at the home of the former Prime Minister? And what if he came face to face with his lookalike? Was the present Earl of Home a member of GB13, or had he simply let them use his house? He remembered the complaint of an elderly nationalist, Harry Lang, a former journalist from his NUJ branch, who had told him about Home intervening at a late stage of the Devolution Referendum back in 1976. In the silky tones of a world statesman, he had advised TV viewers to vote No No, promising that the Tory Government would bring forward stronger devolution proposals. According to old Harry Lang, the Tories then refused to accept the Yes Yes majority vote and dropped plans for devolution. He remembered the phrase Harry had used to describe Douglas-Home was 'yon traitorous rogue'.

Anyway, there was no certainty that there even was a meeting, or that it was in the Hirsel, but here he was, so he might as well do what he could to find out. He looked at his fake Rolex Oyster. It worked fine as long as you changed the battery every now and then. It was 8 p.m. If there was a meeting, would it be before or after dinner? And did the toffs dine at 7 p.m, 8 p.m or 9 p.m? He tried to recall scenes in *Downton Abbey*... could be any of those times.

But the thought of food sparked his own hunger. He zipped up his jacket, swung a scarf around his neck and headed out. In the Co-op he purchased a ready-to-eat pork pie, a Mars bar, a bottle of water and a plastic bag to hold it. He saw some battery pocket torches, bought one and stuck it in his jacket pocket.

The streets were deserted as he turned west down the main road, passing his hotel, and carried on using the pavement as far as the road into the golf club, when it ended. Then he walked at the side of the road out beyond the town lights. Traffic was light but he didn't fancy the prospect of blundering about in dark woodland. He needed a vantage point where he could see people arrive for the meeting… if there was a meeting – and if that meeting was here – at this time. It was all so hit and miss.

Oncoming cars had their full beams on, dazzling him and he had to step up onto the verge to be safe in case they didn't see him. He saw the entrance to Hirsel Drive, to the house beyond and its various attractions, wide enough for coaches, bordered on both sides by woodland. There were lights in the distance. Feeling like a burglar, he walked rapidly on and up the road until it enclosed him in its almost complete but strangely comforting darkness.

CHAPTER SIX

What he dreaded most was big dogs coming at him in the dark. He tried not to think about it, hearing his shoes tapping on the tarmac and the wind in the high trees on either side. He had his torch out now, pointing at his feet as he headed straight for those distant lights that he suspected must be from the big house.

As he turned to look back the way he had come the occasional passing headlights at the road end seemed quite distant as they appeared and disappeared and there was no sign at all of the town, swallowed up by the intervening woods. He practised what he would do if a car came. Stepped into the trees on his left and crouched down. He was sure he'd be invisible.

He studied the map of the estate in the torchlight. He could hardly get lost if he stuck to the main driveway. Quite quickly he saw buildings ahead of him. Closed, dark and shuttered. The tearoom, the craft centre and in the faint light of a thin sliver of moon, the expanse of lake to his left. On his right, the bright lights of the main house.

He walked off the road, stepping cautiously onto grass, and must have come too near the building because a security light snapped on. Cursing, he stepped back quickly and walked more carefully behind the third building which he knew was the Museum of Country Life. He was well out of his comfort zone now! Not for the first time, he thought of his warm flat in safe, quiet Keir Street, even his hotel room a mile away.

He made slower progress in the mushy grass and fallen leaves beneath the trees as he moved to the right, closing in on the big house. Country life? He smiled thinking of a sit-com line he remembered when a louche male character had approached a girl with the line: 'Let me speak to you... of country matters'. It wasn't a sit-com, it was a Shakespeare play. Shakespearean code for sex. He saw a bench on a kind of ridge and beyond it, light from the big house. It was enormous, like *Downton Abbey*. But he heard running water from somewhere nearby.

He observed from behind a tree, feeling the reassuringly rough texture of the bark. Leet Water was six feet beneath him and on the far bank in lights the stately pile of the Earls of Home. The river was uniformly black, its depth unknown, although he calculated it was at least fifteen feet wide. He set off parallel to it, looking for the wooden footbridge he had seen on the map. It was fifty yards down, around a bend. He had to hope it was in good repair.

He stepped out of the trees and approached it. But just then, powerful beams of light swept over him. He threw himself down at the side of the bridge post. But the lights were moving on and he heard the crunch of gravel. A car turned in front of the house and it illuminated others parked in a line, lots of them. The light moved on down the main drive and away.

He switched on the plastic torch and kept it pointed at his shoes as he quickly crossed the wooden footbridge and ran to the corner of the mansion. He was, undoubtedly, now on private property. Reason told him that freely roaming dogs were unlikely, not if there were visitors at the house, if there was a meeting.

He crept around the gable end of the building, stepping carefully in a sea of gravel chips. The windows were high up, but he could just about see in if he stood on tiptoe. Cautiously, he raised himself up and peered in.

There was nobody in the first two rooms but in the third, the windows were open. Light blazed out and discharged the murmur of many voices. He leaned up, holding to the stonework. Many noisy, alcohol-fuelled conversations and the sounds of eating and drinking, laughter. Nervous of being spotted, he drew back.

In the quick glimpse he'd seen about twenty people, mainly men in dinner jackets. It could be perfectly innocent; a bunch of friends, a group of business associates. He had no way of knowing and it was none of his business anyway. He had a crisis of confidence standing there in the shadows, wondering why he had come. What did he think he would gain from it? He could be at home now, in his neat flat in Keir Street, watching crap on TV. Had he really thought he could just swan in among them, pretending to be Gallimont?

He retreated behind some bushes to consider his options and to take some deep breaths. He found the pork pie and ate it, standing behind the topiary. It felt good. He wolfed the Mars bar and had a swig of water, wondering about the bill of fare inside. Probably juicy steaks, foie gras, pâté, Gressingham duck breast and plenty of booze to wash it down. No Mars bars for them! It might be the 15th Earl and some of his cronies from the House of Lords.

Morton had googled him too, a man with four middle names, and knew he was one of the ninety-two remaining hereditary peers in the Upper House, a Tory of course, former Chairman of a well-known private bank. Not short of a bob or two, as his dad would say. Just the kind of chap to be involved in some constitutional pressure group like GB13. Eton and Oxford – where else? And just a few months ago, made a Knight Companion of the Order of the Thistle, to go with his CVO and CBE.

Morton felt the need to urinate and derived pleasure from watering the toff's topiary. Refreshed in body and spirit, he returned to his vigil at the window. The meal was coming to its end, chairs scraping on a wood floor. He looked at his watch in the light falling from the window: 9 p.m. Figures were moving about. It was impossible to identify individuals. Whether Gallimont was there or not, he would never know. Perhaps the meeting had concluded before dinner anyway. Maybe they'd all be heading home shortly. The best thing he could do, Morton realised, was to get into a position to see them coming out. That would give him the best chance of identifying Gallimont.

Suddenly a door opened a few feet from him. Light flooded the gravel path. He fled behind the topiary. Two staff in shirtsleeves were standing in the doorway, one smoking a cigarette, the other vaping. Only ten feet away from him. He could hear their voices but couldn't make out what they were saying. Then he realised it wasn't English. They were Europeans, staff. They quickly finished smoking and went back inside. He drew a deep breath and slowly allowed himself to exhale.

He went back to his vigil at the window but could see only staff clearing away. He crept around the dark gable end to the front of the house. He counted eleven cars, parked outside the front door, mostly limousines or expensive looking sports cars and a minibus which looked rather incongruous in such company. Beyond, he could see lights of a second wing of the house. It was huge and there were lights on in various parts of the building.

'Well, I've got nothing to lose really,' he told himself. 'I can say I was out for a stroll and got lost in the woods. What could they do to me? Nothing.' He pocketed the torch, straightened up and strolled casually, with a confidence he didn't feel, on the noisy gravel between the parked vehicles and the house. Glancing in to the open lighted windows he saw a dozen men seated, eating and drinking at a long wooden table. No doubt the drivers or chauffeurs.

He continued to the vestibule and stepped up the four stone steps under the ivied arched doorway into a stone-flagged hallway. There was a coat rack with coats and jackets hanging from it and several cardboard boxes. The flaps on the box on top of the pile were open. Paraphernalia for the meeting, he wondered.

He glanced in. Yes, stationery, of a sort. Little Union flags on sticks! He couldn't stop himself giggling hysterically. What were they planning to do? Wave these at each other? There were Union flag ballpoint pens, notepads... But, on the bench by the door, under a raincoat that had been dumped in a heap, he saw a red plastic folder protruding.

He heard, above the pounding of blood in his ears, sounds of movement, chairs scraping, feet on stairs, distant voices. He pulled out the folder and fled. In the vestibule, hearing the reassuring murmur of the drivers in the next room, he unbuttoned the stud. It was stuffed with papers, and the first page read: 'Agenda'. This was what he had come for! A door opened and voices came louder, coming his way.

He ran outside, cut back to the corner of the house and peeped back. A crowd of people had come out of the house and stood on the steps, where he had been, smoking, laughing and joking. He felt the encroaching cold night wind slither across the sweat on his forehead and cheeks. There was nothing to stay for.

He ran diagonally across the grass to the footbridge and across it and into the trees. When he felt safe, he held the torch into his jacket and examined his watch. It was 9.35 p.m.

Morton retraced his steps by the black shapes of the museum, craft centre, tearoom, to the main drive. The lake had almost disappeared, had become a sinister void, with occasional watery sounds as a wind-driven tide washed the stones on the shore.

He jogged back along the wide tarmac drive heading for the main road. He had a sudden thought. Car registration numbers. Blast it! Hugh had a police contact who could look them up. Maybe some of the attendees would stay the night, but some would leave, that was what the drivers were doing there.

He found a vantage point behind a bush near the front gates where he could note down the licence plates. They would have to halt at the main road.

It was cold and dark and a rising damp made him uncomfortable, although he was sitting on the plastic bag. He thought about what he was doing. The folder looked good. There could be the whole story inside it. The licence plates would be the icing on the cake. It was the kind of assignment he had done only several times in his career, following a lead that might go nowhere or land him an almighty front-pager. It was all a bit hit and miss. The key was Gallimont. He had to find him and meet him face to face and learn what he was up to.

Finally, after a long half-hour of waiting, headlights came down the drive, a succession of them. He checked his ballpoint pen was working. He was going to have to jot them down in the pitch black. Luckily the headlights illuminated the rear plates of the vehicle in front, as they braked for the main road. Five, six, seven vehicles, the last a minibus with rowdy occupants, then a straggler then another. Nine. Some turned left, some right. He wondered about the occupants. Bluffers like Dardon or Menzies or Spadeworth, or old crackpots like Lord Ashbury or Lord Airlie, waving their Union flags at each other over the port and brandy, singing their old school songs, like a scene from *The Ruling Class*.

But there were no more to come so he stood up slowly, feeling the stiffness of his joints and stretched, then gratefully walked off up to the main road and quickly back to where the pavement began and Coldstream's streetlights, and carried on to his hotel. His stomach was growling and it was just after 10 p.m.

CHAPTER SEVEN

There is something deeply worrying about a telephone ringing in a darkened house in the middle of the night. Ringing and ringing in a cold empty room, where the central heating has long since gone off, where electronic devices; TVs, DVD players and hi-fis sit silently in the red glow of standby mode; ringing, as the red digits flash on the cordless phone base. In some types of housing such a call can disturb people's sleep in neighbouring houses, where sleepers mutter under their breath: 'Why doesn't he answer it?' and try to get back to sleep, ignoring it as it rings on, ever louder, ever more imperious. But in this particular room, where the telephone was ringing, there were no neighbouring houses within half a mile and anyway, a hand was already reaching for the receiver.

'Hullo?'

'Philip?'

'Yes. Who is it?'

'Desmond Thorpe. Sorry to wake you. Something's come up and it can't wait.'

'Really? That important? It's...' he glanced at the big clock on the wall, but without his spectacles couldn't tell whether it was 3.25 or 5.15 or... 'Well, late anyway.'

'Yes, look, I have Commander Smyth for you.'

'Oh! Right. Hello...'

The voice now speaking was grating, forceful, used to being listened to without interruption. 'Now look, Gallimont, there's a problem and I need to speak to you. A security breach, of sorts, anyway. What happened in Edinburgh last week when you were foolish enough to get arrested? I need to know *exactly*.'

'Well, I was… I completed a full debriefing of that,' Philip Gallimont said. 'There couldn't have been a breach of any sort. No loose ends. Not possible.'

'Think back. Did anyone look inside your briefcase? You had it on your person, didn't you?'

'Well, yes, but no-one could have. It was locked and I never gave away the lock code and it was undamaged, so… What kind of security breach?'

Smyth broke in, impatiently: 'Were you in London yesterday?'

'In London? No. I was here.'

'We have a problem then. Briefly, a man passed himself off as you at the British Empire Club yesterday afternoon.'

'*Whaaat?*'

'Twelve hours ago, this man spoke, at some length, to several members about the organisation's activities.'

'Passed himself off? As me?'

'That's what we know. And if you weren't in London, we're dealing with a very serious breach. This goes beyond the level of a prank or an incident we can write off. Someone, some organisation, is aware of your movements and is now in possession of some potentially compromising information.'

'I see. But… how could…?'

'We don't know. But we will find out. In the meantime, you are suspended from duty. Do nothing, go nowhere, speak to no-one. Do you understand? We will send a team up immediately to provide surveillance of your home address and to investigate. Stick to these arrangements until further notice from me. That's all.'

51

And the person whose hand was holding the phone in the dimly lit room, finding that the line was dead, returned it carefully to its base which emitted an electronic beep of thanks. The night resumed all around the almost total silence of the countryside, with one difference. In the cold living room of the house sat a man shivering in a dressing gown who knew he would not be able to get back to sleep, who imagined enemies in the next room and upstairs and outside, silently infiltrating his world, waiting to get their chance to leap out and catch him unawares.

Morton was baffled. He sat on the bed in the hotel room with the curtains closed, the TV muted, and the contents of the red plastic folder strewn on the duvet. His earlier exhilaration had dissipated. He could make no sense of it. Apart from several copies of the single-page Agenda which could have come from any meeting of a body or group – a community council, WRI, even Branch of the British Legion – there was a thick wad of thin tractor-feed paper that proved to be a printout of names and addresses grouped into Health Board areas. Thousands of names and addresses in seven of Scotland's fourteen regional Health Boards: Borders, Highland, Ayrshire and Arran, Dumfries and Galloway, Orkney, Shetland and the Western Isles. Only seven and all, he noted, on the west side of the country.

Most baffling of all, on the final two columns on the right of the page, each name had a unique code and a sum of money. These ranged, he noted, from £8,000 to around £40,000. Was this a donations list? Or a list of bribes paid? Were these supporters?

He leafed through the pages, 142 in total, the names printed in an almost unreadably small font. He couldn't be bothered to count the names, but if there were approximately 100 per page… possibly 10,000 in all. But what was this list for? He studied names and addresses at random. They were not in alphabetical order. They seemed to have no factor in common, though he did begin to suspect there were few obviously Scottish names: no Mc or Mac names at all. Was that a clue?

He sighed and leaned back against the headboard. The only way to solve the mystery was to go and speak to some of the people on the list. Anyway, it did feel disappointing after the exhilaration of his adventure in the dark. What had he expected? A signed confession by the Prime Minister that Scotland's Referendum had been *rigged*? Maybe it was something, maybe it was nothing. He could do no more tonight. He needed sleep.

He looked out of the window, north over the dark woodlands of the Hirsel Park, and lifted it to let some cold fresh air in to the room. Hotel rooms were always stuffy and overheated. He liked a cool bedroom to aid peaceful sleep. He switched off the TV, hearing a passing car out on the High Street. All was quiet.

He folded up the pages of the printout and put them back into the folder. He considered where to put it. His paranoia was kicking in. Under the bed? Nah. He went into the bathroom and finally decided to hide it between folded white towels on the towel rail above the toilet. Then he went to bed and very quickly was asleep, with the fresh night air silently pouring into the room around his sleeping body.

The cause of Scottish Independence is an old one, as old as the Scottish nation itself and although historians disagree on the precise date when Scotland can claim to be a nation, it was around the period that England also became a nation, at the dawn of nationhood within the British Isles. From tribes and clans to statehood, from many regional oligarchs to a single monarch, forming a nation that took its place as one of the oldest kingdoms in Europe.

The intertwined history of Scotland and England included many wars, rivalries and alliances and perhaps one of the most significant events in their shared history was the uniting of the separate crowns under a Scottish monarch, James VI in 1603. This later began to become known colloquially (though never officially) as the monarchy of *Britain* and the die was cast – according to some – that the two nations themselves would be united, made one.

It was originally to be a wedding, a partnership, but in those unenlightened days, the property of the wife and her very person and any decision-making she might have had, became the property of the husband and she his chattel, taking his name and losing her own. James VI or I as he became known, was himself the progenitor of such an idea, even drawing up prototype Union flags and he imagined a complete and happy matrimonial merging of the nations to form one nation state.

In hindsight, that could never happen, there was too much to lose on either side, but what was accomplished, later, in 1707, by mercantile aggression, bribery and political sophistry, was only ever intended as a temporary measure to smash competition from Scottish traders. Nowhere in the document is there any mention of a body now known as *Great Britain*. The document simply unites in equal partnership, the nations of Scotland and England into one state. Both parliaments were to be dissolved and a new one formed, although the new one turned out to be, to the consternation of the Scots' representatives, the very same old English Parliament, Westminster. The tawdry deal survived by inertia, almost in secret, and by the enmeshing of Scottish nobles into the English system so that Scotland was ruled by an anglophile class, keen to participate in the rapacity of an empire overseas. Since partnership would not work, takeover might. And it did.

Now, more than 300 years later, we are able to finally measure the success of the Union experiment by a simple but effective test. Scotland's population at the time of Union was one-fifth the size of England's, but is now less than one-tenth of it. This, perhaps, is the true measure of the success of the Union – for the English.

But the Scottish nation's sense of nationhood did not, as James VI and I fondly imagined, wither on the vine. Instead it has proliferated and thrived and diversified, despite the Union's best efforts. And from these seeds, a modern Scotland emerged unexpectedly from long slumber and found itself wanting. Many have begun to question the creaking, anachronistic, backward-looking state to which they are bound, and have looked abroad to European models of economies and progress, and questioned why better ways cannot be found to feed our hungry, shelter our homeless and promote greater aspiration and ambition in our young.

And why not? There can be only one answer: because of the dead hand at the centre, the institutional inertia, the parochial, stultifying hierarchy and decadence epitomised by the Westminster regime. Used to ruling half the world, it is systematically unwilling, perhaps unable, to change, shake off old patronising and unfulfilling ways.

So the cause of Scottish Independence attracts many of the 'new' Scots and most strongly those with no interest in hearkening back to the arcane rights and wrongs of medieval history, who look instead to the future and to better ways of shaping human society to fulfil the needs of all.

The contrast between the journeys of the two nations grows more striking with each passing year and that realisation has affected individuals on both sides of the shared border. People move up or down for personal reasons: to escape the crowded metropolis, or to seek work there, to find a better quality of life in a more peaceful rural area, or to escape rural poverty and unemployment. Young Scots move south, wealthy retired English move north. And some retain their original dispositions and some go native and enjoy the otherness of their destination, however temporary. The history of every nation is a story of immigration. We have all come from somewhere, to where we are now. And that will always continue, however the two ancient nations decide to rearrange themselves in relation to each other and the islands of Britain.

Morton woke with a start, shivering in the cold breeze on his face and for a second or two struggled to remember where he was. He got out of bed and shut the window. The clicking of the radiators showed that they were going full blast. The bedside clock-radio showed that it was almost 8 a.m. but it seemed still dark outside, or grey at least. He had slept well.

He showered in the small bathroom, noting that the shower water pipes were loose on the tiles, there was dark green mould in the grouting. The water became scalding and he stepped out hastily and grabbed for the towel, dislodging the red folder into the toilet. Blast! He had forgotten it was there. Luckily, it had stuck in the bowl and hadn't reached the water.

He enjoyed a full fried breakfast in the small dining room on the ground floor and checked out at 9.15, strolling along the High Street in his suit and coat, holdall on his shoulder. He had planned to return by bus to Berwick and get the train but discovered he could get a Borders Buses coach to Edinburgh from Coldstream High Street and it would save him time – and money.

By midday, he was unlocking his own front door in Keir Street. He remembered that he had a date in the evening. He hadn't seen Emily since the previous Saturday and knew she had been away at a conference. They had been seeing each other for almost a year, very casually, both stuck in the rut of their respective careers. He liked her fine and enjoyed her company but they both had their own places and it was difficult to see how things would progress. He'd have to think what he was going to wear.

CHAPTER EIGHT

Professor Emily Louise McKechnie was Head of Political and Constitutional Studies at the University of Edinburgh and had risen through the ranks by virtue of being precise, definite about everything she believed in and hard-working. A popular lecturer and senior lecturer, she had been Acting Head during the prolonged absence, through illness, of Professor Odnab Kikollo-Gombally and when the crown finally fell, she had been there to snatch it.

Often on TV because of her precision and her definite encapsulation of what she believed, she had also moonlighted as a Yes-Academic during the Referendum. She wasn't scared to speak her mind, spoke well, looked good and, not to overlook the obvious fact, she was a woman, still under represented in senior academia.

In the dim lighting cast by candles in red glass bowls, Morton timed to perfection his capture of two ricketty chairs and a little table in a stone-walled alcove away from the main route to the bar. The Jazz Bar was a popular basement venue and as usual, crammed, people standing around the walls, wherever they could find a space as all the tables were taken. He glanced over at the trio on the carpeted stage. He found it too loud really, the saxophone breaks were cool and sultry, otherwise it was just crashing guitar chords and bashing drums. Most of the patrons were paying little attention.

Emily came back from the bar with the drinks: a pint of Innis & Gunn for him and a pinkish cocktail with a cherry on a stick and a chunk of lime. 'Good, you got seats. Well done.'

He raised an eyebrow.

'Cosmopolitan,' she told him, 'Vodka, triple sec and cranberry juice. I should have got two. This won't last me ten minutes.'

Morton gave her a sidelong smile. 'Been that kind of a day?'

She exhaled. 'Ooh yeah, department meeting day. But you've hardly said a word yourself. What have you been up to?'

He stared into his pint. The flowery taste on his palate. He actually preferred Belhaven Best, or Caledonian 80 shilling. The candle in the bowl threw out a wavering pink glow.

'Come on then, mister. Spill.'

'Something I'm working on. Not sure if I should bore you with it.'

'I'll tell you soon enough if it's boring,' she said, removing her severe black plastic specs. She reached into her tweed handbag, found a small spray and began cleaning the lenses. Morton liked the fresh, fruity smell of the spray. She had hazel eyes and long lashes. He was pretty sure she didn't need the specs. Her sight was excellent. She referred to them derisively as her 'Academic Armour' and had once told him no-one took a woman academic seriously unless she had authoritatively severe black eyewear. They were a prop to make her look older, more serious, but she'd taken to wearing them socially too.

'Well, okay,' he conceded. 'I'm not sure if it all adds up to anything, at least not yet.' He began to tell her about his apparent resemblance to Gallimont, being mistaken for him, his stint during the legislative statement.

'Yes, I liked that piece by the way,' Emily said. 'Lovely jaundiced tone. Read it online.'

'That was what they wanted. It's my default sourness, I think.' He told her about Dardon, Menzies and Cecil Spadeworth and Chuffy's.

'Chuffy's? Crikey! Boarding school slang circa 1930?'

'The British Empire Club no less.'

'Ye gods. This is like the tale of Jonah inside the whale. Certainly more than a little ironic, you, there, I mean. The type of thing you hate. Reeking of privilege, I mean.'

'Yaas,' Morton drawled, 'One endured it with a stiff upper lip, dear boy. Anyway, it was there I learned of a meeting in Coldstream.'

'In Coldstream?' Emily had a faint puzzled smile on her face and drained her cocktail, looking regretfully at the empty glass.'

'I'll go to the bar, if you like,' Morton offered.

'No, no, finish your story. Information first, booze later.'

'Where was I?'

'Coldstream. Didn't we go there once?'

'We did, last summer. I'd been there before that as well. Well, I couldn't go to the meeting. I didn't want to take the risk but I hung around to see what was going on. And guess where the meeting was?'

'In Coldstream? No idea.'

'At the Hirsel, the former home – or perhaps I should say Hume – of…'

'Of course, Sir Alec Douglas-Whatsits. Good lord. So what happened next?'

'I've a feeling you're not taking this seriously.'

'Oh I am, it's just a little unexpected. A little James Bond-ian, or is it Bond-ish?'

'I couldn't get anywhere near the meeting but I managed to get a folder.'

'Get?'

'Okay, purloin.'

'Steal.'

'Borrowed, shall we say? But it's baffling. I don't understand what it is.' He filled her in on the detail of the file. He could see that she was beginning to be intrigued.

'Well,' Emily sniffed, 'so far, you haven't got much evidence of wrong-doing, have you? It's the sort of skulduggery we suspected, but nothing provable. But what are those lists, and why would they have them at a meeting of GB13? I must say, I'd never heard of this group and yet, you say, it was a listed participant in the Referendum? I suppose the name is an abbreviation of Great Britain 2013? Very imaginative! I could cast a professional eye over the file if you want. Might be able to see a pattern.'

Morton leaned in and held her wrist. 'Nice offer, Em, but I'm not sure I want to involve you. I mean, it is stolen property.'

'You think they're watching us right now?'

He couldn't hear her. 'Sorry, what?'

'I said, do you think they're watching us right now?'

'Who?'

'Well, *them*, of course,' and she laughed. Emily had a mirthful laugh, a sort of teasing laugh that always made him smile. He could imagine many students, male and female, falling in love with her. He wondered what the future held for them. It was a casual arrangement with no agreed rules or certainties. They had slept together but only twice, in a year.

'Seriously, Em,' he said. 'I'm not wanting to get into trouble again, like that time I told you about when I came under surveillance by nasty spooks and nearly got killed.'

'Of course, but that was years ago. You really think…?'

61

Morton finished his pint. 'Who knows? I don't want to stick my neck out more than I already have. I've hidden the file by the way, but okay, I'll let you have a look, in the next couple of days. Your expertise might be useful. How was your conference by the way, Professor?'

'Oh that? *Political Culture and Regionalism: Changes since Devolution.* So-so. The usual. I wasn't speaking. I was just there to smooth the way for a paper I'm contributing to their journal. I knew the editor would be there.'

'Where's *there* by the way?'

'Newcastle Uni.'

'I probably passed you on the train.'

'They wouldn't pay airfares? Things must be tight at the *Standard*? No, we drove, two colleagues and me. I'm thinking we could go on to Paradise Palms. We could try vegan. Or Mother India? Your choice.'

New Waverley in Edinburgh is the flagship hub of the UK Government's Civil Service in Scotland. It is a cluster of buildings in the valley below Calton Hill and the classical magnificence of St Andrews House. The Old Royal High School is on the skyline to the north, and the lower end of the Royal Mile, Scottish Parliament and Holyrood Palace to the south.

In the heart of the historic Canongate, these two interlinked four-floored buildings are ultra-modern and finished in pale yellow sandstone interspersed with huge smoked glass windows. They sit in a site of seven and a half acres and at the lower end is a handsome new public plaza with statuary, bistros, restaurants, cafes, retail. A combined floor space of 200,000 square feet houses 3,000 HM Government civil servants working for HM Revenue and

Customs, HM Treasury, the Office of Secretary of State for Scotland, the Advocate General, the Health & Safety Executive, the Information Commissioner and numerous other departments.

As well as being an eye-catching modern centre, it is something of a political statement, a not-so-subtle reference to the continuing – and ever-to-be continued – superiority of the major parliamentary institution – Westminster – a stone's throw from its upstart daughter-in-law, Holyrood. The ultra-modernity of the centre is no accident. This is Scotland's future: we are Scotland's future, we are going to be here in Scotland for a long, long time and we cannot foresee a time when we will not be in charge.

On the western corner of the North building, on the top floor near Lift C is an office that bears the insignia of the DTI and the title Operations & Investigations Authority, etched into the thick glass front, which incorporates a door operated by a digital keypad. It is a discreet office in a quiet side of the building in which a very small number of civil servants are employed. Two permanent members of staff in fact work the usual hours, though other colleagues come and go infrequently. Because of its proximity to one of the five lifts and the digital door keypad, their movements are unobserved.

There are few unsolicited callers and any civil servants working elsewhere in the New Waverley who may have seen the office must have wondered why the DTI had an office in Scotland at all. Surely the Scottish Parliament has control of trade and industry matters through Scottish quangos such as Scottish Enterprise and the SCDI? But very few would have guessed that the office was actually the Scotland station of MI5.

The first of the team to arrive was Colin Hardwick. Coming out of the lift into the smoked glass atrium with the view over the railway lines emerging east from Waverley, and across to Calton Hill, he put down his briefcase to punch the five-digit code into the keypad. He looked the typical civil servant, in his sharp grey suit and black raincoat. As the glass door opened to admit him into the reception area, he adjusted his steel specs and picking up his briefcase strode in, the lights, operated by motion sensors, coming on. He knew that the permanent staff had already gone home but, by prior arrangement, had left all the systems switched on.

Divesting himself of his raincoat in the outer office, he looked around. He had never been here and the office had only been open for two months. It still smelt new, of screen wash and Windolene. He could see that the door to what must be the main operations room was ajar and he wandered through and stood for a moment taking it all in.

It was impressive and he was not easily impressed. The large room was a compact powerhouse of monitors, screens, computers and multi-functional databases. Hardwick knew he had instant access to shared databases of fraternal organisations such as Police Scotland, Special Branch, the Secret Intelligence Service (otherwise known as MI6), NATO, Interpol and other organisations such as the MOD Police, the Civil Nuclear Constabulary, and of course, a real-time video link to the Internal Comms desk in Thames House, Millbank. Other monitors allowed real-time access to numerous public and private CCTV networks. One had access to satellite images and could retrieve imaging and video footage from military partners across the Five-Eyes intelligence-sharing alliance states.

Hardwick pressed a few keys to check that the systems were live. He knew that the room itself had concealed CCTV footage which was routinely monitored. Everything that was said and done here was on the record. Yes, it was comprehensive and impressive, Hardwick decided. He was used to seeing these tools but not all in one room, more usually spread around on several floors at Millbank. His eye fell on the soft seating area near a coffee machine and water cooler.

As he was making coffee, a soft female voice from the ceiling speaker announced the arrival of colleagues Dennis Cuthbert and Javid Norrow. He went out to the outer office to greet them.

'Hello. You got here. I'm Colin Hardwick.' As they shook hands, he observed that both the newcomers, who were unknown to him, were young. New intake. He'd been in the service for twelve years.

'Coffee's on, guys, in the Ops Room.' He pointed to the heavy door through which he had come.

'Right.'

'Have you both eaten, by the way?'

Dennis Cuthbert, a short squat figure, who looked powerfully muscular, removed his jacket and hung it on the coat rack. 'Yes, Colin, thanks for asking. I got something on the flight. Can't speak for Javid.'

'I have yes. I'll have a coffee though.' Javid Norrow had a ready grin and very white teeth against his smooth brown skin. He looked like an athlete in his navy blazer and grey slacks.

'Come through.' Hardwick led the way.

'Nice!'

'Good big space,' approved Norrow. 'Who's the fourth, by the way? They didn't tell me.'

'Didn't they? Well, it's Carol Harker according to my briefing. I've worked with her before.'

'Old Carol,' said Cuthbert fondly. 'I have too. Not seen her for a while. I think she's been working in Europe.'

'Yes, that makes sense,' Hardwick said, adjusting his specs. 'Moving everybody around. Shakes things up. Anyway, help yourself to coffee. Biscuits here too. As far as I can tell this is to be a short op. Fix a security breach, do obs and then home. Short and sweet, hopefully.'

The three men established themselves in different parts of the room and drank coffee, waiting for the final colleague to arrive. Hardwick moved to the monitor that had the dedicated HD video-conference link to Millbank and tapped the screen. The software used advanced encryption, allowing the signal to safely traverse the internet, and was so fast, conversations seemed almost like real time, very little detectable latency. The screensaver whirled away to reveal the interior of the Irish and Domestic Counter-Terrorism Comms room at Thames House.

Hardwick recorded a short report and after a few moments a cropped-haired young man with large tortoiseshell spectacles, Desmond Thorpe, responded to acknowledge the message. When the screensaver returned, Hardwick went over and refilled his coffee cup from the filter machine.

Dennis Cuthbert paced over to the window. 'Good location, I have to say. Easy access. Five minutes' walk to the rail station, twenty minutes' drive to the airport and about the same to the seafront. Not bad.'

Hardwick was smiling. 'I hear there's a helipad on the roof, if we ever need it. And,' he added dramatically, 'there's a detention facility next door. Two cells, fully sound-proofed, for interrogation, with a video link in here.'

'They think of everything.' Norrow said. He removed his blazer, strolled over to have a look out. 'Big city, Edinburgh, my first time here, actually.' He smiled and loosened his tie. 'God, it's all so compact, so neat.'

Hardwick nodded, smiling politely. 'And there's something else you should know about. In fact, it's the best thing. We have our own secret way in and out. Come and see.'

'Okay.'

They followed Hardwick back to the outer office. Just then, the ceiling speaker informed them that Carol Harker was arriving and they could see her shape outside the glass door, as she completed security clearance. She was in her mid-forties, slender in a grey trouser suit and raincoat, strawberry blonde hair inside the flipped-up collar.

'Hello again, Carol,' Dennis Cuthbert said. 'You know Colin too?'

'Of course, hello.' She had a warm smile, which was one of the things Colin remembered about her. They shook hands.

'Nice to see you again.'

'And this is one of the new intake. Javid Norrow.'

'Hi, Carol.'

'Javid.'

'Colin was just going to show us the unique entrance to Calton Road. That's the narrow road that goes along under the railway lines. We can come in and out that way without being seen, if need be, that's right, Colin?'

'It's not for ordinary use,' Hardwick explained, 'only when absolutely required.' He pointed to the door marked *Storeroom*. 'It's through there. We won't go down now. There's a button on the left just inside that door and a bit of wall slides in and reveals the stairs that go down beside the lift shaft. It comes out to a steel door in the perimeter wall on Calton Road, just under the railway line. Very discreet. Almost no-one uses that street. There's a digital code box there too on the door. Same codes.'

'Cool,' commented Javid.

'Yes. It's surprising there wasn't a Scotland station before, given there's been devolution for years. But the place is cleverly put together. Hiding in plain sight. There are 3,000 civil servants in the centre, we're just four of them, I suppose. Anyway, let's get to it,' Hardwick concluded. 'We've a full briefing with Comms in a few minutes.'

CHAPTER NINE

Morton was up early on the Monday, grabbed a quick cup of coffee, washed, shaved and walked over to the *Standard*, by way of the Vennel steps to the Grassmarket, along the Cowgate to busy South Bridge. On the way in, he picked up a copy and read the headline: *EU Tory Split*. He smiled. No kidding!

The editorial meeting had just broken up and Hugh was in the large meeting room, looking over Johnny Laidlaw's shoulder as they moved text blocks and images around on screen. Hugh looked up, saw Willie in the corridor and waved him in. He saw the front page headline and pointed. 'That story is going to run and run.'

Willie smiled. 'Yeah, they're tearing themselves apart, with any luck.'

'Liked your Westminster piece, Willie. We've had a couple of readers' letters. There's one in today's. One for, one against.'

'Good. Hugh.' He slipped out of his jacket pocket the folded page of the car registration numbers he had jotted down at Coldstream. He cleared his throat. 'Um, Hugh, can you get your police contact to run these down through the PNC?'

Leadbetter grunted and looked at the paper. 'Right. Anything I should know?'

Morton indicated with a silent nod, Johnny Laidlaw still absorbed at his laptop. Hugh raised his eyebrows and led Willie over to the window, where they could see the Castle buildings on Castlehill.

Morton said quietly, 'I'm not sure what I have got at the moment, Hugh, but it could become something.'

'Okay, Willie,' Leadbetter nodded, 'sounds good.'

'But...' Morton frowned. 'Very secret.' He glanced nervously at Laidlaw's back and lowered his voice to a whisper. 'Not a word, please. Email me when you've got the info on those and then I'll come in and tell you about what I've got. *If* I've got anything.'

'You dark horse you!' Leadbetter rubbed at his hairy chin. Morton saw tiny flakes of skin or dandruff escaping in the daylight.

'Beard itchy?' he asked. 'Look, I have some data, if you can call it that, that I need to check out, but I need a car for a couple of days. Any chance?'

Leadbetter narrowed his eyes and made sucking noises with his teeth as if considering whether to run the risk. Morton could see moisture on the thick hairs below his lips. He'd often felt his editor should buy a beard trimmer. 'Hmn, okay, Willie. I'll trust this is going to work out for us. Take the Corsa in the basement. I'll get you the keys. It uses unleaded.'

They both laughed. There had been an apocryphal incident with a young reporter who'd run out of petrol and the boiled-dry car had had to be collected by tow truck.

'Don't worry,' Morton said.

'Ah well, it all goes on the expenses sheet. I get my arse kicked if...'

The grey Vauxhall Corsa was a car Morton had previously borrowed. He sometimes missed his old VW Beetle. He'd inherited it from Sally when they split up and he'd grown to love it, but it had become a liability.

He adjusted the seat and the mirrors and drove the Corsa up the concrete ramp out of the basement into the Cowgate, turning left into Candlemaker's Row and Forest Road and along Lauriston Place, where he found a parking space opposite the Art College and parked.

He walked back to his flat and changed into a more reputable shirt, jacket and long woollen coat and tied a Paisley patterned scarf around his neck. He had rolled up his sleeping bag, blankets, camera bag and the red plastic file and a notebook. Stowing them in the car, he set off, heading south.

He joined the A720 ring road at the Hillend Junction and continued on the A702 to Biggar, a long peaceful road through moors and hills. At first, he listened to BBC Scotland, the Kaye Adams phone-in programme but the irritating callers drove him mad, so he switched to Classical FM, until a commercial break came on, and then to BBC *Women's Hour*, a sane and pleasant driving companion on the lonely road.

A few miles south of Biggar he crossed under the M74 travelling due south into the Lowther Hills. He saw several Saltires and Yes flags flying from cottages on the way and more occasionally a Union flag, reminders of last year's Referendum.

At Thornhill, he turned towards St John's Town of Dalry and approached the trim village of Penpont. He had selected at random several dozen of the names and addresses and intended to start here and work down to Newton Stewart and then round to Gatehouse of Fleet, Castle Douglas and end up in Dumfries.

He parked on the outskirts of the village. There were four names here, only a few streets between them, and several more names in Tynron and Moniave. There was no-one in at the first address. He felt a sense of anti-climax. He walked round to the second and was confronted by the large Union flag hanging limply in the still, cold air, incongruously big, from a stout flagpole in the garden.

He knocked on the porch door. After a few minutes, an elderly man in a V-necked grey pullover, corduroy trousers and slippers came to the door and Morton saw his heavy frown relax as he saw who it was.

'It's you,' said the man. 'Didn't expect to ever see you again.'

'I was passing,' Morton said. 'Thought I'd see if you were okay.'

'Oh yes. They haven't frightened us off yet, the bastards. I've been passing information on, you know. As you said to do, if ever owt's happenin, like. But things has all gone quiet.' He grinned. 'And I wonder why.'

'Yes. Of course, Morton said. 'That's good. And you've not had any trouble?'

'Trouble? Nay, I'm not expecting any trouble. Not now.'

'Great, well must be off. Called at Mr Thridlestane, round the corner. Not in.'

'Aye, happen that's right. They're away on t'olidays. Tenerife, lucky beggars. Want t'come in for a cup of tea?'

'No thanks. Must be getting on. Good to see you.'

Morton went back to the car. What to make of it? He'd better not jump to any hasty conclusions.

He made several more visits. About half of the people were in. The doorstep chats all seemed to go the same way. Though not many seemed to know who he was, they were used to people like him turning up to see how they were. These were people who'd moved into the area, one, two or more years before, all apparently from the south and all of a specific type: well-to-do retired folk, what Morton found himself categorising as *Daily Mail* readers. Some referred to reports or emails they were sending on, information they were providing, but Morton couldn't quite work out what that would be about. One man asked him if there was any possibility of further funding. Morton had pretended to take a note of that, managing to confirm that the sum of money alongside his name on the data sheet, £8,000, had been received by the man, two years before.

'It was very helpful, and of course we didn't expect it,' said the man apologetically, 'but we should have requested more at the time. We underestimated our moving costs. And, since then,' he coughed embarrassedly, 'we have discovered that others have received more, considerably more.'

'Okay, I'll see what I can do,' Morton promised. Back in the car he wrote down verbatim, as far as he could, exactly what had been said on every doorstep. He was starting to get an overall picture and it looked dodgy. The sums of money were not donations, they were funding, support to relocate to Scotland, a defrayment of moving costs. This was 'the Fund' Menzies and Spadeworth had referred to. Every person he had spoken to – and by mid-afternoon, he had spoken to seventeen – was English and there was no doubt they were all of a political hue... strongly anti-Independence.

He had also discovered that some had moved in very recently, one just two weeks before, well after the Referendum. The process, whatever that was, was continuing, it seemed. But none of them seemed to have any knowledge of GB13, though a few had mentioned something called the Ardbeag Agency.

Morton's technique had continually adapted to his audience throughout the afternoon. He found that by using a jokey remark as he left – 'Ah, well, must go. Onwards to Independence, eh?' – he elicited the same jeering response, a shared mockery. The most telling response came in the hamlet of Carsluith in Wigtown Bay, from a large, flabby man, originally from Slough, a railwayman before retirement. He feinted a punch at Morton in response and said: 'Well, we've scotched your bloody chances of that, mate!'

Morton went into a bookshop cum coffee shop in Gatehouse of Fleet and sat lost in thought. Was any of it provable? Such a large-scale scheme was bound to have left lots of public evidence. The funding surely could be traced?

As he sat with an Earl Grey tea and a slice of lemon, he listened to a conversation between the owner of the bookshop and his wife who ran the catering side of the enterprise. He ate his blueberry muffin and looked out of the window at the street. Quiet place. Nice people, southerners of course. But there had always been preponderantly more English people in the picturesque Scottish Borders and Dumfries and Galloway than elsewhere in Scotland.

It was the kind of peaceful place anyone would want to retire to. He knew that many of these new settlers became the life blood of their communities, but they changed them too. Scotland, like England, had long been a place people emigrated to, as well as from. We are a nation of immigrants, he mused, and our relations, for good or ill, with England have helped to shape us. But while he welcomed, with open arms, anyone who wanted to choose Scotland to live in, or retire to, there was something about this... that made it into a conspiracy and not just illegal but a provocative political act. Who was behind it? And how had all these people been relocated so swiftly and on such a grand scale?

In the Ops Room on the fourth floor of the New Waverley North building, the video conference had started with a summary of what was known, or believed, to be hard evidence. Gallimont had been compromised and some of his activities were known about by a third party or group. But not completely because, according to the Intelligence Analysts, the imposter had seemed vague, even unaware of certain aspects, the meeting at the Hirsel for example. Cuthbert and Norrow had been instructed to draw a vehicle from the agency garage and maintain directed surveillance upon Gallimont's house in Aberlady, East Lothian, about fifteen miles away. Their remit was also to trawl his family, known friends and associates and anyone he might have come into contact with during the last ten days.

Hardwick and Carol Harker set to work running the facial-recognition scan, using a low-resolution image of Gallimont, patched into software utilising Edinburgh's live CCTV system. They believed the imposter was based in Edinburgh, although Millbank had commenced an FR scan of the Metropolitan area too, as a backup. Hardwick, whose true metier was Digital Intelligence, or DigInt, knew that the first Metropolitan matches could appear within an hour because of the huge investment that had been made to replace the Tinkerbell tapping service with the giant Preston national database, now located in the basement of Thames House itself.

There had been considerable discussion about the motivation of the imposter and the likelihood there were others involved. Was it a deliberate security breach by an oppositional group, or a more random event, possibly even a prank by someone who knew Gallimont? As they were discussing this with Millbank, the loss of a folder at the Hirsel was reported and the mood changed.

'This is too much of a coincidence,' said Desmond Thorpe, the Admin Officer at Millbank handling the Scotland station activities. 'Must be connected to the Empire Club incident, where, I would remind you, the meeting was mentioned.'

Hardwick agreed. Thorpe, he knew, was a recent graduate and not long through his service-wide induction training, and he had the enthusiasm and haste of the youthful and spoke briskly. Hardwick sometimes felt he was a little impetuous.

'I mean, in my opinion, Colin. He was told at the Club that the meeting was in Coldstream. He learned that from them, *there.*'

'But not exactly where, or when,' Hardwick countered. 'Although, granted, it's not a big place. He could have simply guessed the venue. Does anyone know what the folder actually contained? I mean, how sensitive the material is?'

The next voice was Commander Smyth's. 'Colin, all and any material on this is super-sensitive. Think of the political context here. The cross-border implications. If any of this got into the hands of the media – even social media – well, I can't overstate how damaging that could be. We live in the rapids of the Referendum, lots of sore losers out there, lots of fervent activists. Wouldn't take much to spark real trouble.'

'Quite,' said Carol Harker who hadn't spoken so far. 'We get that. It's ultra-sensitive.'

Hardwick glanced at her and compressed his lips. It had been rumoured that she and Nigel Smyth were having an affair. He hoped it wasn't true.

76

'The missing folder belonged to another liaison officer, by the way,' said Smyth, 'not our friend Gallimont. So he's off the hook for this, at least.'

Hardwick nodded. 'Right. I see.' He disliked Smyth mainly because he felt the older man was a little too sharp and critical at times. He'd suffered a tongue-lashing from him more than once, in the past. Then there was the bouffant greying hair and clipped moustache and suits that were a little too tight, too shiny. He was rather effete, vain. He liked Carol and couldn't help feeling if she was having an affair it was down to the Commander taking unfair advantage of his position.

He looked sideways at her. She'd taken off her jacket. He thought her dusky pink blouse worked well with her colouring. She released her hair from its clasp and sat bolt upright. He remembered a conversation years ago when she'd talked about early retirement, about a fund that had been set up to encourage older staff to go and allow greater diversity. There were few enough good women in the service, he'd told her. The scheme was designed to get rid of middle-aged white males like Smyth and attract a new intake of the likes of Javid Norrow.

Less than ten minutes after the video-conference concluded, the FR scan for Edinburgh had begun to produce facial matches. The first half-dozen were clearly Gallimont but then came a series that could be someone else. He pressed the Millbank Comms button.

'Carol,' he said quietly, 'we're on again. Come over and look at this.'

Thorpe the Admin Officer looked up. 'Ah, you have the Edinburgh FR scan?'

Hardwick held up a print out. 'This is an old friend apparently,' he said, 'someone we've already had dealings with in the past. A journalist, name of Morton, William James. Should be coming to you now.'

Thorpe said. 'Oh, yes, that was quick. He has a file. Good, we're getting somewhere.'

Carol called over: 'Look, the home address is very close to where we are now.'

'Okay,' Thorpe said, 'but it's early doors. We'd better give the scan more time. Looks good though. We'll instruct further action. Later, guys.'

CHAPTER TEN

Morton had planned to sleep in the car and found it wasn't as easy as it had seemed. It was the first time he'd tried it, but he discovered that a Vauxhall Corso wasn't spacious enough inside. He'd had a tiring day but sleep evaded him.

After doorstep interviews on the outskirts of Castle Douglas, he had headed south via Dalbeattie to the touristy Solway coast within sight of Cumbria across the water. There were lovely picturesque coastal villages there and quite a high concentration of names and addresses from his data file.

As it was getting dark and as he had already formed a pretty convincing picture of what was going on, he decided to give it up. People had stopped answering their doors. He felt tired and hungry so he drove on and parked in the centre of Dumfries, in the White Sands carpark facing the Burns' Tower and the historic Devorgilla Bridge.

The River Nith passed over a low waterfall in a pleasing cascade a little further downstream. He strolled up the cobbled streets till he found an Indian restaurant, the Gandhi, in a side street. It looked a bit rundown and there were no diners. But he went in all the same. It was either this or a pizza takeaway. The meal was substandard, derivative, too much and too little at the same time. The curry was a yellowy pink creamy mush with large cubes of tasteless, amorphous pseudo-chicken. He remembered the lovely cuisine and the calm serenity of Chez Mijou.

Later, he stopped in for a pint at the noisy Doonhamers' pub in Friar's Vennel, a rather down-at-heel howff but serving a good pint of Heavy. There were a few noisy drunks but none bothered him. The White Sands was virtually empty at midnight except for occasional taxis coming and going from the taxi office nearby. There were streetlights though so he decided to stay where he was, wound the passenger seat down and the driver's seat and got into his sleeping bag under blankets.

After a while, he realised he could hear the running water of the Nith, and it should have soothed him but he found sleep elusive and only drowsed for a few hours. Too cramped. Eventually, he put on the radio and listened to music and when he felt sleepy again switched it off but it was no use, he was awake, so he gave it up and decided to drive home. It was 2.45 a.m.

This time he drove north to join the M74 near Moffat and continued to the outskirts of Glasgow and the junction with the M8. He found some kind of solace in the long rapid run north on the motorway. There was no way he could face going over the narrow dark roads through the hills that he had come down. It took him two hours and, as dawn was lightening up the sky in the east, he was wending his way along Corstorphine Road, heading for Morrison Street, Lothian Road and Lauriston Place.

He found a space opposite the Art College, almost exactly the same space where he had parked the previous morning. He was exhausted. His most immediate need was sleep. He returned to his flat, dumped all his stuff in the hall and fell into bed. At one point he woke, convinced he had heard the doorbell ring but didn't bother to answer it and slept through till 11 a.m.

When he awoke, he felt rested and rejuvenated. He showered, made himself coffee and toast, looking out over the Vennel steps towards the castle, and checked his email.

Leadbetter had sent him a typically terse email: "Info in, H."
He replied in similar fashion, letting Hugh know he'd be in
about lunchtime and 'had something to show'. He dressed in
warm casual clothes, stuffed the folder and his notes into a
small red and blue daysack, hoisted it onto his shoulder and
set off for the office.

It was a mild, sunny day with a fresh sea breeze from
Leith, Joppa and Portobello. He got into the car and moved
off, manoeuvring into the West Port and Grassmarket and
up the Cowgate, all busy with traffic and clogged with
pedestrians, and as he neared the basement car park used by
the *Scottish Standard*, he pressed the electronic key on the
dashboard and waited for the roll-up door to open. Some
idiot had parked a white Citroen Relay van across the
pavement on double-yellow lines, close to the doorway,
impeding traffic.

He glanced up at the cab, couldn't see a driver. 'Idiot,' he
muttered, adding: 'White vans think they have carte blanche.'
Smiling at his own wit, he drove in and down the ramp and
parked.

He strolled up to the Cowgate and turned to check the
door had closed behind him, then felt movement beside him
and a cloth clamped over his face, eyes, nose, mouth… that
medical smell… chloroform…

When he came back to consciousness he thought he was in
his own bed but gradually as the ceiling came into focus he
realised he was somewhere else. It was bright, quiet and
peaceful where he was. He heard sounds of the sea nearby.
He could move his face but his arms and legs felt like lead.
Then a shadow fell across his face. There was somebody…
He looked up at a grotesque grinning mask, shiny pink with

startling teeth and a bright blonde quiff. But the eyes didn't fit.

'Who are you?' he stuttered. 'Where am I?'

The voice was Scottish. 'Aw in guid time, William. Rest yirsel. An dinna worry. You're in the hands of friends.'

'But who are you? Why am I here? Where am I?'

'Patience. Dinna fash yirsel. I'll be back in a wee whilie.'

The man went away, leaving Willie to twist and push himself against the bonds fastened around his wrists and ankles that anchored him to the bed. He had suspected he had been kidnapped by MI5 or some such, but the cheap mask made that seem unlikely somehow.

The room he was in was very small, a cubicle maybe and painted pale green, like a tiny hospital room. Sunlight came in though the lower part of the window was screened. But the light was strong on the ceiling and in the upper part. Was that a clue? Was the window south-facing? He heard the rustle of the tide, on shingle perhaps. He couldn't be too far from Edinburgh. He'd been snatched at noon or thereabouts, but the strength of the light showed it was only early afternoon. Where was he then? The white van. It must have been them, in the van. And, whoever they were, they had his notes and the data file!

He lay there, frustrated and irritated. He wondered if Leadbetter was wondering where he was, but knew he wouldn't be. He had such a busy day, staff coming in and out and Willie was just a freelance anyway. But this must be something to do with his investigation into the GB13 group and the 'relocation scheme' as he now termed it.

Morton had been kidnapped before, eight years ago, when McGinley and his thugs had taken him to a quarry at Braid Hills. God, that was frightening and he recalled that he had pissed himself. But McGinley was dead and something about the Scottishness of the man in the cheap mask had reassured him. Friends? Well, that remains to be seen, he thought. His stomach had been growling for a while; must be at least three hours since that paltry slice of toast. And coffee. God, he craved a coffee. He tried not to think of it. Shingle, yes, waves on shingle. He heard a car in the distance, voices and footsteps. The door opened and light bounced around the walls.

'William, me again,' said the mask-wearer. 'Right, we're ready for a chat so I'm going to untie your legs.'

'What are you going to do with me?'

'We're just gonnae have a chat. Dinna worry. As I said, yous will be perfectly safe. Ye'll no come to any harm. Just relax, while I cut the cords.'

Morton was helped to sit up. He could see the man's neck and bearded side of his face as the man bent over him to lift his feet onto the floor. The floor was bare wood with scraps of torn linoleum in the corners.

'Now, can ye get tae yer feet, William? Slowly, now. I'll hold yer shoulders. Braw, just follow me. We're only going tae the next room.'

Morton shuffled beside the man who was taller and bulkier than he was, through the doorway into a dimmer but larger room. He had guessed correctly it was a static caravan or mobile home. He found himself giggling, perhaps out of hysteria as he saw two other masked figures sitting there behind a metal fold up table. One was a cartoon pig face, the other looked like Oliver Hardy with a tiny blue bowler hat.

The big man grunted. 'Ah ken, Wullie, at least one of us is a comedian.' The only light in the room came from a barred small window above head height. There was a smell of mould or engine oil.

'Sit down,' said pig-face, the smaller of the two men pointing to the canvas folding chair.

He sat. His wrists were still bound. Anyway, he was intrigued. His journalists' curiosity was aroused and he realised he no longer felt apprehensive. He didn't feel in danger anymore.

'Yes, the smaller man,' was saying. 'It's a static. You probably guessed it. It's completely off-grid. No electric devices of any kind in here. We find it safer that way. I'm afraid we took your mobile off you and we have it elsewhere. You'll get it back as soon as possible.'

'Look, what's all this about?' Morton asked. 'And who are you? Maybe you've got the wrong guy? I'm an ordinary bloke. I'm not important, not involved in anything.'

The big man, now standing beside him said. 'Christ, man, ye'll huv us aw in tears!'

The pig-face man on the left, the smaller guy, who was dressed in a black sweater and black leather coat, said: 'We know a lot about you, actually. Your journalism, I mean, and that's why we're having this chat. We have this, you see.'

He leaned down and pulled up onto the table Morton's daysack and extracted from it his notes and the thick wad of the data file. 'We haven't had time for much more than a quick glance but... it's...' He looked at his colleague. The Oliver Hardy masked man. How odd does that look, Morton thought, smiling, despite himself.

This other man nodded and looked down at the material and began flicking through pages of Morton's notes. He had dirty fingernails, Morton noted, yellowish too, a heavy smoker. And the cuffs of his green sweater were frayed.

The big man standing behind Morton leaned heavily on the chair and patted Morton's shoulder. 'We should say thanks firstly for doing this valuable work. We showed it tae a friend of ours, an expert you could say, and he – we – think it's incredible ye could get hold of something like this. How did you get it by the way?'

Morton sniffed. 'Well, I stole it. It doesn't belong to me, you know, just in case you thought…'

'But where?' asked the pig-faced man in the leather. 'It's dynamite. We've been investigating this for some time and here you've got the proof. Are you likely to be able to get it published in the *Standard*?'

'Published?' Morton repeated faintly. 'Well, maybe, I'd have to work it up into a story first. Anyway, isn't it time you told me who you are? What's your interest in it? And maybe even take off those stupid masks.'

The big man behind Morton laughed. 'Huh! Actually, this thing is a bit smelly, stinks of rubber. I'm taking mine off.'

Morton glanced round at him. A man with a brown beard and blue eyes. No longer a bogey man. 'I think you look better without it,' he said. 'Who is it supposed to be?'

'Donald Trump the billionaire. Can ye no tell? Imagine if the big balloon gets himself elected?'

The other two looked at each other. 'Fair enough,' said the man in the green sweater, taking off his mask.

'That's Oliver Hardy,' Morton said.

'Correct. We didn't know how this would pan out. I think we're going to have to trust you. Not that we have any option. I'm Marco by the way. The big beardie behind you is Alasdair.'

'And I'm Luke – the brains behind the gang,' said the leather-jacketed man who had taken off the pig-face. They all laughed. 'Anyway, what you need to know is we're just three of a larger group. We don't have a name but we're mostly ethical hackers and some of us are media folk and others lawyers, and most of us are – were – Yes campaigners. Since last year, we've kept in touch and we've been monitoring some of the big No campaign money-men.'

Alasdair clapped Morton on the back. 'Aye, man, we're the ones that found out about the money-laundering of some of the No campaign's biggest funders. That was us.'

Luke added: 'Which we released to the media and it got into the public domain.'

Morton nodded. 'Yes, I remember that. Pity it hadn't come to light *before* the vote!'

Alasdair sighed deeply. 'Ah man, aye, that's so true.'

Luke held up his hands. 'Yes, yes, anyway, let's keep to the point. These notes based on the data? Morton, you've clearly worked out what it is: a scheme funded either by the Tory Government themselves or, most likely through some dodgy third-party group or department, to support people who want to relocate to Scotland. Which raises several key questions. How were these folk recruited? Were they vetted, interviewed? How was it ascertained what their political views would be?' And who did all this in the first place?'

Morton nodded. 'That's about the size of it. But very difficult to prove, I think. Don't suppose you'd have any coffee, or anything to eat?'

'Sorry, no,' Luke said. 'But we'll be finished soon then we can take you anywhere you want to go. When you spoke to these people, you didn't record any of it?'

'No, just wrote it down afterwards, as accurately as I could.'

'Pity.'

Morton frowned. 'Well, at the time, I just wanted to get an overview. At first, you see, I thought it might have something to do with donations, unlikely as that seems.'

'Yes, very unlikely, some of these sums are over forty grand,' Marco said. 'Our colleague is presently tallying up the money. Oh, we've scanned the data file. I hope you don't mind.'

'Oh, you have?' Morton said. 'Well, actually, that's a very good idea.'

'We thought so,' said Luke. 'It's an incredible thing for us to have. You must tell us exactly how you *stole* it. I mean, from whom.'

Morton laughed. The others looked at him.

Luke frowned. 'Something funny?'

'Oh, yes,' Morton chuckled. 'You see, I stole it from Hume.'

'Whom?'

'That's right. Hume. Ah, it's a long story. Anyway, yes, it's an amazing document and the people on it are out there, to be spoken to, but how can we prove there is intent behind it, that it's a deliberate scheme? There's also the other aspect, the sensitivity of it. For example, the Scottish Government has made many statements about its desire for inward migration.'

Alasdair grunted. 'Huh, but no boatloads of English Tories, like a slow-motion invasion, just to put the kibosh on our independence.'

Morton ignored the remark. 'They welcome people from anywhere who make the choice to come to Scotland. So no Scottish Government could ever comment on the inward migration of English people without the media making it look like they were in some ways being racist. There are very many English people active in Scottish public life, playing a big part...'

'Yes, I'm one of them,' Luke put in.

'... in public life, and they would never want to make it look like they were somehow less than grateful for their efforts. English people are very welcome in Scotland – that is always going to be the message. But I agree, it was never envisaged that some group or UK Government department would set up a frankly sinister scheme such as this. That's what I meant, ' Morton continued, 'but it will be very difficult to prove. And even without thinking about the people and who they are, here is a scheme where some people are being helped to find nice homes at the expense of other people who might want to live in those homes, but who don't have this kind of financial support. I mean there must be something dodgy about the financial side of it.'

Luke looked at the others. 'Yes, very difficult, but we must find a way. We need to find out about all aspects of it then find a way to stop it. Look, I have to leave you now, and meet up with some of the others, report back. He delved into his pocket and produced a pair of bicycle clips. Nice to meet you, Mr Morton, and apologies for the circumstances. I'm glad you feel you can work with us.'

Morton sniffed. 'Well, I might have done that anyway, if you'd asked. I can still smell that horrible chloroform by the way.'

'Ach, the fresh air will help, Morton,' Alasdair said. 'Come on.'

CHAPTER ELEVEN

When his former captors, Alasdair and Marco led him out of the static home, Morton was glad to get out into the bright daylight and vast open spaces and was surprised to see where he was. The static was raised on bricks in the middle of a rough field. In the far corner, he could see two ponies grazing by a fence 100 feet above the rocks and shingle of the south side of the Firth of Forth. To the east were the two bridges and from the mighty towers of a third, the Queensferry Crossing, decks already cantilevered out, high above the river, inching from the south and north banks towards each other. The grass was wet as they walked up the steep slope to the narrow road. The outskirts of the town of Bo'ness began to appear on the right.

'Nice location,' he said.

Ahead of him, Alasdair replied: 'Aye, we went to a lot of trouble to find a place that is well out of the way. As you'll see, it's tucked under the hill here and hidden from the toon by the bend.'

They reached the narrow road, almost invisible between huge flanks of whin bushes and hawthorns. Morton could see the white van parked further down at a bend where there was a narrow passing-place.

Alasdair was first in and reached into the glovebox and handed Morton his mobile phone. 'It's switched off, of course,' he said. 'Leave it that way until we get into the city.'

'Well, thanks,' he said. He was glad to get it back, even though he couldn't use it. He'd felt bereft without it;

symptom of the times. The three of them squashed up into the front, Morton in the middle.

Marco rolled the van down the lane and into another narrow road. Soon they were back on the M8 and in the outskirts of the city.

'Use your phone now if you need tae,' Alasdair said, as they came into the city by Davidson's Mains. 'Of course as soon as you do, ye'll be back on their radar. But don't worry, we've a few tricks up our sleeve to deal with that.'

'Right.' Morton wondered what the tricks were. They seemed pretty competent, this group, he thought. Not fanatics, not loonies. He remembered he was supposed to see Leadbetter: He gestured with the phone. 'My editor will be wondering where I am. I'd better go there first before going home.'

'Aye, nae bother,' Alasdair said. 'We can be a taxi service. Drop you off, then pick you up and see you safely home.'

The van turned off Hillhouse Road into Queensferry Road, heading down to Dean Village. 'But I live a stone's throw from the *Standard*. It'd be easier to walk.'

'Well, walk if you want,' Marco said, 'but they'll almost certainly be watching the *Standard* to see if you turn up. They'll know you're going there. Email intercept is about the easiest thing for them to do. They'll have hooked in to all traffic from the paper's staff, not just yours. Aw, look at this tosser, come on, move, ye eejit! Right about now, Willie, they'll have us on screen, although the tinfoil panels in the roof will not help them much. Anyway, they know what you have and there's no way they're going to allow you to publish it.'

'Yes, well, I know all about that from a few years ago.' Morton told them about his brush with McGinley and the way the authorities had squashed all publicity about the information he had collated, the illegal radioactive convoys on Scotland's roads.

Marco shook his head. 'Yep, that's them. They're up to it. All the time. But we can keep one step ahead this time. This time, you're not alone.'

'Thanks, guys. That actually makes me feel a lot better.'

They were trundling along Princes Street now, the castle to the south. His hunger had returned with a vengeance. 'Sorry about the grumbling guts,' he said. 'Haven't eaten for hours.'

'We should have thought of that,' Marco said. 'We hadn't planned to kidnap you though. But we couldn't have anyone else interfering. We knew we needed time to have a proper chat.'

'Anyway, don't worry,' Morton said, reassuringly. 'Some minor discomfort but...'

'All part of the service,' Marco grinned. 'But remember only use WhatsApp when you contact us. It uses end-to-end encryption and we know they haven't yet been allowed to hack into it. Of course, eventually, they'll get permission, on the grounds, no doubt, of national security.'

Alasdair who sat behind him, said. 'They won't wait for permission. They never do. But their main efforts the now, is tae get back the data file. They'll have been in your flat of course, that's a cert.' He laughed. 'First place they'd look. However, our guys will have been busy making multiple digital copies and photocopies too and spreading them about, so the spooks will never be sure they've got them all.'

Marco took up the theme. 'In fact, I might suggest, just to take the heat off, we might let them find the original. Only a suggestion. We'll see what the others think.'

'Are there many others?' Morton asked.

Marco looked at him sharply then relaxed. 'I suppose there's no harm in telling you,' he said. 'There's about forty or fifty of us,' he said, 'not including the ethical hackers group. I've no idea how many of them there are.'

'Ethical hackers fur Indy!' Alasdair laughed. 'I love it.'

'They don't use that name,' Marco countered. 'He just made that up and people starting using it.'

'So, what I'm seeing my editor about,' Morton began, 'is to hear what he's dug up on the licence plates of those who attended the GB13 meeting at the Hirsel. He has a contact who was going to run them through the PNC.'

'Sweet!' Alasdair approved. 'That's the kind of contacts to have.'

'I've no idea what they'll find. I'm hoping it'll give us some kind of lead to the connection, if any, between MI5 and this GB13 group.'

'Aye, that'd be nice.'

'Not that I can imagine coming up with a story that I can print. I mean, there's nothing to stand up the story. I don't even have a picture of Gallimont.'

'Well if he looks like you, then you look like him,' Marco said. 'Put on a shirt and tie, coat collar up and we can take a grainy pic in the street somewhere and you could say it was Gallimont.'

'Oh, I hadn't even thought of that,' Morton said. 'It might work.'

'Aye, stick with us, we're the lads with the ideas,' Alasdair grinned.

'Here we are,' Marco said. 'South Bridge, we're getting close. I was just going to pull in past the lights and you can cross the road and you're there. And we'll see you soon, we hope!'

'Huh! You will. No doubt. Thanks!'

And Morton jumped out onto the pavement and the van sped away. He wasted no time in crossing the traffic-snarled street and running in to the *Standard* office. He didn't see any spooks but that didn't mean they weren't there.

Desmond Thorpe, the Admin Officer, was on the phone to Hardwick when the intercept locations from Morton's phone began to come in.

'Oh, he's back in the land of the living. Not far from you. In fact, he's moving towards you.'

'Yes. Got him. Looks like he's on his way home. He must have the material with him. We've already searched there.'

'How is he travelling? Any visual?'

'Not yet, waiting for CCTV to cross-reference. Maybe there's not much CCTV where he is… residential area. We should get that once he comes into the commercial area.'

'Right. Odd that his phone was switched off, for how long?'

'About three hours, really. Last located close to his home.'

'You think he's on to us?'

'Couldn't be. Our team were careful in his flat. And I have visual now. He's in a white van, can't get the registration at the moment. I can just make out the driver's hands, no faces. Maybe that's him, or he may be with others. The CCTV is not well-placed here. It's a Citroen Relay. Waiting for the licence…'

'What's happening at Gallimont's by the way?'

'Dennis and Javid have thoroughly debriefed him,' Hardwick said. 'Nothing new though. They've found nothing untoward in his contacts over the past ten days. In fact, with the new focus on Morton, we can relax on that front. I'd say Gallimont can get back to work, once we've recovered the material and decided what to do about Morton.'

'Yes. Been thinking about that,' Thorpe said. 'It could go a number of ways. We have about three options really. But before we come to that, we'll need some input from higher up. Instructions. Then we can act.'

'Okay, there's the registration coming up now,' Hardwick told them. 'Cross-referencing it through PNC. Oh, it's non-viable. Ooh! Fake number plate.'

'Well, well, what was that you were saying about him not being onto us?'

'It's strange, Desmond. Yet he's got his phone back on. Odd. No, he's not going home, I don't think, too far west now. Turning off Princes Street onto South Bridge.'

'It doesn't look like he's aware. You don't think he's going to turn up at the newspaper do you? That would be…'

'Oh – yes, there he is – right outside the *Standard* offices. We can pick him up easily now. Carol, can you alert Dennis and Javid? They should be on their way back.'

Hugh Leadbetter looked up from the crust of his minced beef pie at Morton. 'Willie! Where have you been?' I was about to get off home. There's fitba the night.'

'It's a long story,' he said, shaking his head. 'I was kidnapped, but by the good guys.'

Leadbetter chewed moistly. 'Jeezo, the good guys?'

He sat down in the chair facing his editor and leaned back. The chair creaked. 'Look, Hugh, I need ten minutes of your time. I'll talk, you listen. But first we have to make sure we're not overheard. I've reason to believe they're listening in.'

Leadbetter swung his legs off the desk and finished his pie in one big bite. 'Naw?' he said or something that approximated to it. 'If I find that tae be the truth, I'll sue the bastards!' He stopped, looked at Willie. 'Who are we talking about? Which bastards?'

'Not here,' Morton said, standing up and taking his arm. 'Somewhere without any devices in it?'

'Devices? Okay, I think I know where.'

'No. Leave your mobile in here.'

'Fucksake, Willie, this better be good.'

In the blustery coastal village of Aberlady, Dennis Cuthbert and Javid Norrow had wrapped up their end of the investigation into the security breach surrounding Philip Gallimont. With the journalist Morton now in the frame, Gallimont was off the hook. They had been given the go-ahead formally to allow him to return to work, but had been advised not to mention to him the further security breach at Coldstream.

They sat in the breakfast diner drinking coffee while Gallimont was dressing for work and packing a bag. They had reluctantly agreed to give him a lift to Waverley Station.

Cuthbert looked up as Gallimont came back in, dressed in a suit and coat, black leather gloves, and swung a leather holdall onto the table.

'Starting right away, I see,' he said, and chuckled. 'Others might have taken another day off.'

'Yes,' Gallimont said expressionlessly. 'Others might. I'm keen to make up for lost time.'

'Well, we're just about ready,' Cuthbert said reluctantly. He had barely started his coffee and had an uneaten Danish pastry on his side plate.

95

'Going far today?' Javid asked, nodding at the bag.

'Short flight to Stornoway. Western Isles. Just for the day.'

'Lucky sod!' Javid exclaimed. 'I hear it's beautiful up there.'

'Yes. My flight is at 10.30,' Gallimont said brusquely, lifting the bag off the table. 'So as soon as you are ready...'

Javid and Cuthbert looked at each other meaningfully. 'Okay, let's go.'

A few minutes later, as they were heading back to the city on the A198, Carol Harker's call came in.

'Right, okay that,' Cuthbert said. 'Our ETA at the location is...' he glanced at the satnav, 'approximately twenty minutes, depending on traffic.'

Javid, who was driving, studied Gallimont in the mirror. He sat in the back seat, beside his holdall. 'That's the fellow who looks like you,' he told him. 'We've located him and will be taking him off the streets today, you'll be pleased to hear.'

'Good,' Gallimont said curtly, looking at his watch. 'I should have set off earlier. Or got a taxi.'

Cuthbert frowned and shared a look of distaste with Javid. 'Well, we have our shout. Sorry and all that, but we can't take you all the way out to the airport. Waverley is as far as we can take you.'

Gallimont sighed. 'I can still make it, I think. It's the only outgoing flight today. I need at least an hour on the island. I've a hire car waiting.'

'We'll do our best.'

They had taken chairs into the staff toilet and in the confined windowless space, Morton had filled his editor in on what had happened to him that afternoon, what they had said about MI5 intercepting all electronic communications traffic from the building. Leadbetter had, in turn, shown him the list of registered owners of the cars Morton had jotted down at the gate of the Hirsel but they meant nothing to either man.

'Could be anybody… or could be somebody,' Leadbetter joked. 'Or naebiddy at all.'

Several times they had been disturbed by other staff coming in to use the loos.

'Use the other toilet,' Leadbetter had barked. 'We're in conference here.'

'What other toilet?' asked Anthony Hope, a features man whom Morton knew slightly.

Leadbetter didn't miss a breath. 'The Ladies. Be a girl for the day.'

'I'm sure this breaches some kind of regulations,' Hope grumbled. 'I only need to use the urinal.'

'Sue me!'

'So,' Morton concluded. 'There you have it, as it stands.'

'I agree with you, Willie. There's not enough at the moment, but by Christ this'll be big when we have it all.'

'My main priority is to keep out of their hands until they realise that recovering the data file from me is pointless because there's loads of copies of it.'

'They didn't give you it back, though? These boys?'

Morton hesitated. 'Well, yes and no. They've kept the original file and all my notes, but they gave me this.' He leaned forward and delved into his sock. He flourished a tiny aluminium data stick.

Leadbetter took it and peered at it. 'Thirty-two gigs,' he said. 'Nice one. And it's all on here? Right, first thing we do is copy this. We can hide it on another removable disk drive, make it harder to find. Then, get you out of the building. Where can you go? I mean, your flat is out of the question.'

'Yes,' Morton conceded, 'they will have been there, may even still be there.'

'You could crash at mine, Willie, but, Katya…'

'No, thanks but that's too obvious. It has to be somebody they wouldn't connect me with. Emily, but she's away on a seminar in York, I think. Wait a minute, I've got an idea. I've got a friend, well, not a close friend, who lives out of the city. Maybe she would put me up. She's got loads of rooms. But how do I contact her and how would I get there?'

'Your friends, the hackers? They have a vehicle.'

'That will be under surveillance,' Morton said.'

'They said to use WhatsApp?'

'Yes, but I'd have to switch my phone on.'

'Well, they know you're in here. In fact, you should use your phone to contact them from here, using WhatsApp. Then switch it off and skedaddle.'

'That's easy to say. How?'

Leadbetter grinned, his teeth appearing through the gap in his thick beard. 'Aha! I have a way.' He tapped the side of his head. 'But first, I want to bring Rod Oliphant in on this. You don't know him, or do you? He's our IT specialist.'

'I've read one or two of his pieces, on the forthcoming legislation, you know. What's it called again? The Investigative Powers Bill?'

'You should hear Rod on that particular all-pervasive fascistic crock of shit. First, we should send out for some pizza. I'm sick of hearing your belly rumbling. And coffee. At any event, let's move out of here, Willie. It's making me queasy.'

Professor Emily Louise MacKechnie had barely switched her phone on after the plenary session in the Ron Cooke Hub of

York University's Campus East at Heslington, when it buzzed with incoming messages on WhatsApp. Her contact Cerberus was requesting a meeting back in Edinburgh. The message was headed 'Urgent'. She thought for a moment or two, imagining her schedule for the next few days, then responded with a date and time, adding 'subject please?' She waited, saw it had been delivered and read. She was due back in the plenary, was the next to speak. She waited, put the phone in her pocket, then it buzzed. She fumbled it out and read: 'UR Friend and ours, WM.' Frowning, she switched the phone off and went into the auditorium to deliver an outline of her paper, *Political Engagement in the Digital Age*. What was Cerberus playing at? Your friend and ours? WM was clearly Willie Morton, then she had a sudden recollection of Willie telling her about… in the Jazz Bar. What was going on?

Philip Gallimont settled back in the seat as the plane took off, gently swinging and banking north, giving him a vista of the Forth and the new Queensferry Crossing under construction close to the Forth Bridge and the famous railway bridge, then curving round over the Grangemouth oil-refinery complex. The Saab 340 twin prop was swift and modern and would make the trip in around an hour, including touch-down at Stornoway.

He glanced at his fellow passengers. There were a couple of dozen, some businessmen, some locals returning, no doubt taking advantage of the Scottish Government's 40 per cent Air Discount Scheme. Subsidy that was what it was all about, he thought, to keep these marginal island flights going. There were quite a few empty seats, about ten. He had a seat on his own, plenty of sunlight to read the file on the way up. It was a new trip for him. Previously, he had been out to

Colonsay, Tiree, Coll, Isla and Barra, but never the main island of Lewis. He glanced down. The Campsies, Loch Lomond ahead. Lovely from the air, on a clear day.

He opened the file. Today he was a developer, using the cover name Ardbeag Holdings and hoped to get at least verbal consent to acquire a large piece of land from a retired minister, the Reverend Alasdair McInnes at Breasclete, which was in a bay just around the shore from the famous Callanish Standing Stones. He'd been told it was a straight drive west over the moor from Stornoway and he could do it in half an hour. He would have to be quick, in and out, do the deal and back to catch the 4 p.m. flight back to Edinburgh. Damn the man insisting on speaking face to face. It was always a nuisance, but then, it was a large development. He was sure, from his study of the site, that he could knock down the manse and the former, now disused church, and create no less than sixteen interlinked modern cottages, all with a sea view and some with a little terraced garden. It was ideal and he was sure Eilean Siar Council would approve it. They were desperate for new housing and a bit of investment. Of course, initially the scheme was for six and retaining the Church, but once on site with full permissions, it could easily be extended.

He glanced down. Big mountains. He wondered which. All so remote, almost no-one living there. And yet, that was what he was mostly seeking out: beautiful hinterlands, for his retired customers. But there had to be reasonable transport access. That was the beauty of this site. Because of the standing stones and busloads of tourists, the road from Stornoway and its hospital and amenities was a pretty decent one and there was a thriving community at Breasclete. His people would soon feel at home. The plane was turning now,

100

the sunlight whirling to the rear of the plane. A wide blue expanse of water below, probably the Firth of Lorn.

He studied the notes he had collected about the Reverend McInnes. He was eighty-six, he noted. Good, that probably meant he was having to leave for a care home somewhere. On the other hand, maybe it meant he would be more reluctant to leave. Ah, his wife had recently died, he read. Jean. Must remember the name. It was what Jean wanted. Time to go. Could he use that, implying he had known her? No, probably not. He would have to play it by ear. At the end of the day, the old man *had* put the place up for sale. All that was to be decided was the price and he had a very clear idea what the place was worth and what he was going to pay for it. The going rate was probably a lot less than the Rev McInnes thought. He sniffed. The stout lady in the seat in front had bathed in perfume of an overpoweringly fruity kind. The plane reeked of it.

The deck crew were bringing complimentary coffee. Yes, he decided, they were over Morvern or Moidart, or Ardnamurchan probably. He couldn't remember which was which. Complete wilderness, really. None of his people would want to be there. Two hours to wait for an ambulance? No way. As he sipped his coffee, he decided to invent a Lewis ancestor. There was that doorman at the Cromwell Club, old Hamish McGillivray, he had a son, be about my own age, Gallimont thought. Lived somewhere down south. He could say he knew him, better still, he could *be* him. Mind you, these people in the islands knew everybody who'd ever been there and this bod was a minister. Better not. Play it straight. He glanced down. Good, that was the Minch, at last. Ten minutes to landing.

101

CHAPTER TWELVE

Leadbetter led Morton down into the noisy print room where the mighty Goss Universal 70 web offset printing machines were running out the next day's paper. The six full-time staff who handled the Goss and the Agfa pre-press set-up were up in the staff canteen having a tea break. There were no windows in the printing room. Morton had been here many times before although he rarely lingered due to the incessant racketing noise of the machines printing, cutting, folding, trimming and stacking, on two floors, like a benevolent giant.

Leadbetter touched his sleeve and grinned. 'I bet you think I've gone gyte, eh? Auld Hugh's going doowally? Na, I'm aware of the Cowgate side entrance. Don't worry, this is something you're not aware of.'

Morton shrugged. 'Right, that's what I was thinking.'

'No, this is only known to me and a handful of others.' He grinned and pointed downwards with his thumb. This building is very old, Willie, 18th century or even earlier. It used to be a tanning works and there was a warehouse where Niddry Street South is now, but the Council widened the main road see, when the South Bridge was built. It's a huge viaduct really, had nineteen arches spanning over the Cowgate Valley, so the clever buggers reused an old tunnel to allow them to pass under the road from the tannery to the warehouse. It's pretty manky, though, Willie, and I've never been more than a few steps inside myself, but I'm told it's in working order. The city architect's department sent some people in a few years ago.'

'Bloody hell. I'd better get a torch. How do I get out at the other end?

'Key,' Leadbetter said. 'A whacking big one.' He grinned. 'One you will definitely not lose. And I've got a torch for you. Come on.'

He led the Morton into the printer's store, which was filled with huge ink cylinders and mighty rolls of white paper on axles like giant toilet rolls, sitting on wheeled trolleys. He pointed to a wooden panel at the back. He pushed it and it swung open easily. At once there was a cold musty breeze.

'Good lord!' Morton swore. 'It's unbelievable. It's much wider than I would have imagined.'

'Aye, isn't it? Built to allow donkeys to carry up the hides,' Leadbetter said, switching on his torch. 'As I believe anyway. I'm going to come down at least part of the way with you. Just tae see what it's like.'

'Well, brilliant,' Morton said.

'I think that's only fair.'

'In which case, after you. Oh, where's the key?'

'I have it here.' The editor produced a huge, rusty mortice key, fully a foot long, from a hook on the inside of the door. 'Can you believe the size of this thing?

They stared at it in wonder. 'Fuck me,' Morton exclaimed. 'That is one serious key!'

'Right, get your torch on. Let's see what this tunnel is like. Pull the door behind you.' And they entered, or rather, stepped down, into the tunnel.

Everything panned out just as Gallimont had planned. The plane landed at the small airport close to the dunes and the sea, a mile out of the town, and the CarHire Hebrides vehicle was waiting for him. A white Vauxhall Corsa. It was a bright and sunny day on the Western Isles and soon he was driving south on the A859 to Leurbost to join the west road for Callanish. The quality of the sunlight was extraordinary, he thought, almost tropical somehow and made the marram grasses waving in the wind look exotic, even Caribbean. Four miles down, he turned off onto the main A858 and eight miles later, passed the signs for Callanish. It was only two miles further, according to the satnav. It took him through the hamlet of Breasclete and about half a mile further towards the Dun Carloway Broch, with a view of Little Loch Roag and the island of Great Bernera, according to the satnav. He knew the views and the birds, the diverse wildlife here, were the main attraction for his customers. He saw the manse, and behind it the church, a low, grey-stone mass on a small hillock and the stone walls of another structure, heading down to the rocky inlet and the sea. 'You have arrived at your destination,' the satnav told him unnecessarily. He was glad it was in English and wondered idly if they had Gaelic versions.

He parked off the road and put his coat on and took out the inner folder from his file. The rest would stay safely in his car. Wouldn't do to let the old man see that! As he picked his way up the stony track to the manse and the even smaller church, he saw the church was roofless. Even better – the price would be lower. He also noted gravestones, or what might be gravestones, very old and very dilapidated. Blast! That could prove tricky. But they didn't look too extensive. The builders could work around them, somehow.

He knocked on the door and stood waiting. There was no reply. He began to stress. What if the old man had forgotten the date? What if he had been taken ill? He heard the slow lash of the waves on the rocks. The sunlight was strong and somehow brighter here. Everything he could see – stones, walls, machair grass – seemed to be bathed or blanched by it. It was extraordinary. *Tropical* was the only word he could think of to describe it. Of course, it got the Gulf Stream up here. He knocked again. He wasn't in. The old bastard! He'd come 200 miles and the old man had snubbed him. Then he had an idea. He walked around the gable end and there he was, the old man, in shirtsleeves, digging or turning over the sandy soil on his vegetable patch, or whatever it was. Christ! Did he not know he was leaving? And he must be deaf. Careful, Gallimont thought, better not spring out and give him a heart attack, at least, not yet! He grinned.

'Excuse me.'

'Och, it's yourself arriving.'

'Reverend McInnes, I presume?'

'Well, the very same.'

Two hundred miles south, Colin Hardwick and Carol Harker sat side by side staring at their monitors. 'What do you think, Carol?'

'He's a freelance. Okay, he works often for the *Standard,* but I would imagine that usually takes the form of emailing in his work and perhaps the occasional visit, but he's been in there, for two hours. It seems odd.'

'I agree. Question is, should we report it? We still have Javid and Dennis in situ and direct camera surveillance of both entrances. Perhaps he's rumbled us and is planning to stay the night in there?'

'We can't go barging in there anyway.'

'No. I wouldn't think they'd authorise that,' Hardwick said thoughtfully. 'And I'm beginning to wonder if Morton is our man. Maybe we should get back to basics? There were several other matches in the Edinburgh and Lothians area. Maybe we should look at them, make sure we've not made a mistake.'

'If we do that, we'd better not let Millbank know till we've evaluated that possibility.'

'I agree. It's just that, as you know, sometimes facial recognition technology can fuck up. Create false acceptances. After all it's not quite able yet to scan in real time, there's always a bit of a delay. That can lead to error. As you know, I'm sure, Carol.' He looked up at her, smiling.

'Yes, so I've heard, Colin.'

'Also where you're patching between lots of different CCTV networks, like we've been doing, there can be function creep, you know, where the biometrics seem to be convergent but have got a bit mixed up. The system thinks it's got the right person because it's confused what it's looking for. I mean some of the biometric points get skipped over somehow.'

Carol smiled. 'Yes, Colin, I've heard about that too. But in this case, I'm pretty sure. I mean, the fact that Morton is already known to us. His connection with a well-known subversive, Professor McKechnie, is pretty conclusive. We know he was in London at the right time.'

Colin nodded. 'On balance, yes, you're right. But something about this is bugging me.' He frowned.

'I think it's time we ate, don't you? That Italian place in the plaza is apparently quite good. Come on!' She got up and smoothed her blouse. 'Even James Bond needs to eat sometime. And Jane Bond too.'

Negotiations with the old man at Breasclete had been more difficult than expected. First there had been endless questions about the background of Ardbeag Holdings. He had wanted

106

to know how they had come by the name and if they truly were a Gaelic company. Gallimont had found his patience wearing thin. And then there had been the arrival of his nephew. Or a man calling himself his nephew. If a name like Murdo Gilleasbuig McLeod could actually be real. And a whole farce had ensued about the sale of the croft and the scale of the proposed development.

The newcomer had insisted they walk down to the bottom of the croft to the machair, almost on to the rocks, purportedly to 'get a sense of the historic scale of it' and between the two of them it was as if they were exorcising the entire history of the place, while he stood by, smiling politely as they conversed in Gaelic, no doubt discussing him. And this Murdo was playing a game with him, he felt, encouraging the old man to prevaricate and ask endless questions, caveats. Every time he produced the documents, there was something else 'most urgent' to consider. He saw the hour go by on his watch, imagined the 4 p.m. plane taking off without him on it. And this Murdo, who was 'friends with someone on the Council' but wouldn't say who, seemed to have come along just to frustrate the signing of the deal. He tried to close the deal several times but by 5 p.m. he was no further forward.

And then an odd thing happened. A young woman arrived. He didn't see her arrive, but suddenly she was there with them in the vegetable garden and she had a camera.

'Och, Eilish is from *The Stornoway Gazette*, Mr Gray,' Murdo told him. 'Ye'll no mind if we have a wee photo taken?'

Of course he bloody minded! But he couldn't easily refuse and it was done. A picture of him, masquerading as Philip Gray of Ardbeag Holdings, was out there. But *The Stornoway Gazette*? Could he have it stopped? The readership was

107

probably only a couple of hundred, including the sheep and sheepdogs. He wouldn't mention the picture in his daily report. Maybe it was the sort of thing that happened here. A man from the mainland coming to speak to a local minister about the sale of a miserable piece of scrub land was probably front page news here.

As Eilish and Murdo took their leave, and from the way they were with each other he guessed they were fond, as the phrase went, he was thinking fast.

'Actually, I'll have to be getting back, myself,' he said. 'Not needing a lift to Stornoway, are you?'

Eilish glanced at him with a definite look of disfavour that he found strange. 'Ach no, I have my car here.' She smiled coldly. 'That's how I got here. In case you thought I came by horse.'

Gallimont stuttered. 'Oh, of course not. Look, I think I will have to defer discussions on this for another day. There are still too many,' he coughed, 'unexpected and unresolved, issues. I thought things were further along than they seem to be.'

'I was thinking the very same myself,' said the old man. 'I will be having the confabulation with our Member of Parliament, Mr Angus Brendan, to see what he thinks himself.' He straightened up, holding his sore back. 'So that when we meet again, we can resume our discussion with less unploughed ground between us.'

And that was where it was left. No signature, no deal, no verbal agreement, nothing achieved. Two and a half hours of tosh about heritage and preserving the Gaelic language and the 'generations to come after us', as if that wasn't the same everywhere. So he got in his hired car and drove back to Stornoway, cursing the old man and Murdo with every mile and when he arrived at the airport, all was ominously quiet. There were no more flights to Edinburgh until the morning. In the end, he'd returned the hire car and got a taxi to a small hotel at the harbour, the Royal Hotel. He hated having his time wasted and felt certain he would not be coming back to Breasclete. There were other easier developments to exploit. But he had a sneaky feeling that he had been tricked in some way, although he couldn't put his finger on it. And Stornoway was grey and undistinguished, like a battered Council Estate and it stank of fish.

The team had reassembled at 9 a.m. in the modern offices of DTI Operations & Investigations in the New Waverley office, refreshed after a night's sleep. For the first time, they met the two permanent staff, Crispin Hayes, a bespectacled public schoolboy, a Harry Potter lookalike, Hardwick thought. But pleasant and with excellent manners. Very young though.

Kirsty Haldane however, was an athletic-looking redhead in a grey skirt suit and white frilly blouse. Hardwick wondered about her age. Twenty-three? He noticed that Hayes deferred to her on almost everything and he found that he was smiling as they all helped themselves to coffee.

'As far as it goes,' Dennis Cuthbert said, leaning back in the beige corduroy sofa, 'and I know it's subjective and not for noting down anywhere, but I found Gallimont to be a pompous ass, an absolute total uppity twerp.'

Javid Norrow smiled. 'Yeah, me too.'

Carol Harker shook her head. 'Boys, the thing is, he's back at work while Morton is still at large. That's the issue for today, right, Colin?'

Hardwick tore his eyes away from Kirsty Haldane's face. 'Um, yup, that's today's job. Get a hold of Morton. Can't be hard. Chances are he's still in Edinburgh.'

Crispin Hayes put down his coffee cup. 'Right, we'll leave you to it. Kirsty?' He began to move through to the outer office.

'Okay.' Kirsty smiled at them all, Haldane knew, but it felt as if her smile was mainly for him. The door closed behind them and he felt the mantle of responsibility once again descend upon him.

'Okay, team. Assignments.' He chuckled, 'But first, a word from the team leader.'

They took their places for the HD video conference. The system used 128-bit AES encryption which meant that its content was scrambled over the internet and then decoded at either end without any significant latency, or time-lag. It was the essential tool of the SIS, virtually hacker-proof. And they used, as back-up, an ongoing counter-espionage programme on all video-conferencing content to ensure no unauthorised 'check-ins' had occurred. The screen saver whirled aside and revealed Commander Smyth sitting alongside Desmond Thorpe and he was the first to speak.

'Listen up,' Smyth instructed. 'A further development we've only just learned about, deepens the shit crisis we're already in. The facts are, based on several reports we've just obtained, that our target was 100 miles away in Galloway on Monday talking to people listed on the data file he stole. I don't think I have to spell out how serious this is.'

Carol and Colin looked at each other incredulously. Javid, sitting behind them, sought clarification. 'So he – the target – has managed to impersonate Philip Gallimont *again*?'

Smyth was undeniably irritated. 'That's what it comes to. Twice. This is not the amateur our intelligence analysts suggested. He is able to act with impunity and evade us at will. It is vitally important that he be stopped. God knows what he will do next.'

Carol said: 'What we need is a proper analysis and evaluation of what he has, what we think he has and whether it could be published, I mean coherently, as a story. He has information, but is it publishable?'

'Good point, Carol,' muttered Colin. 'He's been working closely with one paper, the *Scottish Standard* and it's reasonable to expect that if he's writing something, it will be for them, exclusively. He's their man.'

Smyth came back: 'Yes, we can't be sure though. If we come down hard on that paper, Morton will then feel free to offer it elsewhere. I'll get our Analysis boys onto it, Carol, that's something we can do, but in the meantime, the best thing is to get hold of the rogue, preferably with all his stuff, and take him out of circulation. Bring him in. Keep him there and question him properly. Find out what he knows and what he plans to do with what he knows. That's top priority.'

'Agreed,' Cuthbert said, winking at Colin Hardwick. 'We'll pull out all the stops. We think he's still in Edinburgh and so we'll have him by the end of play today.'

'Absolutely,' Hardwick agreed, nodding.

'Good,' Smyth said. 'Now, I've been in contact with Roger about getting Home Office approval to raid the *Standard*, on the grounds of stolen material that will prejudice national security, but as you can imagine I want to hold off on that until it's absolutely necessary and you know why.'

Hardwick said: 'Yes, there's a certain amount of tension already up here as it is.'

'Yes, but that's not quite it,' Smyth told him sharply. 'The public are less tolerant these days of raids on newspapers. It creates waves, causes problems for a long time afterwards. We simply don't like to do it. But if we have to, we will.'

'Okay. Thanks,' Hardwick terminated the call and the screen saver whirled back into position. He stood up and turned to his team. 'Assignments. Carol and Javid, trawl the known locations: home, his parent's house, the *Standard*, Professor McKechnie, the other friends. Intercept any WiFi activity you can, and await special instructions as and when, okay?'

'Okay,' Carol smiled. 'You drive, Javid, if you don't mind.'

'Cool.'

'Dennis, can you man the Ops Room today? Maintain the FR scan and liaise with Desmond.'

'Sounds fine to me.'

'And I'll take the second vehicle, and Kirsty, who has good local knowledge, follow up on the other names on the list.' He noticed Dennis was avoiding his eye and Carol was faintly smirking. Oh, well, privileges of rank.

CHAPTER THIRTEEN

What had most surprised Morton about the tunnel was the warmth. It was dry and smelt quite pleasantly of clean antiseptic soil and there was surprisingly little dust. After the initial descent it had levelled out and Morton could see that it extended an amazing distance straight ahead. It was quite wide, not wide enough to extend his arms fully, but he imagined laden donkeys in a long line making the journey many times a day from warehouse to tannery.

'Well, Willie, nae point in me going any further,' Leadbetter decided after about twenty yards. 'Looks good enough. Keep the key safe. I'm not sure what it'll be like at the other end. The architects didn't say if it was a viable entrance.' He chuckled, 'I suppose they were just more interested in the antiquity of the thing. There's probably loads of these kind of things about, but I can imagine they dinna want the public to get tae hear of them. They'd affect the income of the Edinburgh Dungeons tour guides! Anyway, good luck.' He turned back, his torch flashing up onto his black and white face and his weird, beard-muffled grin. 'Watch oot fur the ghouls!' He cackled lugubriously.

'Very funny!' Morton said. 'Anyway, if this gets me out, I might be able to come and go as required.'

'Yeah, keep in touch by WhatsApp. Okay, best of luck.'

'Bye.'

Then he was alone, walking forward, stepping over occasional lumps of detritus and several times what looked like corpses of rodents, long-dead, fully ossified. Soon the tunnel was climbing steadily and there was the door. The city architects had covered it with yellow and white sticky tape. Warning. Dangerous Drop. Do Not Enter. He could feel fresh air. Could that really be true? There was a faint spot of light, when he switched off his torch. The keyhole. He peered through but all he could see was a stone wall beyond.

He inserted the huge rusty key and turned. It was stiff but he exerted pressure and felt it give. He pulled the door to him and peered around it. It was in a derelict building. He was at street level, he judged, but the floors and ceilings had been removed. It was a four-storey building at least, but it no longer had floors and there was a drop of... he peered down... almost twenty feet to the rubble and earth of what had been a cellar floor. There was a piece of ancient rope on a hook at his feet. He reached down and pulled it up, and leaned over and saw a ladder attached to the end of it.

He pulled the ladder and propped it and carefully checked it was secure at ground level then stepped on to it and pulled the door behind him, locked it and tossed the key to the ground. It clattered on concrete. He descended gingerly into the cold, damp-smelling cellar.

Morton carefully laid the ladder flat by the wall and took out his torch and examined the cellar. It was long disused and a green slime, gleaming in the torchlight, revealed water penetration. At the far end, soil and rubble and spoil had been mounded to provide a walkway over the remnants of concrete foundations and demolished brick walls. He saw shoeprints in the soil. Probably the city architects. Who else would be creeping about around here? So, he reasoned, there must be a way out.

It took him a few minutes of scrambling about in the damp, uneven terrain to find his way in the derelict building. Then he saw daylight outlining the frame of the door and

114

made for it. The ground was uneven but had once been flat. He had no idea where he would come out. He came up to the door and saw that it was steel or iron. There seemed to be no lock. Eventually, he discovered a small catch halfway down on one side. He pressed it. Nothing happened. He held it down with all his strength and felt it start to release. The heavy door creaked open. Daylight flooded in. He was in a quiet, sloping side street. He stepped out and the door swung back behind him and clicked. He examined the front of it, grey painted. No sign of a lock or the catch. It opened from the inside. There was no indication of what lay behind it. He saw that he was on a steeply sloping alley, blind at the top to his right and it was laid in bricks or paving stones, not tarmac. At the bottom he could see the Cowgate. It was Niddry Street South. And he had been here before. There was a club he'd visited, years ago.

There were no pedestrians, although he could see cars passing along the Cowgate. He was free to go and glad to get back to the 21st century. He descended the lane and saw on his left, the club he had been to. The Caves. He read its brass plaque: *He who is without mathematics shall not enter.* And underneath, the Scots translation: *Nae eejits.* Yes, he'd been there. Interesting place. He noted the street had two names, the other was Whisky Row.

He crossed the narrow Cowgate to the pavement on the north side and began to walk east as he had been instructed. After a couple of minutes, a small car pulled in to the kerb. He peered in. Alasdair. He got in, and Alasdair drove off, after flipping down his sunshade.

'Nice one, chum,' Alasdair said. 'Put this hat on and lean back, behind the sunshade.'

115

Morton looked at the hat. It was a nondescript black beanie. He sniffed it and grimaced. 'Well, if I must.'

'Now, let's find this pal of yours. She disnae ken we're coming, I take it?'

Morton grunted. 'I couldn't use my phone and I don't think she's on WhatsApp. She might not even be home. I've never been there myself, you know. On the other hand, she could hit the roof. She's just a friend, it's a bit of a liberty.'

'Well, we'll just have to give it our best shot. We need to get you out of circulation for a while. Now, Muirhouse, was it?'

'Yes, off Marine Drive,' Morton told him. 'Go round by West Granton Road.'

'I've a rough idea. I'll have to go down round Dynamic Earth the now and then up Abbeyhill to London Road, and then mebbe Leith Walk. Long way round. Pity, we've no satnav in this.'

'Just as well, we'd be tracked for sure,' Morton said.

'Aye, suppose.'

'I thought it'd be the old van,' Morton said.

'Oh no, they'd have clocked that, even though we changed the plates,'

'Ah. Right, good idea. Is that legal?'

Alasdair looked at him oddly, frowned. 'Naw.'

Twenty minutes later, they had reached the roundabout at the start of Marine Drive that separated Pilton from Muirhouse, with large new housing blocks on the right.

'Okay, slowly now,' Morton instructed. 'We're taking the next on the right. Should be West Shore Road. Should be going uphill.'

'There,' said Alasdair. 'You're not wrong, chum. Never been here before, me. Trees. Looks like a wood coming up.'

'That's right. She's second house on the left.'

Alasdair drove slowly upwards in the shade between thick trees. As they breasted the hill, they could see the wide Firth of Forth through gaps, and some rocks at the shore. 'Nice area. Let's hope she's in.'

Morton felt anxiety at the thought of arriving unannounced and throwing himself on the mercy of Celia Thornton. 'This is it, he said. 'Pilton Mains. It's quite a long driveway. Go up.'

'Jeezo!' Alasdair muttered. 'Stately pile? It's a bloody castle!' He parked in front of the grand portico. 'Okay, Willie, ring the bell. Summon the butler, or whatever they do hereabouts.'

As Willie walked over to the front door, he could see Pilton Mains was perched among ancient trees on a hill above a wide recreation area, with a view of Cramond Island, and beyond, miles of water; the wide expanse of the Forth estuary and beyond that, the towns of Fife. The city felt far away. As he knocked he realised how little he really knew about Celia even though he'd known her for years. They were acquaintances really, not even friends. Her brother had been two years older than her, four years older than Morton, the captain of the First XV. Merchant banker now. He looked through the engraved glass of the inner door, and pulled the mighty lion's paw bell handle again. He could hear it jangling throughout the ground floor. He felt, rather than saw movement, a shifting of shadows and Celia appeared. She was wearing green dungarees, a wax jacket and black wellies, not to mention a pink bush hat. Her hair was tied back and her face was pale, un-made-up.

117

'Cripes, crivvens and help ma boab!' she exclaimed, laughing. 'Look who it is? William James Morton! What on earth are you doing here?'

'Celia, um… it's quite a long story.'

'Well, Willie, you'd better come in. Oh, and who's this hunky fellow?'

'I'm Alasdair, Mrs…' He shook her hand. 'We're sort of a pair at the moment. We need your help.'

'Goodness, you wait years for a man, and two come along. And you need my *help*? How intriguing. Do come in, it's a bit of a mess at the moment.'

'Right, thanks.'

Willie and Alasdair followed her through a large hall into a green-tiled room at the north of the house which was a kitchen-dining room. Willie noted a large window facing the wide Firth. At the centre of the room was a majestic red Aga with a black lum of its own. There was a wonderful smell of cooking and onions. It was a comfortable busy space, leeks and potatoes in a basket on the marble-topped table. An industrial-sized steel sink, a large oval dining table with six chairs. Nearby sat a large Labrador, which briefly raised its head to look at them then sank back with a snuffle into its heat-induced lethargy.

'Sit yourselves down, boys. I wasn't expecting visitors so I'll just be back in a second. There's coffee on the go. Help yourself. Milk in the fridge, biscuits in the tin.' She disappeared.

'You didn't tell me she was so good-looking,' Alasdair said. 'And no husband on the go?'

'I don't think so. I think she *was* married. I don't know.'

'Well she's bonny. I might marry her myself.' He grinned at Morton. 'Since you're already spoken for.'

'She's a Tory,' Morton said. 'Well, used to be.'

Alasdair chortled. 'That makes her human. We all have faults. Politics is not so important when it comes to affairs of the heart, I find anyway.'

Celia bustled in again, completely changed, in a blue chambray shirt, tight faded jeans and white moccasins. The Labrador got up eagerly and came forward, tail wagging. Celia had put on some lipstick and her hair was brushed and hung loose around her shoulders. Morton saw Alasdair's jaw hanging slack and frowned angrily at him.

'Got coffee? Good. Another sultana biscuit? They're homemade. Now, let's have the story, boys. Fire away.' She leaned against the Aga, folded her arms and looked down at them, smiling expectantly.

'Well...' Willie cleared his throat. Where to begin? 'It all started with the Philip Gallimont thing, you remember? My look-alike?'

'Of course. Were you able to contact him?'

'Not quite.'

'Oh, okay, I won't interrupt... tell me the story. Are you wanting a top-up?'

'Yes, please, Ms Thornton.'

'Och, goodness, it's Celia. And you're Alasdair? With a d?'

'With a d. What's the doggie's name?'

'Digby. Sit.'

The Labrador, who was of robust size, sat on its haunches looking up at her, clearly expecting food. Alasdair rubbed its head and ears.

'Anyway, I'm working on a story to do with him, Gallimont,' Morton said, 'and I've got into trouble with the authorities somehow.'

'Oh, Willie, I like this story. And how does Alasdair fit into this? Is he your bodyguard?'

Alasdair looked up. 'I'm just a heating engineer!'

'Hmn, useful man to know.'

Morton nodded. 'Alasdair and others are helping me. But when I said the *authorities*, it's not the police, it's some kind of spooks, MI5 types. They are trying to stop me running my story, although I'm not sure if there even is a story, as yet.'

'All very cloak and dagger. And you want to stay here for a few days?'

Morton reddened. 'Well, yes, if that's possible?'

Celia clapped her hands together. 'Possible? There's heaps of rooms. I have damp in some of them and dry rot too, but there's a couple of spare bedrooms that are comfortable enough. No-one will bother you here. Stay as long as you like. No, really, it's rather exciting! Anyway, the soup's nearly ready if you are interested. Onion and leek.'

Alasdair beamed. 'Celia, you are an absolute darling!' he burst out.

And Morton was mystified to see her blush ever so slightly, before she pinned on an apron and began to stir the soup.

CHAPTER FOURTEEN

Emily kept glancing up at the clock in the room on the tenth floor of David Hume Tower, while the last few minutes of her supervision ticked away. Both of her MPhil students were competent but lacked overall familiarity with their subject. It was as if they knew it all but lacked empathy. They were looking at it in a detached manner as if it was a beetle pinned to a corkboard, not as if it meant anything to them. Polite but distant. There needed to be human warmth. She wondered about them and how well they integrated with the rest of the students. They hadn't volunteered to do any teaching of the undergraduate classes. Maybe they were waiting for her to suggest it? Other MPhil candidates had practically bitten her arm off for a few paid hours here and there.

Finally, she was able to see things to a conclusion. It'd be a month before she saw Jeng or Dolores again. The room was quiet as she heard them outside waiting for the lift. She glanced at her watch. The clock was three minutes fast. She heard the lift arrive and depart. There was a light knock on the door. Luke. She waved him in. He looked just like any student with his satchel and his leather jacket. Still fresh-faced and youthful, his hair needed the attentions of a barber. She remembered him as a student, just a few years before. *Quite brilliant*, his IT lecturers had said.

'Hello, Emily. Forgive this intrusion.' He glanced around at the books and papers on her desk in an empty room and looked out of the window. Edinburgh spread before him in the afternoon mist. 'Cerberus insisted I come in person.

121

We've something to arrange. First, I need to bring you up to date.'

'Right.' She glanced at her watch. 'I've a departmental meeting in half an hour.'

'Oh, I won't take ten minutes. Now, the laptop is off, and your phone?'

'No, I'll...' She closed the laptop lid. 'Left the phone downstairs, as usual. Is it really necessary, all this switching off?'

Luke's face was grave. 'Oh yes! As you'll hear.'

Emily adjusted the position of her spectacles. 'You said it was something about my friend WM? Am I to assume that's Willie?'

Luke put his finger to his lips and examined the coffee percolator, the projector, the DVD player and checked the laptop was off. He felt under the lamp socket behind her desk.

Finally, he straightened up. 'Okay,' he smiled. 'And this is not your usual room?'

She watched him, frowning slightly. 'Normally I see students in my own room downstairs.'

He sat down opposite her and took out an envelope from his jacket pocket. 'Okay, an update. Your friend and ours, Willie Morton, is in a safe location but he can't use his phone or laptop or send messages. Our colleague who's with him can communicate with us by fully encrypted messaging, WhatsApp. Things have taken a serious turn, you see. We believe Morton's in danger.'

'Oh! Poor Willie!' Emily expressed concern. 'Is there anything we can do? Where is he?'

'He is safe for the moment. Which is where you come in, if you will. We need your help. We want you to put a message out there, indirectly, to MI5.'

'Right?' Emily frowned. 'How?'

'The data file Willie obtained,' Luke told her, 'is now beyond their reach and there are many copies and many people who now have access to it. Once they – the spooks – realise he's no longer in sole possession, he should be out of danger, you see.'

'Yes, I see.' Professor McKechnie sat back and looked at him. 'Good grief, poor Willie. It's come to this that journalists in Scotland cannot pursue a story without MI5 breathing down their necks. It's intolerable!'

'That's good,' Luke said, 'righteous indignation. Use that.' He slipped the envelope over to her. 'Here's the briefing from Cerberus – what we need to get out there. Carefully worded as you can see. We're going to accuse the UK Government straight out, even though we suspect it's this rogue group, GB13 behind it. We don't yet know how they join up, whether the funding comes from Government or from some private fund.'

Emily opened the envelope. 'I was worrying about him. I'm certainly happy to help out, if I can.' She unfolded the single typed page inside and read it quickly. 'I see. You want me to break Willie's story on STV? Is there no other way? Won't he be a bit miffed? I imagine other papers will then run the story, *his* story.'

'True, but he can't get it published. What he's got won't stand up at the moment, and we have extra material he doesn't have. Anyway, you're only going to raise the alarm, not give away enough for the public to realise what's going on. So we – the media – can have a hook to hang the story on, if that makes any sense. And in a way that keeps Morton safe.'

'Might work.' Emily reread the text. 'Leave it with me. I'll contact *Scotland Tonight* right away, get that ball rolling. I can probably get on tonight if I'm quick.'

'Good. And there's an emergency meeting this evening too. Usual venue, 11 p.m.'

She frowned. 'The timing will be tight, I should make it back from the studio in time, if I get them to pre-record a couple of hours earlier than usual. We'll see.' She looked up at Luke. 'And Willie will be there?'

Luke stood up. 'Oh no. That wouldn't be… and we can't risk it anyway. Not till you've done your stuff. Righteous indignation and outrage. There's plenty of other stuff happening, but that'll keep till this evening. I'd better be off.'

Colin Hardwick and Kirsty Haldane sat in the black Mondeo hallway up Buccleuch Street within sight of the entrance to David Hume Tower. They were using a laptop to intercept email traffic in the vicinity, equipment interference as the manual described it, though more colloquially known as a 'drive-by download'. They had a working range of thirty to forty yards. Carol Harker and Javid Norrow were outside Morton's parents' home in Merchiston Crescent and Dennis Cuthbert was in the ops room monitoring several temporary cameras that'd been installed outside Morton's flat and across the street from the *Standard* building.

'Doesn't seem that long since I was a student, myself,' Kirsty mused, tucking a stray lock behind her ear.'

'Here? Edinburgh?'

'No, Glasgow. Computer Science.'

'My field too,' Hardwick told her. 'Although I was an Arts man, originally. You must have come into contact with a lot of radical types there. In Glasgow, I mean?'

Kirsty laughed, a melodious sound, he thought.

'How long have you been in the service now?' he asked her.

'Coming up for two years, Colin. I was recruited at the Uni actually. My professor had connections, he set it up. After the general service induction, I was off to the Middle East more or less straightaway.'

'Baptism of fire? This was Six, then?'

She smiled at him. 'Something like that, Colin. Yes, then I was transferred. But it's strange, working in your own backyard.'

'How do you mean, Kirsty?'

She thought for a minute and took a deep breath. 'Well, isn't this a little odd, Colin? I mean we're not exactly dealing with terrorists here, are we? These are ordinary people, not any kind of extremists.'

'That thought had occurred to me a few times during the last few days. Chasing journalists… It's not exactly *Al-Qaeda*.' He sniffed. 'But we do what we're told.'

'Of course, Colin, but if Scotland were to become Independent, they might set up their own Intelligence Services.'

He smiled warmly at her. 'Well, you'd be sure of promotion then. Oh! There's a known face – look – leather jacket crossing the street, four o'clock. Luke Sangster. Come on, let's get moving. He's heading towards the Library or the Meadows. We need to turn the car.'

Ensconced in the large room Celia referred to as her library, with the magnificent view of the Birnie Rocks, the sea and the Fife coast beyond, Morton had worked up the story of his escapades while impersonating Philip Gallimont, writing it in a deliberately cloak and dagger style reminiscent of John Buchan's *The 39 Steps*: the pursuit leading him from Chuffy's and the sinister GB13 group to Coldstream, trying to overhear dinner jacketed guests at the Hirsel, then out into the wilds of Galloway – very much as in the plot of Buchan's perennial thriller, paraphrasing his interviews with the residents of Dumfries and Galloway and what they had said. The working title was: 'Is UK Government relocating No Voters to Scotland?' He hoped Hugh could think up something better. It was as strong and powerful as he could make it, though he wished he could have got some UK Government rebuttal, even a comment from a Scottish Government spokesperson. Maybe Hugh would add that in. Anyway, it was gone, posted to Hugh on a small USB stick, by Celia on her way to the supermarket. Alasdair had gone with her and he was amused by that – they seemed to be getting on very well, had a jokey kind of relationship, not exactly flirting but it took the pressure off him. Alasdair was also planning to have an exchange of messages with his colleagues. Morton felt a bit left out. He just had to sit and wait.

Although STV's five-nights-a-week current affairs magazine programme was broadcast from 10.30 to 11.30 as if live, segments were pre-recorded beforehand, some just ten minutes ahead of real time, others several hours in advance. Emily was a strong supporter of the programme as opposed to the higher-budget competitors on the BBC, which she privately referred to as 'Biased British Conservatives'. She'd been asked to appear on the BBC several times during the Referendum and each time had become embroiled in ridiculous spats, set up deliberately, in her opinion, to smear her credibility as a Yes-supporting academic. *Scotland Tonight*, though quite low-budget, home-grown and heavily featuring local accents was helmed by a male and female presenter who played up the chattiness as if to shake off the 'boring politics' tag and convince browsing viewers they were all about vital urgent *new* news.

As Emily pushed through the swing doors and walked in to the small, ultra-modern reception area of STV Studios at Fountainbridge, she was intercepted by the purple-and-blue-haired Kate Bridie, one of the production administrators.

'Professor McKechnie,' she cooed, coming forward with a big smile for the customarily effusive hug and kiss on both cheeks affected by media folk. 'I wasn't aware you were coming in.'

Emily smiled faintly and muttered something unintelligible. It was not beyond the bounds of possibility that Kate Bridie was a spy of some sort.

'If I can help in anyway? Is it Sally you're in for?'

Emily smiled. 'Thank you, Kate, very kind of you. It's just a brief... meeting. All set up. Nothing to worry about.'

'Okay, if you're absolutely sure.' Frowning, she turned to the poor reception girl and as if to exert her authority, quite sharply said: 'Perhaps the Professor would like a coffee?' and she went out.

'No, no thanks!' Emily called to the girl who was already at the coffee machine. 'By the way can you let Simon know I'm here, thank you.'

She sat down to wait. The STV *News at Six* was on, muted, with subtitles. David Cameron's troubles with bolshie Tory Eurosceptics. Boris Johnson acting like a big chump who'd somehow lost his school cap.

Simon Fane appeared, in shirt sleeves, his sandy hair sticking up, a little red-faced and flustered. 'Emily! Great!' He kissed her on both cheeks. 'Come ye through.' He led her through into a windowless, empty pinewood-lined studio with green carpeting that smelt new. They sat side by side on a carpeted bench at the side of the room. The interview set-up was on standby, cameras at two angles focusing on a pair of chairs with a large colour photograph of central Edinburgh at night behind. 'Firstly thanks for coming in,' he said.

Emily smiled. It was an interview she'd pushed for.

He tucked one leg under another and leaned back, smiling. 'Okay, so, you've got something for us, an additional one-to-one segment.' He put on a mock-baffled look. 'That we don't know anything about. Help!'

'Don't worry, Simon, this is kosher,' Emily reassured him. 'It will run fine. You're getting this on an exclusive basis, a wee scoop for you.' She took out a page from her file. 'Here's the questions you need to ask and here's notes for your wee preamble to camera. Don't...' she paused, smiling, and laid an admonitory hand on his shirt sleeve. 'Don't deviate from the script. And I'm going to be careful with my answers too. If this goes fine, the papers tomorrow will pick it up and you'll get a spin-off for your news team tomorrow and we'll see where it goes from there.'

As Simon scrutinised the page, the door open soundlessly and Sally McElhone beamed in at them, looking mischievous. 'Oh, hello, hello!'

The bubbly blonde was Simon's co-host on *Scotland Tonight* and her manner and make-up made her seem a little lightweight, which was unfair, Emily thought. Funny to think she was the daughter-in-law of former SNP Leader Donald Stevenson. It was just her cheery style, Emily decided. Nothing wrong with that. Her heart was in the right place. Women were under such scrutiny which their male colleagues were not. Just because she wore red lipstick…

'What are you two plotting?' Sally McElhone demanded with a lugubrious grin.

Simon cleared his throat. 'Ah, Sally, we've an additional segment now for this evening, but I'll handle it. Don't worry, that'll give you another five minutes for your shoppers' survey.'

Sally pulled a face. 'But that's already been edited and cut to eight minutes. I know, we could squeeze in that piece from ITV about Boris getting stuck up a tree… Seen it, Emily? It's hilarious!' She began to mime the Mayor of London climbing like a dysfunctional panda…

'Go away, darling!' Simon said, gently. 'We're busy. I believe there's a bottle of sherry in Studio A… '

'Ooh! You villain!' Sally exploded. 'You know fine there isn't! Anybody would think you wanted rid of me.'

'Now where were we?' Simon said, a little discomfited, once Sally had gone, although he couldn't have seen Sally pulling a gruesome face behind his back. 'Ah yes. Okay, Emily. Let's do this. I'll just let the techies know we're ready to record. You are ready?'

Emily stood up. 'As I'll ever be.'

CHAPTER FIFTEEN

Willie Morton was sitting at the large dining table in Pilton Mains with Celia. He could hear wind in the trees and rain on the open window pane. Alasdair had gone to bed. They'd nearly finished a bottle of a warm, spicy Chilean Merlot, and the small TV on the angled stand above the wine rack had *Scotland Tonight* on, volume down low. He hadn't been expecting to see Emily suddenly appear, being interviewed by Simon Fane.

He jumped up. 'Oh! Oh! I have to watch this. Turn the sound up.'

'Is that Emily?'

'Yes. Isn't she...?'

'Magnificent? Yes, I can see what you see in her. More's the pity.'

'Hey, it's my story they're doing! Gallimont. They're not naming him, I notice. God, this'll set the cat among the pigeons!'

After the five-minute segment ended and the programme went into its ending sequence – *Five Things Happening Tomorrow*, narrated by a gleeful Sally McElhone – Morton punched the air.

'Ye gods! I've just realised. I'm in the clear. That's what it was for. To let the spooks know that other people, not just me, have the data file. Someone must have told Emily, put her up to it. I wonder if Alasdair's still awake.'

'Ah leave the poor man be,' Celia said fondly. 'He's needing his beauty sleep. He was out chopping logs for me today. He must be exhausted.' She smiled. 'Let's finish this.

And I must say, Willie, it's delightful to have a man come with me to the supermarket. He's very attentive, you know.'

Willie grinned. 'How much of this wine have you had?'

'Well, less that you, but then I've always been a toper.'

'*Toper*? What a good old word. You seem to get on well together.'

She threw him a fond glance. 'You think so, Willie?'

'I do. You're…. like an old married couple.'

Celia threw back her head and laughed. 'I can't believe I've only known him for three *days*. It must be fate that you came around, brought him. I mean that you both… oh, dear, I'm slurring my words, now. I was thinking…'

'Well, what were you thinking?'

'If it's time to open another bottle of this lovely Merlot?'

'Celia, dear, I think so.'

'I'm so pleased you found Emily, though. I remember when you and Sally Hemple broke up. She was so wrong for you, mercenary little bitch. Never did like her.'

Willie reached over and pulled out a second bottle of wine, took a bread knife and sliced off the metallic cap-protector and unscrewed the cap and filled the glasses. 'Sally? A mercenary little bitch? Surely not? This is news.'

The next day, Morton rose late. He had slept very well, aided by the alcohol, the somnabulence of rain and the sighing of the wind in the leaves. When he went downstairs, the house was empty and Celia's black Citroen Berlingo was missing from the driveway. He made himself a coffee and sat down to wait. He was on his second cup when he heard them returning. Celia had bought several papers and brandished the *Standard* as she came in.

'Who's on the front page, then?' she chirruped.

'It's in? My story is in?'

Alasdair grinned, as he laid down several plastic bags of shopping on the table. 'Oh yes, and it's mega!'

The headline shouted: 'Uncovered: Westminster Plot to flood Scotland with No Voters.' Underneath was his byline. Good old Hugh. The story was continued on pages, 2, 3 and 4, but some of it baffled him: there was a second story, under a joint byline of Hugh Leadbetter and Eilish McHarg titled, 'Mystery over Lewis Property Deal', with a large picture of Gallimont. It had captioned him as Philip Gray, of Ardbeag Holdings, a company it described as 'mired in controversy' and in the text he read that Gray was the name used by the man who had attempted to conclude a property deal in Lewis, but evidence pointed to his real name being Gallimont.

Morton looked at the picture they had used. Gallimont, or Gray, was in a car parked beside what appeared to be an old church. It was a grainy picture but Morton didn't think he looked like him. Superficially perhaps.

He reread both stories and tried to get the gist of how they were connected, apart from Gallimont being the link. There was no mention of GB13 in either story. The funding for the relocation scheme was assumed to be UK Government money. But how did Ardbeag Holdings connect with GB13 anyway? It was unexplained. There was more to be revealed. The details of the source was assumed, not confirmed. And who was Eilish McHarg? He couldn't do anything about it, until he was given the all-clear. Still, Hugh had done him proud.

There was nothing of any substance in any of the other papers but the *Record* had a two-para story titled, 'Mystery over Misuse of Government Funds in Relocation Scheme', which simply quoted Emily from the STV programme as its sole source.

Alasdair came into the library as Morton gazed out at the Firth, *Standard* spread out on the table in front of him, feeling a warm glow of self-importance. 'Good, eh? The story is finally out there. The shit has hit the proverbial. And what it should mean is you're aff the hook, because it's moved the story up to politician level. The spooks will no longer be bothered about you. They'll have mair tae bather aboot.'

'You think? I'll be able to get back to my flat?'

'Aye. But caw canny just now. They'll give us the all-clear. Luke says they'll be forced tae go on the defensive. Explain, or at least try to deny, misuse of Government funds, deny or disown Ardbeag Holdings. Your evil twin Gallimont or Gray will be for the high-jump anyway. He'll be for the disappeared, you can bet, taken out of circulation. Anyway, Luke says, watch FMQ today. He thinks it'll come up there.'

Morton sat up. 'Oh. FMQ? Really?'

'Celia says you can borrow her laptop tae watch it,' Alasdair said. 'Is that no good of the lassie?'

At 12:30, the holding picture of the Holyrood online TV channel gave way to scenes of MSPs moving to their seats in the spectacular pine and steel debating chamber shot through with streaming sunshine. The picture cut away to shots of visitors seated upstairs in the public gallery. Then cut to the team of three staff sitting at their podium in the chamber, including the Presiding Officer, who banged her gavel and announced: 'Next item – First Minister's Questions.'

'And we're aff!' Alasdair said, sitting beside Willie on the sofa as they peered at the laptop screen. Celia was out doing a mystery shopping assignment in various branches of the Bank of Scotland for her market research company.

133

The weekly jousting event followed a clearly defined format. There were the standard questions asked by the party leaders, the formal replies by the FM, then the backbenchers asked questions, all previously tabled, and the FM responded with the answers worked out in advance. Then all hell broke loose with supplementaries 'off the cuff'. So it was past the halfway mark of the session, when an SNP backbencher, Annie Ross, of Angus North & The Mearns, stood up to ask: 'Is the FM intending to question the UK Government on today's media story about funds being misused to support people from England to relocate to Scotland? And, was the FM aware of such a scheme operating?'

'Here we go,' Alasdair crowed.

Morton could almost see excited anticipation sweep the chamber as all eyes switched to the diminutive form of the FM, clad in a scarlet skirt suit and matching high heels, who had risen to answer her backbencher.

Poised and waiting her moment as the hubbub died away, the FM half-turned to her own MSPs and said: 'Today's media story relates circumstances of which I am unaware. We will therefore be taking an early opportunity to request a ministerial-level meeting between the two Governments to demand an explanation. But, and I stress this, our Government welcomes *all* who choose to come to Scotland, from wherever they come, to make Scotland their home.'

And the FM sat down.

At the end of FMQ, the First Minister returned to her office suite in the Ministerial Tower, and coming out of the lift on the fourth floor, beckoned Sean Kermally who sat hunched over his computer in the L-shaped open office space allotted to the SpAds. He picked up his iPhone and followed her through the outer office into her inner chamber. Liz Farrell, her top SpAd, was out.

In the inner room, which had a great view north, of Calton Hill, she turned to Sean. 'What's all this about? Who is Willie Morton? What's going on?' She sat and crossed her legs and, stretching out, kicked off her red shoes.

Sean sat opposite her. 'Willie's a good reporter. I remember him well. Neutral politically. Some story though!'

'Sean, I want Fiona to take this on, urgently and I'd want you to go with her, and keep Liz in the loop of course. But before that, let's organise a briefing here. Can you ask Professor McKechnie and if possible, the journalist too, and of course Fiona and both you and Liz should sit in.'

'Right. We might be able to set that up for Monday. I think you've a slot then. I'll check.'

'Good,' the First Minister said, frowning. 'It's odd, isn't it, Sean? What on earth possessed them to do this? I mean, we expected dirty tricks after last year but this? This is crass.'

In the detached former farmhouse on the outskirts at Aberlady, where ivy swarmed the gable ends, competing with Virginia creeper, Philip Gallimont had packed his suitcase and it was sitting in the boot of his black Volkswagen Passat on the drive, ready to flee at a moment's notice. He'd had no communications from any of his contacts. He felt very exposed, his picture having been splashed across the media, looking like a convict on the run. But he knew that a big story in Scotland might not ruffle many feathers down south. Not many people in London read the *Standard* or the *Daily Record*, or viewed STV. And so far, BBC Scotland had not covered either story. Of course, Smyth and his lot would be aware of what was happening, but many others might not. And Smyth and Co. were not his paymasters or his boss. Yet, his monthly salary had appeared in his account as usual this morning. Could he carry on? Should he carry on? Or contact his head office for advice? He looked at the low sun over the stone sundial, the hedge beyond and the woods, and drawn by the light, went out into the garden. The house was his, of course, bought and paid for, under his real name. And there was no reason to suppose that anyone other than his boss and Smyth and Co. knew its location. He'd heard that politicians were now interfering in the media story, but what they were doing was, to all outside eyes at least, perfectly legal. They were a Trust, all above board, with clients seeking property in a rural location and he was the one who found such properties for them. The support offered was a private matter between the Trust and its clients. Very few could be aware of some of the methods employed to secure those properties. That aspect of things, for which he had a distaste and a complete disinterest, was completely secret. He stopped, listening, by the hedge.

A car was coming along the road. It carried on towards the village. Even he was not entirely aware of what occurred, or how it occurred. Properties became available and he concluded deals in due course with the deceased's agents. There was a bit of a premium on his side because of the rather sudden nature of the property becoming available and in the usual chaotic state one would expect of an elderly person struggling on alone, pottering about pointlessly into futile old age. He was used to seeing these properties and the state they were in. Fumigation was the first requirement, and of course, they came to the market cheap because of it. He'd acquired his own place in this way, but that was even before he joined the company. The phone was ringing. He hastened inside, to the study.

It was the person whose voice he least wanted to hear: Smyth. He felt a little panicky.

'Philip? How are you bearing up?'

He wasn't in the mood for small talk. 'How do you think? I've had my picture splashed across…'

'Yes, we're aware of all that. Best thing at the moment is to go on holiday. For two weeks. Keep out of circulation. Wait till all the political hoo-hah has died down.'

'Right. I'll have to let…'

Smyth cut in: 'No. That's all been done. You're clear to go. Two weeks and we'll contact you after you get back, once we know where we are. In the meantime, we're shutting up shop, as far as possible.'

'Right.'

'Is that okay with you, Philip? Any questions?'

Philip thought. There was one. 'What about the meeting of the liaison committee in three days' time?'

Smyth cleared his throat. 'No problem, old boy, we'll handle that. Enjoy your holiday, Mr Mayberry.'

Philip put the phone back in its cradle, a shiver running down his spine. Why had Smyth used his service name? Was he being told the truth? Were they, even now, planning to make him disappear… *permanently*? He picked up the phone and made a call, made a flight booking. Half an hour later, Philip walked out the front door, locked it and got in the car. He had booked flight tickets to somewhere warm, but was not driving to Edinburgh airport. His flight was from Newcastle. No-one, not even Smyth could know that.

Willie Morton turned the key in his lock in Keir Street. The air inside was a little musty and he felt the old familiar feelings of being home. He looked around in the rooms suspiciously, looking for any sign of things in the wrong place, things having been moved, or removed. He just had an instinct that they had been here. He remembered that old mantra that if you think you're being bugged you probably are, but if there are any signs of it, then you probably haven't been.

He went into the kitchenette and opened the fridge. The milk was off. He flushed it down the sink and looked at his wristwatch. Too late for black coffee, anyway. Bed. He needed to catch up on sleep. After four nights at Celia's he had had found himself unable to sleep properly. Oh, it had been comfortable, but it was not his home. He liked his own things around him.

He prepared for bed. Turned on the radio – BBC Radio Scotland: *Mr Anderson's Fine Tunes*. Rarely a dud tune played. Across the spectrum of folk, country and western and acoustic music. Some old favourites, Steve Earle…. He got into his bathrobe and took off his watch and ring, showered, did his teeth, opened the bedroom window and got naked into the double bed. He could sleep safely till morning. He was glad to be back in his own bed.

As Morton slept gratefully and fitfully in his bed, new nightshift operators got to work. They had travelled up from London specifically for the job. The intention had been to complete the job during daylight hours, but instructions had come late and by the time, Bob and Rob arrived in situ, they discovered that the empty premises they had been ordered to enter were no longer unoccupied. It was not a problem. Bob and Rob were specialists and each had a different speciality, each from a different section, although they often worked together. Bob, from section A1(D) was the skilled burglar, able to spring any lock, circumvent any security device and if necessary repair any damage. He had originally been a carpenter.

Rob's skill set was different. He was a radio engineer, and specialised in devices, specifically in the optimum placement of such to ensure maximum surveillance as required. Bob could instantly see the potential in any room. He was the older of the two and for his first decade had specialised in the humble infinity transmitter, or induction devices inserted in telephone handsets, but with the move away from landlines he had had to diversify. Technology had improved so rapidly that he now found the equipment he used so incredibly small and yet so powerful that it was, in his words, like 'taking sweets from a baby'.

Bob and Rob not very reluctantly repaired to the nearest hostelry in the Grassmarket, where they sat unobtrusively, quietly discussing Premier League football, the merits of Chelsea over Spurs and Man U, till closing time. Then they returned up the Vennel Steps to Keir Street and without any sound or difficulty at all, entered the target premises and efficiently completed their business, in less than two minutes.

CHAPTER SIXTEEN

There was something of the glamour of 1960s movie star about Fiona Temperley MSP, the Cabinet Secretary for Constitutional and External Affairs in the Scottish Government. Sunglasses often perched on her thick, glossy blonde hair helped to convey that image, and she usually wore strong colours and exquisite perfumes. She had a grand manner, but this belied sharp acumen and political *nous*. First appointed a minister in Donald Stevenson's minority administration, she had remained a minister under Alex and now Nicola and that said a lot, thought Sean Kermally, as he walked to meet her along Marsham Street. He had taken the sleeper train down, while Fiona, her PS Daniel Cunningham, and Liz Farrell had flown down on the red-eye to London City and come by Tube. They had arranged to meet at the Caffé Nero directly opposite the Home Office main entrance.

'Ill-met by moonlight,' Fiona quipped as they met up on the pavement outside the small cafe. 'We haven't much time. It'll have to be a very quick review of strategy.'

'After you,' Sean held open the door for them. He was a little nervous, mainly because of the presence of Liz Farrell. She was Top Dog and they both knew that he was a poor third, jostling for second spot with Seonaid Nicol who, very well-connected with all sections of the party, was lead liaison with the Westminster group of MPs. He smiled to think they were both redheads but so different in manner and method. He knew his place, and took their coffee order over to the bar.

140

'Oh, and a Danish for me,' Fiona called, 'if they have.'

'I'll have one too,' Liz said. 'And... Daniel?'

'No thanks.'

'Good boy,' said Fiona, warmly. 'You're adhering to the Government's dietary advice. Wish I could.' And Sean could see the trace of a blush on poor Daniel Cunningham's face. He'd only been in post a year and Fiona was one of the most hyperactive ministers around.

They barely had time for a quick chat before they had to get out and cross the road, passing a single tree in the middle of a small patch of grass. The modern concrete and glass building with its narrow horizontal slats resembled an unfinished jigsaw puzzle in light grey. Sean quite approved of the coloured glass sections of roof high up that swung out and overshot the facade.

The party arrived at the front door and were ushered inside by door staff to where Jason Schwarthman, the Home Secretary, and his PS and PPS, were waiting, all smiles. It was a feature, Sean thought, of political meetings that everyone was so cheery and excessively polite, until they got behind closed doors when the knives came out. There were two lifts and when Fiona and her opposite number went into the first, Sean dived in with them and the doors closed.

'Nice flight?' inquired the Home Secretary idly. As if he cared, thought Sean.

'Apart from the chaos at the terminal,' Fiona said, patting her blonde hair to check it was in order. She smiled archly. 'When *will* you decide to build that new runway?'

'Ah, well...'

Sean smiled. She'd discomfited him and the meeting hadn't even begun. The room they were shown into was clearly also used as a venue for press conferences. There was a dais flanked by Union flags on either side. He smiled grimly. No accident, Sean thought. Reminding us who is boss. He almost laughed aloud then as Fiona strolled casually to the far end of the extended rectangular oak table and sat down facing back into the room so that the flags were invisible to her, forcing the others to do likewise! Then she took out her folder and a bright yellow *I'm with Nicola* SNP pen.

The two parties of four settled into their chairs, facing each other across the wide table and, without preamble Fiona went straight onto the attack. 'You'll have seen the media reports of the last few days?' she stated, pushing a dossier of press clippings across the table to the faintly smiling minister.

Schwarthman's smile wavered. 'I haven't. Our media down here hasn't featured the story, but I've been fully briefed about the stories in your local media,' he said shooting his cuffs to reveal sapphire cufflinks. Sean winced at the emphasis he had ever-so-slightly dropped upon the 'local'. Metropolitan snobbery, nice! The toothsome smile returned to the Home Secretary's shiny brown face. 'And I can reveal, that, fortunately, there is very little truth in them.' It was a perma-smile, Sean thought, frozen to perfection and he had undoubtedly worked hard to learn how to keep it intact during the most febrile confrontations.

'Oh come on,' Fiona snapped. 'The stories are based on actual documents and witness statements. Chapter and verse. We didn't come all this way to have you try to deny it. We want you to *explain* it.'

In any other politician, such a direct style as Fiona's would be seen as abrasive, counterproductive even, Sean thought, but as he watched her over the shoulder of Daniel Cunningham, he was reminded again that Fiona, even on the attack, exuded charm and style that, with a younger male opponent, could be disarming. And they had been briefed fully by Professor Emily McKechnie, one of the sharpest commentators around, and by Willie Morton, who had stressed to them the need to pin-point the links between UK Government funding and personnel, and this pressure group or bunch of loonies called GB13. Morton's point had been to force these two apart to see what crawled out from underneath.

Light flooded into the small office on the ministerial floor of the Queensberry Tower as the First Minister drank a cup of tea, the day's papers piled on the table, along with a social media digest and the printout of the report from Fiona Temperley.

'So Fiona got nowhere with the Home Office,' Nicola said. 'That's a surprise. I had thought there would be some admission of guilt, even by omission. It's not like Fiona to come back with no scalps, Sean.'

Sean frowned. 'It was obvious Schwarthman had been instructed to stonewall. As Liz would have told you…'

'I haven't seen her. She's on other business.'

'Well, that's what he did. He admitted nothing, gave nothing away – I mean, to the point of actual rudeness. My feeling… he was uncomfortable about it. He knows he could have been more cooperative. They're hiding something, and it can only be one of three things: one, they actually have no involvement but think they can shut the whole thing down; two, they are up to their necks in these activities; and three, which I think most likely, is they have some involvement, there is some crossover of Government funds, personnel or services in kind with this group, and they don't know how to clean up, or *if* they can clean up.'

Nicola nodded. 'Interesting, Sean. I'll touch base with Liz later today, see if her observations coincide with yours. Thanks.'

Sean returned to his desk to collect his jacket and headed down to the Refectory. As he stood in the queue behind some female assistants to Labour members, he wondered what Liz was up to. They were a team, the eight SpAds, and Liz was one of the team, but she was on a different level somehow. She had been the party's Senior Media officer years before he had been in the post, and they had both made the same journey from Comms to SpAd. If Nicola had the reputation of being the sharpest politician in the UK, then Liz was due a big part of the credit. Simply, Sean knew, the two were intuitive, flexible, fast on their feet and blessed with the ability to see the best line right away, at first glance. And they were rooted in common sense, two working-class girls, the same age even. As a team, they were unbeatable, you couldn't see the joins. He sighed and moved up to the serving area with his tray. He envied them their closeness, the strength of their shared thinking. The FM had an almost talismanic belief in Liz's advice. As a mere male, he couldn't ever be a part of it. And yet, he could learn from it. What made them great? How could he discover it for himself? He knew he had something else to offer. His asset was his strong analytical skill, an ability to see things almost as if from the outside.

He joined a couple of MSPs at a table that looked out into the Garden Lobby and desultorily joined in their conversation, exchanging a few remarks about nothing special. When he returned upstairs to his desk, Liz came over. He wondered where she had been.

'FM wants us for a chat,' she said. 'If you're free.'

'Oh yes.'

In the FM's office, Nicola stood at the window. 'Right, I think we've made a decision, Sean, but I wanted to share it with you first, before we announce it.'

'Okay.' The significance of the order of the pronouns: *we, I, you, we* was not lost on him.

'Based on what you've both told me,' Nicola began, and Sean felt a wee glow at his inclusion, 'and from speaking to Fiona of course, I think we need to take this further – right to the top. I'm thinking about moving a request to meet the PM on it. Does that sound…?'

Liz and Sean nodded. Liz said: 'We can't be seen to be treated like idiots.'

Sean frowned. 'They gave us nothing, but we know they're not clean.'

Nicola brought her hands together and did that thing with her face. He could never decide if it was a reflective face or a rueful face or a decided face. 'Yes. That's about it,' she said. 'Okay, so we do it and I want both of you to come with me. Cameron's a nice guy but he tries too hard to be nice, wants to be fair. He has a big drawback. His upbringing and his life of privilege has made him, at certain key moments, entirely unsuited to move forward in the national interest. He lacks the killer instinct at crucial moments and he can't see that, but I can.'

Liz coughed discreetly and in the silence, added: 'And by the time of the meeting, we'll try to have something more – some new aspect that they can't deny.'

Sean looked at her. 'And do we have that at the moment?'

Liz laughed and shared a smile with Nicola. 'Don't be silly, Sean, that's where you come in.'

Although the air was still on the cold side of fresh, the sun occasionally put in an appearance as Willie Morton struggled up the hill track at the side of the Salisbury Crags in Holyrood Park. The track was known as the Radical Road, and to his shame he didn't know why, although he had been up it umpteen times. Emily was just up ahead at a bend and when he caught up with her, they had a terrific view, south, west and north over the city, the Canongate, the architect's jumble of upturned boats of the Scottish Parliament, Holyrood Palace beneath them, and beyond, New Waverley, St Andrews House, Calton Hill, Princes Street, the Scott Monument, the Castle on its rock.

'Grand to be out!' Emily said.

'Out of breath, you mean,' Morton said. 'I feel old.'

'Good for you, clear your mind of all that nastiness. Come on, let's put a spurt on.'

It had been a while since he had worn his walking boots, Morton reflected. He had once been a keen hillwalker. A few years back he had replaced his aging fleecy and walking trousers with a black Berghaus Argentium lightweight technical top, grey and black OEX Strata softshell walking trousers, which he wore with a grey micro-fleece and a black Jack Wolfskin down jacket as required. He liked the functionality of the kit: the layering principle, kit that was adaptable to all circumstances. He was becoming a bit of a techie. Emily had joked that he looked like 'the man from MilkTray!'

There were always walkers and joggers and tourists on the track, Morton knew. And some looked ultra-fit. He stopped to let a young woman in pink neon lycra and dazzling white trainers speed past him, tuned in to her MP3 player.

They reached the turn in the track which diverged. They took the left which began to ascend to Arthur's seat, the volcanic plug that was the highest point in the city. Soon they saw rock faces and felt a stronger wind, and shortly were on the top among jagged rocks and the trig point on the summit, where tourists were taking selfies against the Edinburgh skyline.

'Made it!' Emily said, unzipping her orange puffer jacket. Her hair was held in a white hairband and he could see some drops of sweat on her forehead. 'We should do this more often. Out on the hills.'

He took a drink from his water bottle. 'I have always meant to get around to doing some big walks. The Pyrenees, the Alps. Well, I did a little bit in the Austrian Alps once, years ago.'

'Well, I'm your man,' Emily said. 'My work is so sedentary. Let's see if we can set up something for the big vac in the summer.'

'Hmn, let's.' He felt at that moment, a big lifting of his spirits. He always felt that, on every summit, even Arthur's Seat, which was only 800 feet.

'I'm so glad we've put all that stuff behind us,' she said, as if reading his mind. 'It is over, isn't it?'

'Yes,' he said, though he wasn't sure. He had not told her about the text message he had just received from Sean Kermally.

CHAPTER SEVENTEEN

Sean Kermally was in his one-bed flat off Leith Walk watching the early evening news on TV when Willie Morton phoned. He had both his mobiles beside him on the sofa. He muted the TV, switched on the subtitles and picked up the mobile that was ringing. He was of the generation that had never had a landline phone number. 'Willie? Thanks for ringing. You got my message then?'

'I did,' Morton said. 'But what's this about?'

Sean paused, thinking. 'Consequences… or maybe loose ends.'

'That sounds interesting. There *are* loose ends and I was hoping someone would be pursuing them.'

'Oh, we are, Willie, we are. Look, have you got time for a pint? I could meet you in Deacon Brodie's in half an hour. That's close to you, isn't it?'

'Not too far.'

'Okay, see you.'

Morton put on his jacket and brogues and set off down the Vennel Steps and along the Grassmarket up Victoria Street to George IV Bridge and into the Royal Mile, or the High Street, as he preferred to call it. As he walked he was trying to decide if he should make contact again with Luke, Marco and Alasdair. He wondered if Alasdair was still in residence at Celia's.

The lights flared out of the leaded windows of Deacon Brodie's one of Edinburgh's most tourist-friendly pubs. It looked exactly like a historic howff should, black pitted timbers and vaulted ceilings and leaded glass, and upstairs the restaurant was highly regarded for posh nosh. He'd taken Emily there on one of their earliest dates. It was a pity she'd had an evening meeting. He would have been able to take her along with him. She and Sean knew each other because Sean had taken his degree in Politics at Edinburgh. Surprisingly, there were vacant seats inside the door. He got a pint of Belhaven Best and sat down to wait for Sean at a black-stained wooden table. Although it was a relatively quiet night, the background racket of English Premier League football on the TV high above the gantry rose and fell as tiny figures swarmed back and forth on the bright green pitch. He liked to wait before sipping his beer, watching till the frothy head was white and all the beer was still. He lifted it off the beer mat. That first mouthful. It was only when you sipped it you realised how much of a drouth you had. He exhaled in satisfaction and leaned back.

He was half-finished his pint before Sean appeared, in jeans and parka. 'Another?' he inquired.

'Aye, okay. Best, thanks. And crisps, cheese and onion.'

When they'd settled in the quiet, gloomy corner, oblivious to the noise of customers coming and going, the TV football, and food being brought to tables, Morton said: 'Okay, what is going on?'

Kermally split open a bag of crisps and helped himself. 'Well, Fiona Temperley spoke to her opposite number on the subject the other day.'

Morton laid down his pint carefully on the beer mat. 'No? That's a surprise. I didn't see anything on the news.'

'There wasn't. They didn't put out a statement and we didn't either, for different reasons, I suspect. But the meeting was a total whitewash. The boss is furious. I was present, heard everything.'

149

'Well. So, what? He denied it was funded by the UK Government?'

'Yup.'

'Denied any involvement in the activities of GB13?'

'Yup.'

'Let me see... claimed GB13 was a perfectly legal group?'

'Absolutely. His hands are clean. Gallimont is not, never has been, a Government employee, or a civil servant or anything, if he even *exists*.'

Morton sat back, frowning, then he took a sip of beer and wiped his lips. 'So we're at an impasse?'

Kermally flipped his beermat and caught it. 'Not quite.' He grinned.

After a minute, Morton was forced to ask. 'Come on, don't leave me in suspenders.'

Kermally leaned forward and spoke quietly. 'I know two things, Willie. First, that Gallimont or Gray, whatever his real name is, has been taken out of the picture.'

Morton put down his pint carefully. 'You don't mean done away with... murdered?'

Kermally scoffed. 'I don't think so! Just *disappeared*. Probably gone abroad. And the second thing is that the core group of GB13 are unabashed. Business as normal, old boy.'

Morton was mystified. 'How do you know that? How could you know that?'

Kermally tapped the top of his nose. 'It's who you know, old chap,' he said. 'And I know a lot of people who know people who know.'

Morton grunted. 'Mystical bullshit now?'

Kermally smirked. 'Okay. Somebody I know knows somebody who works in Westminster and they know somebody who's a member, or at least a person who chucks in the odd tenner here and there, to GB13.'

'Woah!' Morton exclaimed, impressed. 'You're kidding me?'

Kermally assumed a saintly pose, hands held out, palms together. 'It is so. Truly, grasshopper, the path of righteousness is a twisted one full of sudden U-bends...'

Morton grunted. 'Huh! Well, no, I am impressed. So what does this mean?'

'The word on the street down there is Gallimont has caused a stink and done a bunk. Some ordinary members want him to appear and explain what's going on. There's even rumours he's ratted them out somehow. And his being Scottish doesn't help his case.'

Morton shook his head. 'Really, your informant knows all this?'

'Yes, but more than that. They're expecting him to appear to explain himself and reassure them things are okay, business as normal. That's one reason why we're scaling down our Comms on the issue, so as not to alarm them.'

'That doesn't follow. You want them to carry on?'

'In a way.'

Morton began to feel a shiver coming on. 'Oh no! You're not meaning...?'

Kermally nodded. 'We need *more*. The FM wants something big to hit Cameron with. She wants to meet him face to face. But we need something, and this is probably the best chance. We'd back you up, minimise the risks,' he said. 'We can help to prepare you for it. If it comes off, you'll have a huge scoop. We can bust them wide open.'

Morton drained his pint. It was exciting, the thought of being once again in the belly of the beast, Jonah in the whale, as Emily had described it. 'You said that was one reason. What was the other?'

Kermally put down his mobile and frowned. 'Oh, the reasons we're not doing a media release? The FM is not keen to pursue the… let's call it the *relocation scheme* because it might make our Government look anti-English. English people in Scotland are vital to the nation's success and she wouldn't want to do anything to put off English people from moving here. However, there seems to be genuine grounds for prosecution, possible property fraud, so we're pursuing that angle and leaving the nitty-gritty of the other thing for now.'

'Letting them off the hook a bit?' Morton suggested. 'The scheme bears all the hallmarks of an aggressive political act.'

'Maybe, but you could see how it might be made to look if the FM pursued it. "We must rise above it," were her actual words.' He grinned. 'Anyway, Willie, while you're thinking about it, I'll get us another couple of pints.'

'Right. And more crisps!'

While the rest of the team had been reassigned to Thames House, Colin Hardwick had been instructed to remain working in the Edinburgh ops room. Javid and Dennis and Carol had flown back to London. There was always a feeling of regret when a team split up after an op, but also one of relief. With new colleagues you had to be on your best behaviour and although he got on with Carol, he'd found Javid and even Dennis a little irksome. It was easier on his own, although Kirsty and the boy wizard, Crispin, were just next door. As far as he could comprehend, the op was completed, but he had been instructed to maintain a 'discreet' surveillance on Morton and the reason for that, Desmond Thorpe had told him, was Morton was likely to try to

152

continue his investigations, despite the reassurances of which they knew he was aware – that the UK Government was not involved and the group GB13 was, in any case, a legal group. That puzzled Hardwick. It contradicted some of the information he believed to be true. There was no doubt that Commander Smyth had been in direct contact with Gallimont, and so had Javid and Dennis. There was a working liaison there which had been denied at the political level. From what he knew of Morton he would not be surprised the journalist would want to sniff that out. And in a way, he'd be right to. Should there be a link in the first place? What was Smyth doing involving the service in the activities of Gallimont? He aired some of his concerns to Kirsty Haldane over a pizza in Prezzo, on North Bridge, three minutes' walk from the Scotland station.

It was a light, airy place, done out in pale green, with huge plate-glass windows and sleek, low-profile modern furniture. They had a seat with a view over the undulating light grey roofs of Waverley Station. There was still a bit of light in the sky, the dying remnants of a sunset over the New Town.

'I think you're right, Colin,' Kirsty agreed. 'We can't question our orders, but there's something funny going on.' She cut another wedge of their shared Tropicana, a delicious mix of prosciutto, pineapple and mushrooms. 'And you'll remember my misgivings about the entire assignment.'

Hardwick sipped his lager. 'I remember, Kirsty. You know, I suppose we could take a trip down to Gallimont's place. The address is on the log. There have been no FR scan hits for a couple of days and his mobile is either off or he's out of the country.'

'And I suppose,' Kirsty continued, 'if you are right and Morton intends to continue his investigation, we'll have an easier time following him. *His* mobile is back on and we have the transmitter inside his wristwatch.'

'We'll check that when we get back, although he seems to have returned to his normal schedule. What time is Crispin on till tonight?'

Kirsty checked her watch. 'He'll be packing up about now.'

Hardwick swirled his beer in the glass. 'He doesn't say a lot, does he. You and he get on okay together?'

Kirsty smiled. 'Well. We did. But I think he had a bit of a crush, and that kind of put a bit of tension into our working relationship.'

Hardwick raised his eyebrows. 'Oh dear, I did wonder. Maybe, it's time one or other of you was reassigned.'

'Him, hopefully,' she laughed. 'I like working in Scotland, among my own folk.'

'Bit of a holiday for me too,' Hardwick mused. 'I like the slower pace. Actually,' he said, 'I think I will have another drink. Or we could move on somewhere else, if you fancy? At any event, I don't think we need to go back to the office now.'

'I'd be up for a pub crawl,' Kirsty smiled.

'Which is *not* what I'm suggesting, you mischievous person,' he scolded. 'One drink. Then I'm heading off home. I'll get the tab here, by the way. No, really – privileges of the senior officer.' As he said it, he wondered where Carol Harker was. He hoped it wasn't true about her and Neil Smyth. Maybe he'd be back in London in a few days and then he could engineer a meeting with her. Ask her straight out. He smiled. And then ask her out. Well, she could only say no.

Willie Morton walked down to Waverley Station just after 11 p.m., feeling cold and a little hungry. He had drunk four pints and snaffled lots of crisps, but by the time he'd got home to change, didn't feel like eating anything.

He changed into a suit and tie and his warm overcoat and threw his toilet bag and a spare shirt and underwear into his small leather holdall, thinking he might get something at the station. His mobile was switched off and he hadn't been able to let Emily know where he was going. He suspected she'd gone for a drink after her meeting. The Caledonian Sleeper for London left just after midnight and his berth was booked.

The cavernous interior of Waverley was echoingly empty and cold at this late hour and he felt the chill through to his bones. Nothing was open either. He'd better order breakfast on the train. He found his sleeper compartment easily enough after walking for miles along the end platform. It was the longest train he'd ever seen.

He was reassured to find, from talking to the steward, he would have the compartment to himself. Solo occupancy. But when he got into Coach C, Room 8, he found there would have been very little space for anyone else anyway. It was tiny! He unclipped the metal stairway and tossed it onto the top bunk. That made it a little bit easier to manoeuvre. He filled in the breakfast form to order a bacon roll, coffee and a wake-up call half an hour before the train got in to London. He walked back along the narrow corridor to the next carriage, found the steward in the lounge car and paid for his breakfast. Back in the tiny compartment, he undressed and got into the narrow bunk bed and tried to put thoughts of his work and where he was going out of his head.

He felt the train leaving the station, imagined it clattering down beneath the London Road, past Craigentinny Sidings, the freightliner terminal near Portobello Park, Brunstane and into Midlothian, Tranent, Haddington, closely following the A1. At last, the regular side-to-side jogging of the wheels on the track lulled him to sleep somewhere between Dunbar and Cockburnspath. He awoke somewhere in the north of England and wondered where he was. The alarm on his wristwatch showed it was 2.45 a.m. He remembered, and fell asleep. And the train clattered south, through the remote fells, Newcastle upon Tyne, Durham, Darlington, York...

CHAPTER EIGHTEEN

Willie Morton awoke when his phone alarm went off, and he lay for a further minute feeling the rhythm of the steel rails humming, just like in the American folk and country songs he loved, and remembered: Pete Seeger, 'The Hobo's Lullaby'. A pale light was filtering through tiny perforations in the corrugated paper blind. The compartment was warm, already too warm, and his throat felt dry.

He coughed, cleared his throat, blinked a few times and swung his legs out of the bunk bed. He reached to the bottle of water and uncapped it, swilling his mouth round with lukewarm water, then swallowed.

He needed to go to the toilet, which was at the end of the carriage. He dressed loosely in trousers and shirt and put his bare feet into his shoes and went out into the corridor. But there was a woman there and Morton, befuddled, could not comprehend that the corridor was not wide enough for two people. He dithered but the woman, a very large woman in grey pyjamas, with untidy grey hair, was in no mood for waiting. Morton was smeared all over her as she forced herself past him heading to the toilet.

He followed and went into the Gents. An entire packet of paper towels had burst all over the floor. He returned to the compartment and rolled up the blind. Urban landscape. Houses, fields, a park, flats. He'd slept well, considering. Then the dread returned. He was heading into the mouth of the beast – the meeting. He picked up his wristwatch: 7.35 a.m. In three hours he'd be there, among the faithful, risking his life, playing James Bond. He didn't feel remotely like the type of man who could pull it off. He sat on the bunk and remembered what he had to do.

Sean had given him a mobile phone. It was a reconditioned Samsung Galaxy, unlocked to operate as a Pay As You Go. It had Bluetooth and that was why he had it. It worked in conjunction with the silver ballpoint pen. He reached up to his satchel on the upper bunk and found the pen, still in its Platignum Papermate presentation box. It did work as a pen, Sean had demonstrated, by scribbling with it on a beermat. But more importantly, it had a recording device concealed in the silver double heart Papermate logo on the clasp.

The camera was the top one of the two hearts motifs, the microphone the lower. Both undetectable. To turn on recording he simply had to press the clasp downwards till it gave a single, almost inaudible, click and then simply ensure he was facing towards what he wanted to record. It transmitted the AV recording by Bluetooth to the Galaxy, with the usual buffering delays, to an app called CineMaker. Even if the phone was switched off, as long as it was somewhere about his person, it would record.

Sean had instructed him to switch it on well in advance, when safe to do so, and let it run. It could record up to 360 minutes continuously.

'But even a meeting of GB13 shouldn't last that long, Willie, so you'll be okay.'

'You can laugh,' Willie said sourly. 'Are you sure they won't be aware of Gallimont's troubles?'

Sean was relentless. 'If you stick to the script you'll be okay. Then, when you come out, and it's safe to do so, switch it off again and go to the Terrace Cafeteria and you'll see

Susan Havilland. This is what she looks like.' Sean had showed her on his mobile phone.

Morton nodded. 'Presume she's a researcher?'

'Don't worry about that. She'll be hanging about waiting for you. Simply hand her the pen and phone and you're free to come away. We'll take it from there.'

'What will you do with it?'

'First we'll clean up the AV file, to remove any references to you, any traces of you speaking on it, then we'll see what we've got. Assuming it does have some nasty stuff on it, it'll go to everyone who needs it. Let David Cameron try to talk his way out of this. Nicola will have him by the short and curlies. Conspiracy in the heart of the Palace of Westminster? Nice.'

'And if they rumble me? If I get any trouble?'

'Come right out of there, at once. Get that on tape too. That'll look good!'

'You cold-hearted sod! I mean, is there nowhere I could go?'

'Well, the Scottish MPs and staff are based all over the place now. Some are in Portcullis House. I've put Susan's mobile and office phone number in your contacts.' He grinned. 'She's the only contact in there so you shouldn't have any problem. Willie, this is going to work out okay. They're not going to rub you out.' He laughed. 'Not in Parliament, heaven forfend! As far as we can determine, they're not aware of anything more than some intrusive press interest in their activities in Scotland. You can reassure them on that, according to the script I've worked out for you.'

Willie washed his face in the tiny sink, dressed and put the pen in his top pocket. There was a knock at the door.

'Steward.'

He opened the door and accepted his small cardboard tray with a bacon roll and a cardboard carton of coffee.

'We'll be at Euston in twenty minutes.'

'Thank you.'

He opened the ketchup and inserted it into the roll, which was very hot. He took the cap off the coffee carton and sat down on the bunk to eat. The train was still moving but slowly and he guessed they were already in central London, moving through the complex spaghetti of railway lines to the station at Euston. He practised switching the pen on, recorded himself standing in front of the mirror, speaking to himself. He switched it off. He found CineMaker, an unobtrusive white square on the second page of the Home screen of the phone. He played back the file, turned up the volume. The picture was pin-sharp and the sound was clear. It worked. The miracles of modern technology. He deleted the file and looked out of the window. Without any fuss, the train had come to a halt. He finished his coffee and looked at his wristwatch. It was 8.05 a.m. He pulled on his coat and picked up his holdall and stepped out of his sleeper compartment onto the platform.

In her bedroom in Lochend Grove in Restalrig, Emily was up and about, making coffee. She checked her mobile. There was an enigmatic text message from Willie. Brief, and, she noted, sent at twelve minutes past midnight. *Am on the trail again. Speak soon, Luv W x.* What did it mean, on the trail? She wondered if it might have something to do with the meeting in the Parliament that she'd been invited to. Apparently, it was to be a meeting with just herself, the First Minister, the Cabinet Secretary for Constitutional and External Affairs Fiona Temperley and a couple of special advisers. She'd thought the whole thing was over – apparently not. Well, she could fit it in. She had an easy morning anyway.

After breakfast, she got out her mountain bike from the shed round the side of the flat and cycled the two miles to the university. It was a lovely route, down to Marionville Road, round the Meadowbank Sports Stadium, Ann Terrace, onto the Queen's Drive around the edge of Holyrood Park. She cut off into Beaumont Place, Crosscauseway and across to George Square. It generally took about twenty minutes, including waiting at the traffic lights at the busy junction of West Richmond Street and Nicolson Street. She chained up her bike in the rack, collected her mail and entered the department. She was about to pour herself a coffee in her room when there was a knock. A slight, red-haired young woman stood there, smartly dressed.

'Hello, Professor McKechnie?'

'Yes, that's me.'

'Have you got a moment?'

'Well, I suppose so. I don't think I've met you before? Are you…?'

The woman laughed. She was very pretty, Emily noted, frowning, and slim too. 'Oh, I'm not a student. I was… years ago.'

Emily sighed. 'Right. Then how can I help you?'

The woman offered her hand. Emily shook it. 'I'm Kirsty,' she said, but please don't ask me who I work for!'

Emily laughed. 'What? I don't understand.'

'I shouldn't be here. My bosses wouldn't like it. But can we just talk?'

'You're very mysterious, Kirsty. But have a seat. Coffee?'

'If you're making it. Black, one sugar.'

Emily poured her a coffee and added sugar.

'Right. Why have I come here? You must be thinking that. I'm assuming you've worked out, more or less, who I work for.'

Emily smiled. 'God, it's like policemen, they get younger every year. I can't believe you're a... well, a spook.'

'I'll deny it of course,' she smiled. 'Anyway, I just want to pass something on, that I think needs to be passed on, which concerns your friend Mr Morton.'

'Oh? Fire away.'

'You need to know that he could be in danger. Not from us of course. We don't behave like that, at least not on British soil. But there are some dangerous people in the murky waters that he has dipped his toe in. Some really unhinged types. That's the first thing. But the main thing I want to pass on is that you should keep pressing to find connections between the UK Government and its departments and the GB13 group. Those do exist. There are close links, working links, daily liaisons. The evidence is there to find.' She stood up. 'Sorry to be so mysterious.'

'Oh right, really? There's no more you can say?'

'I would, but honestly I don't know more.'

'I'll mention what you've said to Willie but I can hear him now saying what you've said is no more than hearsay.'

Kirsty sighed. 'I can understand that. I feel that we – and I can't specify exactly who *we* are – have got it wrong on this one. There is no danger to the safety of citizens from journalists like Mr Morton. But there is, in my personal opinion and some of my colleagues, an unhealthy symbiosis developing between those paid to guard the safety of the citizens of the UK and some of these British nationalist groups like GB13. What you might call *undue influence*. I'm sure you already have these suspicions. I'm just hoping to persuade you to have the courage of your convictions. But I have to run, and of course, I'm relying on you not to disclose that we had this meeting.' She smiled. 'Thanks for the coffee.' She stopped in the doorway. 'And not all of us are opposed to the idea of an independent Scotland, you know, if it should ever happen.'

For Willie Morton, the two hours he had to kill before turning up at the Portcullis House Visitor's Entrance were long and filled with anxiety. It seemed a far cry from his reckless impersonation of Gallimont in Chuffy's, only a fortnight before, even though he had a back-up plan this time, people who knew what he was trying to do, and of course the secret spy pen. And reason told him there was little they could do to him, in such a public place.

He wandered into the newsagents in the busy Westminster Tube station and purchased a copy of the *Guardian* and walked the nearby streets and sat in the wan sunlight on a bench inside St James Park. He saw the gang of pelicans on their rock taking turns to stand up and do early morning wing-stretching.

He strolled round by the Duck House, the funny Swiss chalet and its neat and productive little garden and turned round over a bridge watching funny ducks that he read on a noticeboard were Egyptian. He looked into the shallow khaki water and was surprised to see an aluminium crutch. Seagulls flew, pigeons were everywhere and a heron stood close to the fence, motionless, intense. It was real, alive, Morton finally decided. The thing was, he was going to be getting his visitor's pass under his real name but once inside, would be impersonating Gallimont.

163

He looked at his watch. Still more than an hour. He dumped the newspaper into a paper bin near the entrance to Churchill's War Office and went up the steps into King Charles' Street. He walked down Whitehall, crossed Westminster Bridge and walked to the base of the London Eye, then turned and came back across the bridge, admiring the ornate gold-painted lamp standards, which were catching the morning sun. He strolled up and then down Victoria Embankment.

He was still too early and turned up Parliament Street, walked up as far as the Cenotaph, and back: 10.20 a.m. Time to go in. He had to do it. It felt like it was all down to him to find out the truth.

He presented himself at the unobtrusive side entrance of Portcullis House around the corner from the main entrance. He had been told it was rarely used but would be a quick way in. It was. There was no-one but him using it. The glass door opened and he went in and passed his shoulder bag to one of two security staff, who put it through the X-ray machine. He took off his watch, and put coins, his wallet and the jacket with the spy-pen in it, into the plastic tray and was frisked and had the letter from the MP scrutinised. He could see through the glass into the ground-floor atrium and he could see there the MP whose name was on his letter of authorisation. He didn't know the man at all, but recognised him from TV programmes. He was one of the new intake, quite young, maybe ten years younger than Morton, slim and bespectacled, in a dark suit, waiting patiently for Morton at the end of a plexiglass-sided rampway. The white-shirted security man was enormously bulky, the pockets of his serge trousers revealing the white lining as he stretched forward to hand him back his shoulder bag.

164

'That's all fine, Mr Morton.' He handed Morton a Visitor's Day Pass on a white lanyard. 'Put the lanyard round your neck please. You're free to enter.' He was in, the thick glass door sliding open to admit him to Westminster.

The MP came forward, unsmiling. 'You're a little late, Morton. However, no problem.' They shook hands. 'As explained to you, I think, I can only escort you into the main building, then you're on your own.'

'Yes,' said Morton. 'Thank you.'

The MP indicated the busy sunlit central atrium, where politicians, staff and visitors held meetings. There were some trees, Morton noted, that looked exotic and, he noted, several food stalls and coffee bars.

'This is more like Holyrood than Westminster,' Morton marvelled.

The MP smiled. 'Yes, isn't it? It's rather different from the creaky old palace, isn't it? There's actual daylight. Smells nice, feels open, warm, comfortable even.'

'Is your office upstairs?'

'No, I'm in a different building. We're all spread out. There's some in here, some in the Norman Shaw buildings, North and South, some in Dover House and some in 53 Parliament Street and all these are connected, like a rat run. Anyway, look, I'm sorry I don't have time to offer you a coffee here.'

'Yes, that's a pity,' Morton said. 'It's a nice interior. Those trees...'

'Twelve fig trees and water features no less. There's a coffee bar and two restaurants, the Debate and the Adjournment Brasserie. Upstairs has committee rooms and of course offices. I think there's about 210 MPs and staff here. Anyway, Morton, you're not here for the guided tour, though I've not been informed exactly what you are here for, and I don't wish to know. We'd better be moving.'

The MP led him into a corridor, swiping his pass on almost unobtrusive contact points and then down carpeted stairs into a tiled corridor. There were lots of staff and members moving to and fro.

The MP spoke confidentially in a low voice so that Morton had to strain to hear him. 'We're under the road, now, Morton. This tunnel is also reached from Exit 3 at the Tube station. It brings us up in New Palace Yard.'

Morton nodded. He felt like a fugitive but he wasn't. He had a Day Visitor's Pass which he had obtained in his real name. He was legit. But it didn't feel like it, somehow. The MP ahead of him swiped his pass again and they exited the tunnel into daylight and Morton realised they were at the start of the open Colonnade. To his right, he could see the railings and the armed policemen and even the Cromwell Gate Entrance. But he was already inside.

'You'll be alright from here, Morton?' the MP asked.

Morton nodded. 'Yup. The Press Room is just up here. The Moncrieffe.' He handed his holdall to the MP. 'And thanks for taking care of this.'

'Okay,' he smiled faintly, 'I'll pass it on to your local member so you can collect it in a few days. I'll leave you here. Good luck!' He walked away in the direction of the Terrace.

Morton looked at his watch. He was going to switch now from Morton to Gallimont. He felt the letter inside the left pocket of his jacket. The one with the invitation from Edgar Kellett MP to the meeting of GB13. Then he folded the other MP's letter and shoved it into the back pocket of his trousers. Mustn't get them mixed up!

He was pretty well acquainted with the corridors and labyrinths of the place, having been based here yonks ago, when he had explored all the nooks and crannies in his spare time. The thing was never to look lost. Even if you went wrong you just turned and tried again.

As he walked along the narrow corridor, a man passing by in the other direction nodded at him and said, quite distinctly: 'Hello, Philip.'

Morton froze. 'H-hello,' he stuttered. But it was okay. It was. In fact, it was a big boost to his confidence. It was funny that he was better known here as someone else than as himself. But the mere existence of this meeting here, was evidence of a sort of collusion, at the very least, between some parliamentarians and this nasty little group, using – or misusing – the official resources of State. He hoped he would be able to find out more about the links, the funding, the people involved, uncover misuse of Government resources, find out what they were up to.

He had reached the tiled Lower Waiting Hall near the Members' Dining Room and ascended the stairs to the Upper Waiting Hall. Two members of staff barely glanced at him and he turned into the committee corridor that he knew extended the full length of the river side of the Palace of Westminster. The carpet was a colour-clash of red, blue and green. The corridor was quite empty but he passed a few people who sat nervously outside a committee room on a sofa, waiting to appear before a hearing or a tribunal. He noticed that each committee room had two doors: one for the members and one for the public. Morton saw a Gents toilet and went in. He was feeling last-minute nerves. Could he go through with it? He'd need a big dose of luck. He planned to be invisible, stay at the back and video the proceedings and get out as quickly as possible. There were two urinals, one cubicle and one sink and towel dispenser. He went into the tiny cubicle and clicked the recording device on.

When he came out of the toilet, he followed some other people ambling along and saw a wooden signboard on which was a small piece of paper: Meeting (Edgar Kellett MP) This Way. He couldn't back out now. Halfway along the corridor, he saw a knot of people and knew that was the Trafalgar Room. Liveried staff members of Parliament were checking the invitations list outside the Public Entrance. That was a relief. He had imagined GB13 thugs giving him the eye. It was far more civilised than he had expected. As he waited in the doorway, he could see the magnificent bright interior of the Trafalgar Room. It was probably the most expensive venue in the place to hire. He could see catering staff laying out a buffet lunch over to his left.

He showed the invitation letter in his turn, the one from the jacket pocket on the left side, his false name under the letterhead of Edgar Kellett MP. The flunkey searched for him on the list, barely glancing at his Visitor's Day Pass. 'Mr Gallimont… ah yes, welcome to the Trafalgar Room.' And he was in.

It was a flaw in the security that the Visitor's Day Pass did not have a name on it or a photo. Once you had one of those round your neck you could get more or less anywhere in the Parliament and be anyone. You could be someone different from the person you had declared yourself to be when you passed in through security.

The room was laid out theatre style, facing a raised dais, with a large Union flag hanging at an angle from a flag stand at the front. The chairs had the gold-embossed House of

168

Commons portcullis on green leather. There were about thirty men and a sprinkling of women, mostly at the bar. At a quick glance he knew none of them. He sauntered around one of the ornate white-painted pillars, beneath the hanging chandeliers, to the bar area and waited to be served. Sunlight, reflecting off the River Thames, sparkled in the window frames beyond the lacy window screens. He tried to smile affably, and relax. Nothing could happen to him here, in the heart of government, surely?

'What will you have, sir?'

Morton wondered if Gallimont was the champagne type. Probably. He smiled and indicated the pale green flutes. He hated champagne but it seemed to be all that was on offer anyway, that or orange juice, and he couldn't imagine Gallimont swigging fruit juice. He caught snatches of conversation and some meaningful glances but he couldn't make out who was who. He should have looked up Kellett, a Labour MP. Was he the little man with the very bald head? He felt out of place, talked to no-one. Gallimont would have been known and spoken to. He was already looking suspiciously out of place. Then he saw a familiar face. Gordon Menzies.

'Hello again.'

'Philip? Wondered if you be here, old boy.' He shook hands. 'Heard about your troubles.'

Morton made a deprecating gesture with his free hand. 'Ah, it was a temporary problem. We can take these in our stride.'

'Quite so. Want me to get you another bubbly?'

He frowned. 'That's okay, old man. One is sufficient. Now if it was a single malt...'

'With you entirely there. I think I'll skip it myself.' He looked at his watch. 'Should have been started by now. Wonder what's causing the hold-up. I have to be back in Whitehall by 12:00. Let's grab a seat.'

CHAPTER NINETEEN

Morton's luck was holding. The meeting was under way. He was sitting in the second back row and had been barely noticed. He had filled in the time by chit-chatting with Gordon Menzies. Not for the first time he had wondered why such a manifestly decent chap was knocking about with GB13. He hoped Sean and his friends could erase Menzies from the recording. He felt gratitude towards him.

The meeting was dull, the kind of meeting any group might be having, a grind of annual reports and financial matters with very little clues to anything. He had caught several references to Lord Ashbury, who was resigning on the grounds of ill health.

Menzies whispered knowingly to him: 'Parkinsons, poor sod.'

There were several references to Crail and just as he was wondering what a small Fife coastal village had to do with it, he heard another reference… it was *Lord* Craile, not a place, a person. He remembered the name. Former Chairman of the Independent Scotch Malt Whisky Producers' Association. Famous for taking Tony Blair to court over his reform of the Lords, subsequent to having not succeeded in his bid to remain one of the ninety-two *elected* hereditary peers. He had made a lugubrious farewell speech in the Lords prophesying utter doom for the British way of life that was often quoted as an example of hyperbole. Lord Craile, he now learned, had stepped up his funding of GB13's activities because of pressure put upon 'our normal funding sources'. Morton began to listen intently. The speaker, the Hon Secretary,

Wilfred Wilkins, looked around the room, nodding, his expression grim.

'You may have heard of some unfortunate publicity stirred up in Scotland upon some of our activities there and,' he pointed his finger in Morton's general direction, 'some of our staff have come under intolerable strain. But we have been able to rise above these temporary setbacks.' The rest of what Wilkins was saying was mush in his ears as he felt people turning around to look at him. Inwardly, he was quailing, sure the moment of retribution had arrived. What if he was asked to speak? He felt a hot flush in his hands and at the back of his neck.

But Wilkins droned on. 'With this shift in our funding,' he claimed, 'we will be free and less restricted so that we may redouble our efforts to strengthen the bonds of our great British Union.'

Morton joined in the polite applause and gradually felt his stress subside. Wilkins was no orator and his voice had a monotony to it that grated in his ears. He began to refer to 'our legislative group' and Morton learned that it was chaired by Edgar Kellett MP. It was building support in the House for a motion which it hoped to pressure the Government to accept. If they didn't, it would be introduced as a private member's bill. Morton listened intently and perked up his ears when he heard Wilkins say that, as yet, the press had not got wind of the move. Wilkins felt that as there was a strong chance of the Government accepting the motion, or at least of both main parties putting it in their manifestos for the next election... they didn't want to diminish the prospects of its eventual success when it was announced. Morton was mystified until a voice from the floor questioned Wilkins and he responded:

172

'Yes, that is correct, Lord Bloater, it is our Constitutional Change Bill that I'm referring to. Any vote affecting the constitution will be required to gain seventy-five per cent of the vote for it to succeed – and a seventy-five per cent vote of the full House will be required before any referendum can be held in any part of the UK.'

Lord Bloater stood up and cleared his throat. He was a stout man, of considerable girth and his white shirt belly extended far beyond the confines of his grey suit. Morton smiled to think how aptly he was named.

'Well, thank you, Mr Wilkins, ahem. Ah, some of us are new to all this. It is a highly sensible piece of legislation, which I'm sure the present administration will be amenable to and wish to proceed with.'

'Thank you for your support, my Lord. We are making considerable headway.'

Morton felt his face heating up. They were going to legally prevent any possibility of a second referendum on Scottish Independence! Locking Scotland inside the Union forever. No wonder they didn't want the press to get wind of that! Wilkins sat down after a final rhetorical flourish.

The next speaker was even less distinguished, to Morton's mind, though as his speech was shorter and he ended by announcing the buffet lunch, he received hearty applause. People started to get to their feet and there was movement towards the sides of the room, to the bar and the buffet, spread out gloriously on tables. There was a revived sense of bonhomie within the room and Morton, lulled by it, headed over to the buffet. He was unaware that he had become an object of fascination for several men standing in front of the dais. He was their subject of conversation; their eyes followed

173

him as he made small-talk with several of Menzies' acquaintances.

'Gallimont?' A hand touched his sleeve. Morton turned from Menzies to see two men studying him. One was the MP, Edgar Kellett, an unprepossessing, wizened, bald man, the other, a distinguished-looking man with bouffant grey hair and an efficient moustache. He wore a dark burgundy waistcoat, a shiny grey suit and suede shoes. He was the one who spoke.

'Philip,' he said silkily, pulling on his arm, 'a word, if you please. Over here.'

'Oh, of course,' Morton said, trying to keep up the pretence of being affable, smiling faintly.

'You know me, of course?' the taller man said.

'Of course.'

'When was the last time we met, can you remember, Philip?'

Morton realised it was a trap. They were onto him. 'Um, not for a while,' he said. 'You normally telephone me.'

The man smiled triumphantly and closed his eyes momentarily. 'Of course I do, Philip. And how was your holiday?'

Morton kept his fixed smile. 'Lovely. Very nice, thank you.'

'And what was the weather like, Philip?'

'Warm, lovely and warm.'

'Hear that, Edgar? Perhaps we should have gone with Philip?'

'Do a lot of sunbathing, did you?'

Morton said nothing. He had realised he was in a swamp and was disinclined to provide more amusement for them.

'I'm surprised you have come back so soon, or maybe you never went at all?' He narrowed his eyes. Ah yes. But you have never met me either, have you, Philip – or should I say, William?'

Morton was thinking fast. He had to leave. But he was surrounded. He couldn't make it to the doors without having to fight his way out.

The man with the moustache was beaming triumphantly at his success. 'Yes, you have been most inventive, William. Plucky, and a little bit cheeky, too, would you say? Edgar?'

'Cheeky blighter, Neil. Coming here, supping our bubbly and spyin' on us all the time, no doubt, the beggar.'

'And what have you found, William? That we are a legal pressure group operating in the best interests of the British State, to weed out troublemakers like you and protect the unity of our wonderful country. I would not imagine you could have found anything in the least bit... what was your word? Subversive.' He smirked. 'Imagine, you coming in here, to the Mother of Parliaments, believing you could... no, don't try to run, Morton. You can't possibly escape.' Commander Smyth had made a slight movement of his forehead and Morton realised he had been silently flanked on either side by two large men in blazers.

Smyth said: 'Take this unexpected guest to where we can speak to him at our leisure after the meeting. Use whatever means are necessary to prevent him leaving.'

'Yes, sir. Come on, you.'

Morton was forcibly escorted from the room. He saw the crestfallen look on Menzies' face as he passed. 'Philip?'

Then he was out in the corridor, being frogmarched roughly along between the two silent bullet-headed thugs. 'Where are you taking me?' he asked.

175

'Shut it, you!'

They had almost reached the end of the corridor but the two men pushed him out through a glass door into a stairwell. It gave access to a carpeted stairway and they propelled him towards the narrow steel-railed stairway. It was too narrow: They would have to be in single file, Morton saw.

He pretended to slip on the carpet then and one of the men lost his grip of his arm. He twisted and evaded the other's hand. As they rushed forward, effectively blocking each other, he tripped lightly up the steps.

They came up after him, cursing. He was in a narrow carpeted corridor, with striplights all along it. He ran to the end hearing the men charging after him. There was another stair down. But it only went a few steps and continued into another corridor. They were close behind.

'You can't get out!'

Morton had intended to continue along the small corridor but saw a narrow iron staircase almost concealed behind a pillar and ducked into it, hearing the thugs thunder past into the small corridor. He went up and up, two floors and came out under a skylight.

The floor was bare, uncarpeted. The doors were locked – he tried one or two. He went along the corridor. Another narrow circular iron stair. He saw an empty bottle of champagne on the bottom step. He picked it up – a useful weapon. It was darker, weaker lighting, as he cautiously ascended. But there was no-one there. His breathing was coming back to normal. He'd lost his pursuers, for the moment at least, but where was he?

At the top of the stair, there was a small corridor, blind, no way out. Two small grey-painted doors. Both locked and they had the look of being disused. He was beyond the public area, even the area used by functionaries. It was colder up here, beyond the range of the heating too, maybe. He noticed a loose panel in the wall, and knelt down and peeked through it. Beyond was completely dark. The panel was a concealed door.

He pulled out the mobile phone from his jacket, and switched on the torch function and held it out, then gasped, lost in wonder. It was a frighteningly vast empty space, rising up to the underside of the pitched roof, almost the size of a football pitch.

In the dim light he could not see far into the void but near at hand were mouldering heaps of plaster or stone. He could hear trickling sounds. Mice? Or rats? It was dusty and yet it also smelled damp.

He carefully stepped over the oak skirting board into the space and pulled the panel behind him, and squatted there in the complete dark broken only by the pale beam of the light from his mobile phone. He was safe, for now. But where was he?

He knew there were 1,100 rooms on seven floors in the Palace of Westminster and he was clearly above all of them, somewhere in the roof space. He could see damp patches and there was one place where a hole let in shards of daylight in which clouds of dust danced in a frenzy, intersected by falling droplets of water. He heard the faint rustling of mice, the sound coming in waves. He even wondered if he heard their squeaking. It was like Castle Gormenghast, a damp Gothic ruin, rotting, mouldering – this building that Churchill had praised, with a fine irony or sense of self-delusion, as 'the citadel of British liberty'. He smiled at the grim irony of him being here, given the piece he had written for Hugh a fortnight before. It was actually more dilapidated than even he had imagined.

He stood up, plaster or dust crunching under his shoes, shining the torch around him to check the bare wooden floor was safe to walk on. He left the champagne bottle standing by the door panel as a marker so that he would know the way back, and began to walk carefully around the perimeter. There were wet patches where the wooden floor had become slippery with slimy fungus, where he had to watch every step he made.

After about ten minutes of this slow progress, he came up against brick wall that extended as far as he could see on either side of him. He wondered if this was the Elizabeth Tower, whose spire contained Big Ben. He continued to walk around the perimeter at a right angle to the side he had come in by, and examined the first of a series of rectangular vents in the floor and cautiously peeped down over the rim. Ventilation shafts, connecting to extractor fans in the House of Commons, no doubt, or the Members' Dining Room or the kitchens.

He suddenly remembered the ballpoint pen in his top pocket and pressed the clasp to stop the recording. He wondered if it had worked, whether there was anything on it that Sean could use.

He reached an ending, a corner of sorts, and turned ninety degrees. The roof beams had descended and he had to duck down to avoid banging his head. He became disorientated, trying to remember where he was in relation to the panel he had come in from. He believed he was now on the far side, opposite where he had come in. But where had he come in? The phone's torchlight was dimming, now too poor to see more than a few feet in front of him. He wondered if there would be more doors concealed by panelling on the side he was on. He wished he had a proper torch.

Eventually, as he walked, his eyes became used to the dark and he saw ahead a line of light on the side and crouched down to feel with his fingertips inch by inch all around it. It was a similar panel door to the one he had come in.

He pushed it once, twice, and it swung outwards. There was light. He found it dazzling and narrowed his eyes against it. When they had adjusted to the light, he could see green, red and blue carpeting – a corridor.

He straightened up, brushing dust off his shoulders and blew his nose to clear his nostrils of plaster dust. Finally, he stepped out unsteadily, holding the wall and placed one foot then the other on carpet. He looked bemusedly at the white footprints he was making then began to move quickly along the corridor.

Two men were coming towards him, talking loudly. Politicians or civil servants. He ignored them, noticing the funny looks they gave him as he passed. He continued till he came to an iron circular staircase in a narrow well and descended, all the way down, one, two, three, four levels, to come out on grey carpet, opposite a grey door marked, Cavalry Officers' Hat Store. He laughed silently, incredulously. Really? A further wooden stair turned and descended ten steps down to a door which opened out onto a well-lit, green-carpeted public corridor.

Morton realised he was in a part of the building that he knew, somewhere between the Commons' Debating Chamber and the Members' Dining Room. He knew it was a Member's Only area and so he wasted no time in hastening to the Terrace Cafeteria, unchecked, unimpeded, glad to be among people again. He breathed more easily when he made it to a door out onto the Terrace, with the Thames ahead of him and the bridge to his left.

It was busy, serving a lunchtime crowd and smelt agreeably of hot food. He looked around. No waiters, good, because, as a Day Visitor, he knew he was supposed to be accompanied by someone with a pass, but his cover story was that he had simply gone out to the toilet and was returning to his table.

He knew he was safe here and breathed more easily, forced himself to walk more slowly down the aisles of tables in the fresh air under the awning.

He spotted Susan Havilland halfway along.

He leaned over her. 'Hello, Susan, is it?'

'You must be Sean's friend, Willie?'

He sat down opposite her. Glancing around quickly, he unclipped the pen and handed it over with the phone. 'You wouldn't believe the trouble I have had.' He was glad to be rid of it and briefly told her what had happened. 'I just need to get out of this place. Now.'

Susan stood up. 'Right. Follow me. We can be there in two minutes.'

Susan led him quickly down to the Lower Waiting Hall, along into the Central Lobby, which as usual was thronging with political fixers and their hangers-on. He saw a couple of media people he knew vaguely.

'Thanks for doing this,' he murmured.

Susan smiled. 'No problem, Willie. Did you really get chased about by…?'

'Yes, and some of them must still be about.'

'Well, you'll be safe here, surely?'

They passed up the stone steps into St Stephen's corridor. Willie glanced at the huge painting that was supposed to

180

represent the passing of the Act of Union, with a line of aristocratic supplicants and a bishop presenting something to the matronly Queen Anne. All the stone statues in here, he remembered someone telling him, were in cricketing poses. He could believe it. An English in-joke. He recalled that the English, as well as the Scottish Parliament, was to have been dissolved by the Act of Union. But that had never happened. A promise not kept. Westminster was the English Parliament continuing with a few Scots added to it. Not quite the equal partnership of nations promised. Then they were into the cavernous wooden-beamed St Stephen's Hall.

'You'll be safe here now, yes?' Susan asked.

'Yes. I'll get straight out.'

She touched his sleeve. 'Go out the Carriage Gate, Willie. You just push yourself through. No need to go back through security. Quicker.'

'That's a good idea. Thanks – and for that, bye!' Morton passed out of the stone-flagged hall, without further incident, to the fresh cold air of New Palace Yard and went swiftly up to the narrow black steel gate and he pushed effortlessly through the bars and arrived on the pavement. He felt, strangely, exultation and relief in equal parts. He seemed to have got away with it. After that, came a wave of angry resentment at the danger he had been put in and what he had heard of attempts to stymie democracy in the very heart of the 'Mother of Parliaments'.

CHAPTER TWENTY

Colin Hardwick and Kirsty Haldane, in the ops room at New Waverley, had tried to solve the puzzle of what Morton was up to. Their intercepts showed that he had travelled to London on the train during the night. It was outwith their jurisdiction, yet it had been twelve hours and they had still not been informed whether Millbank was following up or whether they were to stand by for new instructions.

'I hope we were not exceeding our authority, implanting the transmitter in Morton's watch,' Kirsty said at last. 'But we did let them know. They must be acting.'

Hardwick looked up from his study of the printout. 'It was our initiative. Can't see how there could be any problem about it. Clearly, Morton was in London on business of some sort and is now returning by train. They should, by rights, be keeping us informed of what he was doing there. All we can do is wait for further advice.'

Through the exertions and stresses of the day and out of a sense of relief, Morton felt sleep creep up on him as the train travelled north, every mile taking him further from his enemies. He tried not to think of the meeting, his desperate escape from the thugs and the shit storm that would result if, or when, the recordings he had made found their way onto TV or social media. He had helped to let the public know what was going on. It had been stressful, but in a strange kind of way, enjoyable too. He had gone up close and personal with the kind of person he most abhorred: men who believed that they were the ones with authority, who believed they had carte blanche to push people around, because of some racial or ethnic superiority, or because the history of the Empire was in their blood and made them feel entitled to absolute obedience; men who sneered at and mocked other nations and their aspirations and the very concept of equality or diversity. The purring superiority of the man called 'Neil' who had casually ordered his thugs to detain him was typical of the kind, or the caste. He had acted as if he was in India in the 1940s dealing with some 'boys' in dhotis. His life had been imbued with a self-belief that he was born to rule, that he had an entitlement. Morton's mind wandered off. He remembered, oddly, a conversation a few years ago with a boy who had been in his class at George Watson's. They'd bumped into each other at a dinner in the Royal Hotel in George Street. Hugo, the toast of the glitterati, whose dad was in the House of Lords. After a few minutes of conversation, Morton discovered Hugo hadn't changed since school days. His politics were repellently right wing and he still had a snobbish attitude.

'I'd actually forgotten you were in my class, Morton,' he said blandly. 'It was a good school, was it not?'

Morton had agreed it was. It should be. Had cost enough.

'And, Morton, you *sound* like you went to a good school. You could be one of us, Morton, you really could.'

Was that all it was – attitude, manners, a confident front? But Morton knew the social divide owed more to the denying of emotions, the blunting of compassion. Empathy was for cissies. Hugo and the rest of them belonged to a different world where harsh realities were never allowed to intrude, where each day began and ended with entitlement.

But the conversations of the other passengers in his carriage, the pleasant and reassuring sussurrance of their

183

voices and the warm bulk of the large man sitting in the forward-facing airline seat next to him, with an occasional baby's gurgling cry, nudged him imperceptibly over the line towards sleep. He pulled his coat around and used a sleeve against the window as a pillow. He was fast asleep as the train stopped at York, Darlington, slept through Durham and was only briefly aware of Newcastle as the bulk of the person in the next seat got off. He dimly heard the sounds of doors opening and closing, the change in tone of voices as they left the train or joined it. He was warm and sleepy, safe, he thought, soon to be home in Edinburgh.

When he awoke – or was being shaken awake – he at first imagined he was at his destination. He blinked up at a man's face staring intently down at him. Peripherally, he was aware the train was still moving through countryside. The man stared down and kept shaking him.

'What is it?' Morton asked testily. He didn't like the look or the smell of the man. A shaven-headed, cruel face, tattoos on the neck. Reminded him of the thugs in the Trafalgar Room.

'You're Morton?' the man whispered hoarsely, leaning over him. His breath smelt bad, and Morton now saw that he had a small black gun protruding from the front of his jacket, aimed at him.

'What?'

'Are you Morton, the journalist? Or should I call you Philip Gallimont?'

'What *is* this?' Morton blinked, sitting up, under his coat. He saw that everything in the carriage was placid. No-one was looking. His sleepiness left him suddenly. 'Who are *you*?'

'I ask the questions.' The man palmed a mobile phone with his left hand and looked at it, showed Morton the picture on the screen and nodded. 'Yep, you're him. You've got some nerve. But your time's up.'

'I don't know *what* you're talking about,' Morton said, faintly. 'You're not going to use that on a train. You wouldn't get away.'

'That's my business,' the man said abruptly and grabbed Morton's arm. 'Come with me, you!' He began to pull him out of the seat. Morton reckoned his best chance was to stay put, but the man was strong. 'Come out of it,' the man growled. Morton could sense that other passengers had started to become aware.

Before he knew what he was doing, he'd shouted: 'Help! This man has a *gun*!'

The man had pulled him to his feet. He'd interposed his coat between them. The gun was somewhere underneath it.

He pushed forward, as if he was in a scrum, ramming the man onto the edge of the empty seat across the aisle and pushed the coat over him.

Passengers were standing up to look, alarm on their faces. Then the gun went off with a wet sound like someone snapping a tree branch. Nothing happened for a second. The man pushed the coat off angrily. The gun reappeared.

Someone started to scream. The gun was still in his hand, as he struggled to get upright.

Morton saw horrified faces as he jumped clear of the man. Despite his peril, he was aware of the blue North Sea, a row of quaint cottages. The automatic sliding doors flew open, he fell through in his haste, fell onto the floor of the corridor, the man charging after him, tripping over a holdall that'd rolled out of the luggage rack, falling, and the gun clattering loose on the floor.

185

Morton scrambling to his feet, terrified, shouting, the man scrabbling along the floor for the gun. The train starting to slow. He saw houses, a town approaching. Tweedmouth, nearly at Berwick.

He tried to run down the corridor but the man caught him by the legs. They struggled together. The man was short but stocky. He stank of sweat, Morton realised, hands covered with tattoos, dirt under his fingernails, an assassin or thug of some sort, a criminal – GB13 no doubt. He must have got on at Newcastle. Somebody phoned him up, instructed him. The train was slowing.

He got to the carriage door, pulled down the window. The man was still on the floor, one hand holding Morton's leg, the other scrabbling for the gun. The train was braking hard, he dimly heard people rushing about, shouting. He thrust his hand around the outside of the door, feeling for the brass handle, the onrush of cold air in his eyes and hair. The door wouldn't open. Of course not, the train was moving.

The man was on his knees. He had the gun. As time stood still for him, Morton's life hung in the balance.

'Don't be a fool, Morton!' the man shouted, and fired. The bullet shattered a hole in the door where Morton's leg had been. But he was holding onto that door. He was out of the train. He was flying in the wind, swinging in mid-air, gasping to get his breath. Cold, rushing air, the door knocking back against the train, his legs dangling, holding on tight, wheels, braking, violent movement.

The man's face appeared, leaning out, trying to shoot at him. He couldn't do anything but hold on. The door swung away then from the train, far out, away from the train. Morton was stopped, hit by something rough and thick and, uncomprehending, fell off, let go, dropped down.

186

He heard the gunshot but it was far away. He was alive. He saw the man jump out.

The train carried on. Morton was stationary. Stuck inside a bush, he slithered down slowly, flopping forward onto his front into soft grass. Then he began to feel the pain in his legs and across his arms. The train was gone, its brakes slowly screaming out of sight, metal on metal.

He waited till the dizziness passed and raised himself to his knees to see the end of the train disappearing up the line. He heard it slowly crossing a bridge and then remembered – there was a bridge just before Berwick.

He got to his feet. He felt okay, pain in his legs and arms. He had scratches on his hands, his knees were wet. He laughed. So what if they were? But where was the man? Was he nearby? He moved forward jerkily, anger building in him, and just a few yards further along at the tree line, saw that the bank gave way to the sudden drop of the start of the famous Royal Border Bridge. It was 120 feet above the shallow River Tweed. He slowly began to realise that the man who had attacked him had jumped, but had jumped too late.

Morton looked down but could see nothing. It was unreal. Five minutes of a completely unbelievable experience that he couldn't quite take in. The shock of seeing a gun pointing at him, bringing back to him all the horror of the Glen Orchy Distillery and McGinley. The mad struggle, jumping out of a train, swinging in the rushing wind, being shot at… His legs and hands began to shiver and shake. The man had had a picture of him so there was no doubt of his motives.

Once the shaking and trembling and shivering stopped, Morton felt his legs and arms and realised he only had a few scratches and bruises. It was incredible. He walked unsteadily back along the grass verge below the track. He saw the bush that had saved his life – a thick broom with a few yellow petals remaining from last year and noted that a branch had snapped under his weight. He thanked it silently and stood there, getting his breath back. Then he continued unsteadily by the railway line and down to a field edge and a gate to join the main road under the railway bridge leading to the town. A hundred yards further he walked across the Tweedmouth Bridge into Berwick, where he had been two weeks before. Everything seemed bright and colourful and the air smelt fresh and wonderful. He was alive! He shivered and then he realised that he was in his shirtsleeves. His jacket and coat were on the train.

CHAPTER TWENTY-ONE

The fresh sea breezes of Berwick-on-Tweed sifted through Willie Morton's shirt and caused him to shiver uncontrollably as he hurried across the Tweedmouth Bridge. The city centre seemed almost deserted under yellow streetlights. He could feel the pain of the scratches and little cuts on his legs and the backs of his hands and wrists, and even a line of smarting pain across his cheek and forehead, which was a little damp, perhaps blood. He saw many charity shops displaying coats in the window but all were closed. He looked at his watch: 5 p.m. Too late. He was freezing. He saw warm, golden lights in The Coffee Place, behind a pattern of whorled glass panes. He could see no-one inside but the door was open. He stood there out of the wind, letting the warm steamy atmosphere enclose him and heard the sound of hoovering. He walked towards the toilets and a girl, bending over a hoover, stiffened in alarm.

'Sorry, sir, we're shut!'

'Oh! Sorry I startled you.' He waved his hands. 'Could I just use the toilets?'

'Of course. They are through here.' She indicated doors leading to stairs and he found the Gents on the upper floor. His face, he saw in the mirror, was scratched on the left side and laced with a thin trickle of blood. He dabbed at it with a paper towel. Other than that, he was not too bad. He wondered about the other man. Where was he? It was unreal, what had happened. The shock was wearing off. He luxuriated in the hot water, washing his hands and face. He

189

had got off lightly. He directed the warm air blower at his face, enjoying the warmth.

When he got back downstairs, the girl was waiting for him, standing protectively in front of the till; freckles, lots of dark hair. He winced. 'Thank you so much. I've been in an accident,' he told her. 'Lost my coat. It's freezing outside.'

'Oh,' she said. 'Wait a minute. We've a couple of coats here – lost property. I'll have a look.'

'You're so kind… Hannah,' Morton grimaced, reading the name on the badge of her uniform tunic.

'Been here for yonks. Hang on, I'll fetch them.' She disappeared into the kitchen area and shortly returned with a zipped-up pale cream cotton jacket and a dark belted raincoat. 'This one's probably better – warmer,' she suggested, holding up the raincoat. 'Look, it's got a lining.' She wrinkled her nose. 'Could do with a dry-clean, but…'

'Beggars can't be choosers,' Morton smiled. It hurt to smile. 'Hannah, you're an angel,' he told her, pulling the coat on.'

She flushed and he felt a strong urge to hug her. He was feeling new waves of elation or delayed shock. It was making him a bit giddy.

'How do I look?' he joked.

She frowned and the freckles congregated. 'It's a bit small, but not too bad. That coat's been here longer than what I have. You look like a policeman, a detective, now.'

'Well, thank you so much!' He took out a tenner. 'No, no – for your kindness, Hannah.'

'Well, okay. I'm just happy to oblige.'

She waved as he walked away and he was thinking how much he would like to kiss her. There had been an intimacy of sorts between them. He wondered if she was a student.

190

Probably married with three kids. He looked at his watch. 5 p.m. Frowning hurt too, he discovered. The watch wasn't working, yet he had only replaced the battery a couple of weeks ago. He'd have to take it in for repair. Maybe the fake Rolex was finally giving up the ghost. He remembered buying it in Barcelona with Sally. On the big clock on the Old Town Hall, it was just after 6 p.m. Had the watch broken during the attack on the train? Was that really an hour ago? He saw a reflection of himself in a shop window. The coat was okay, rather old-fashioned, but he didn't care – it was warm. Thank god he still had his wallet.

The next train to Edinburgh was 6.24 p.m. He noticed a phone box in the station cafeteria and bought a cup of tea and a sandwich at the small takeaway, Café Express. The phone box accepted debit cards. He made three calls – to Hugh, to Sean and to Emily in that order – then settled down to wait for the train, with his cup of tea. It had been an extraordinary day. And someone had tried to kill him. But he was alive.

When he got off at Edinburgh Waverley, just after 7 p.m. he walked home and gratefully entered his key in the familiar Yale lock of his first-floor flat in Keir Street. He'd had an intensive dialogue in his head about whether it was safe to go to the flat, given that someone had already tried to kill him. But he would have to take a chance. And besides, he did not really believe that they would try again, not here. The flat was as he had left it, a little musty. He opened a window and looked around, enjoying being reunited with the comfort of the familiar. He showered, changed his clothes and put the raincoat into a plastic bag to drop off at a charity shop. He placed the broken watch on the mantelpiece. He looked in

191

the kitchen to see if there was anything to eat. He was out of bread and the milk was off. There was some food in the freezer compartment. But apart from tins and biscuits and crackers, there was nothing he fancied. He zipped up his hoodie over a tee-shirt and shirt and pulled on his leather jacket, tied on a scarf, clapped a beanie hat on his head, pulled on gloves and set off walking to the *Standard* office.

In the old days, when he had first worked with Hugh and the *Scottish Standard* team, they had been crammed into two-floors and a basement in an old warehouse that had a rear entrance off Candlemaker Row and a front door on George IV Bridge. The team had come together to build a new title in the blood-stained aftermath of a failed attempt by a media consortium to amalgamate the *Scotsman* and the *Herald*. The new team had voted, against all logic and advice, to continue. The title had come from a quip an embittered hack had made about 'keeping up our standards' despite the mass sackings. And it had worked. By adopting a supportive line on Independence, the *Standard* had thrived where the others continued to decline. And they had gathered around them the best, the most committed, the most enthusiastic. After five years, they had flitted further up the Cowgate to larger premises on South Bridge.

The nightshift team was spread out on both floors of the building and the sweaty, gone-to-seed news editor Michael Donnelly was there too, but Morton ignored him and went into Hugh Leadbetter's office, hung his jacket and scarf on the peg, switched on the anglepoise lamp and typed non-stop on his boss's Hewlett Packard desktop PC for thirty minutes. The news story about his day came out complete, in an organic shape, requiring little editing or reshaping. He titled it: 'Journalist Survives Assassination Attempt on Train'. He

192

forwarded it to Hugh's mobile and to Sean then left the building. It was a big relief to him to be able to walk away, out and anonymous in the chilly night air, mingling incognito with other pedestrians beneath the street lights. He flipped his jacket collar up and pulled the beanie down over his ears and set off, walking to Restalrig, to Emily's flat in Lochend Grove. A decent walk. He needed the exercise.

Emily had prepared a lasagne which was baking in the oven.

'The warrior returns,' she said, when he turned up at the door, but he could plainly see the concern on her face.

In the kitchen, she uncorked an Argentinian Malbec while Morton took off the coat. 'Oh, Willie, I was so worried, when you phoned. These people are nasty! I really think you should go to the police.'

'Well, I am, that's all arranged. I'm meeting them with Archie McDonald, at 10 a.m. But I had to make sure my piece was in the paper for tomorrow.' He beamed. 'Front-page lead you know. But has there been anything on TV or radio?'

'Come on. Sit down. Here, I'll pour you a glass of this nice red.' She grabbed his hands. 'Ooh, you're freezing!' She had tied a folded kitchen towel around the neck of the bottle to prevent drips.

'That's nice,' he sipped his wine. It was rich, deep and fruity. 'Just what I need. That smells good. I haven't eaten for ages. I've literally only had a croissant today.' He made a face. 'Not counting a sandwich at Berwick, or I think it was a sandwich. Fish paste, maybe. Yuck!'

'Well, it's nearly ready. No, there hasn't been much on the radio. Just a brief report about a man falling from a train near Berwick and police looking for another man who jumped off to escape – that's you, isn't it? And something about a gun

193

being found on the train. Anyway, forget about that now, if you can. Come through and let's eat.'

'Emily, you're a saint!' He felt the warmth of the wine spreading throughout his veins. It still seemed incredible that they were together. What on earth did she see in him?

'And you'd better stay here tonight.'

Morton smiled gratefully. 'I was hoping you'd say that.'

'Well, they won't know where you are. You can lie low here until tomorrow.'

'Yes, that's why I wanted to get my story out first, before going to the police. Then there'll be follow-ups and developments over the next day or two, some of it coming from the police, some from me – or Sean, I should say.'

They sat down to eat and he told her the whole story of his day, from the sleeper train and his briefing by Sean Kermally to the anxiety of his attending the meeting in the Trafalgar Room and his flight through the dusty, upper floors of the Palace of Westminster to the roof space.

'It was surreal, you know, Emily. Like something out of Mervyn Peake's *Gormenghast*. Mice and spiders and dead pigeons. Being up there in the dust and the mould, several floors above all the pomp and dignities. Like a cathedral of emptiness. Felt like I was a long, long way from anywhere, but I was right in the heart of London all the time. I walked right round it, and I didn't know how I would ever get out, get back to the real world. Anyway, I found a narrow iron staircase that ran all the way down about four levels to a little door: The Cavalry Officers' Hat Store. Can you believe that? I didn't see any cavalry officers. Luckily.'

'Unbelievable,' Emily murmured.

'And from there I got to where I had to meet Susan, and to where I had to hand over the recording I had made. Sean was still editing it when I phoned him from Berwick by the way.'

'I'm amazed you managed to go through with it, Willie! A spy pen?'

'I know. Actually I forgot I had it on me. I don't know whether there's anything on it, apart from dust and dead pigeons of course. But Sean says some it is okay and some is good.' He accepted another helping of lasagne. 'This is great, Em. But the worst of it was what happened on the train. I honestly thought I would die.'

'I don't want to think about it!'

'It was all so… I was sleeping and suddenly, I didn't have time to think. The door swung open and I was holding on, swinging in mid-air, hanging from an open door of a train!'

Emily closed her eyes. 'Don't tell me any more. I don't want to have nightmares. At least you're safe now, and it's over. It is over now, isn't it?'

Morton shrugged. 'God knows. But when the story is out there, maybe I'll be a little safer. There's safety in the limelight. This is the second time I've had this kind of trouble just for doing my job. I don't even know *why* they tried to kill me. What is it that they think I know? Sean said the best bit is when they began to interrogate me and then threaten me. Well, that and this bill they're trying to introduce – the Constitutional Change Bill – and stuff about funding from this Lord Craile.'

She looked at him over the rim of her glass. 'I've only vaguely heard of him but then again there are what, about 800 peers in the Lords? Far more than the number of MPs anyway. We'll have to look into him. Or someone will.'

'But, Emily, the man questioning me, who seemed to be in charge, was some kind of Government official or that's

195

what he seemed like. Sean's investigating that. But he reckons the few seconds where the man starts to threaten me and then the two thugs grab me is good footage and he'll feed that to the networks at the appropriate time. Connecting that incident with the... god, listen to me. The attempted murder on the train... well, that's going to drive the media bananas! I'm stuffed now, Em. I somehow got through the whole day on a croissant and coffee that I had on the sleeper and then a cup of tea at Berwick!'

They gravitated to the big sofa in Emily's living room and he had another big glass of wine and began to nod off.

CHAPTER TWENTY-TWO

When Crispin Hayes entered the DTI Investigations and Inspections office on the fourth floor of the New Waverley North building the next day, just after 9 a.m., he found his colleague Kirsty Haldane already in and working in the inner ops room. A spread of that morning's newspapers lay in an untidy heap on the desk in the outer office and there was the smell of coffee brewing. As the ops room door was open, he put his head around.

'Morning.'

'Morning, Crispin,' Kirsty called. She was typing up a report. 'Be with you in a minute.'

He hung up his coat and began the routine tasks of the day. It was twenty minutes before she came through to the outer office. 'Hi,' she said. 'Sorry about…' She indicated the mess of newspapers.

'That's okay. Looking for anything specific?'

'The incident on the train at Berwick yesterday late afternoon.'

Crispin looked up, eyes bright behind the tortoiseshell spectacles. 'That was on the news late last night. Man fallen from train? It's all over the radio this morning. There were two men and a gun.'

'Thing is, Crispin, one of the men, the one who jumped and got away, was the target of our op.'

He sat up. 'Right. Wow! And Thames House is aware?'

'They must be. But they haven't passed on any new instructions. And there's this. I've had it confirmed by the police, about the identity of the man who attacked our suspect. He works, or used to work, for the service.'

Crispin blinked and resettled his specs. 'Really?'

'Yes. No-one told us that formally, of course, although we also know that our target did get back to Edinburgh.'

'You know that? How?'

'Transmitter that was fitted in his wristwatch. So we know he got back to Edinburgh. We know he is staying with a friend, at an address we know about. But what's puzzling is Millbank has kept us in the dark about the whole incident and about the man who tried to kill him on the train. Something funny is going on.'

Crispin sighed. 'It's at times like this that I'm glad I'm only a junior Admins Officer, not Intel. Call me unambitious, but...' He removed his thick spectacles and became a little less like Harry Potter. Kirsty saw that there was something unguarded about his face, like a tortoise out of its shell.

'But you're still doing your General Induction Training, Crispin. Plenty of time yet,' she smiled. 'Once Colin comes in, I'm going to do a video call to Desmond. Find out what he thinks is going on.'

Crispin looked up at the clock. 'He messaged me earlier. He'll be in in at 9.30, he said. Well, he's overdue.'

Ten minutes later, Colin Hardwick came in, carrying a travel case and a briefcase. 'Guess what? I've just been reassigned to Millbank,' he said, bluntly. 'Email, first thing this morning. I'll get the lunchtime train.'

'Colin, what is going on?' Kirsty asked.

'What do you mean? My reassignment?'

'No.'

He frowned. 'You mean specifically?'

198

Kirsty nodded and glanced at Crispin who was on his computer. 'Well, let's go into the ops room.'

'Good idea.' As Hardwick closed the ops room door behind them, he added, 'We should not discuss ops in front of Crispin. Anyway, what's concerning you?'

In the ops room, Kirsty moved over to the window. 'The person who tried to kill our target on the train,' she said quietly, 'turns out to be a serving officer, or former officer.'

Hardwick did a double-take. 'No! That's definite, is it?' He joined her in front of the window. They could see Calton Hill Observatory and St Andrew's House and, to the west, Edinburgh Council HQ and the sea of roofs that was Waverley Station.

Kirsty sighed. 'Well, Colin, Millbank hasn't updated us on what's going on. We need to tell them – remind them – we are still conducting surveillance on Morton and have the transmitter in place. Maybe they're unaware of that?'

Hardwick made a deprecating noise halfway between a snort and a grunt. 'Kirsty, maybe we should quietly forget about that,' he said. 'I mean, reading between the lines, this could all be a bit of a cock-up. You know – left hand, right hand? After all, we don't know what Morton was up to in London yesterday. Presumably they do. We need to tread carefully, in case we're cutting across some other op we don't know about.'

She glanced at him. 'I have a bad feeling about this, Colin. Think about it. We were in close two-way contact practically on an hourly basis over the last week. Now we seem to be totally out on a limb. We deserve to know what's going on. It's our op, or it *was*.'

199

Hardwick nodded. 'Okay, I agree. We'll call Comms on it before I go. You dial up and let them do the talking. See if they volunteer any info.'

As the live images of the Comms room began, they waited for Desmond Thorpe to talk to them. Finally, he appeared and took his seat. 'Apologies for the delay, people. What is your status, please report.'

'*Our* report?' Kirsty said. 'We have nothing.'

Thorpe looked baffled. 'I see. Well?'

'We're waiting on an update from you.'

'From us? No, I have nothing either.'

Kirsty glanced at Hardwick, who nodded, so she continued. 'Well, our target was the victim of an attempted hit yesterday by a service operative while returning from London on the train.'

'Right. Yes. Heard that on the news. And how do you know he was a service operative?'

'Local police,' Kirsty said. 'I had to check with them. That was standard procedure. What's going on, Desmond? Was a hit on our target authorised?'

Thorpe seemed disinterested, Kirsty thought, wouldn't look her in the eye. 'Most unlikely, I should think. He wasn't on any danger list. But, frankly, I don't know any more than you do.'

'You're not serious?' Hardwick said. 'You're the first point of contact. Can you at least tell us if there's another op ongoing, involving the same target?'

'Ah, that I can't tell you. I would if I could, but I don't know. Colin, you're coming home today, I believe?'

'I am, but I'd like to know there's no loose ends up here.'

'As far as I know the op is regarded as complete. By the way,' he said, 'and this concerns you particularly Kirsty, how did you know that the target was in London? We understood that he had stopped using his mobile phone.'

'We were continuing to maintain surveillance on him, as instructed.'

'Right. But we were not aware down here that he had travelled to London. You didn't inform us.'

Kirsty stood up. 'Yes. I did. I discussed it with Commander Smyth.'

'Ah, that explains it. He must have overlooked that detail in his log. He had several days annual leave due and he won't be back until next Monday.'

'I see,' Kirsty said. 'Well, he certainly did know Morton was in London because I told him.'

'Okay, no sweat. I'm sorry I don't know any more about the Berwick incident. Bit odd, but there it is. I'd be surprised if there was another op involving your target, but then again, I'm only the Admins Officer.' He laughed. 'Low down the pecking order.'

Hardwick weighed in. 'A hit on our suspect and there's no briefing about it? That's odd, surely, Desmond? You can see how it looks.'

Ignoring Colin Hardwick's warning frown, Kirsty interrupted him. 'I informed Smyth our suspect is in London, somewhere in Westminster, and the next thing, someone with possible links to the service is having a pop at him.'

Thorpe's face elongated with acute concern. 'Ms Haldane, careful what you're saying, please. These conversations are monitored. And how *did* you know he was in Westminster? What method of tracking did you use?'

Colin Hardwick spoke: 'We had a transmitter inserted in his wristwatch, Desmond.'

'Ah! And presumably Commander Smyth instructed that? I didn't know about it.'

'Come on!' Hardwick protested. 'The instruction was to maintain close surveillance, so we took an initiative. He had stopped using his mobile.'

'And you reported your initiative to the Commander?'

'No, Desmond,' Kirsty said. 'And you know what? He never asked. He just presumed we were carrying out our task by using our own initiative.'

Thorpe reeled them in: 'Okay, okay, people. I think we've got to the end of this one. I'll look into these various issues and get back to you, Kirsty, and Colin, we'll see you here later today, yeah?'

'He never asked?' Hardwick said, once the line was cut. 'Smyth never asked how we knew?'

'Colin, I got the impression he was taken by surprise by the information. I don't like the sound of this. I wish you hadn't been recalled. I'll be left up here to deal with the shit storm if it turns out this hitman is one of ours. As far as I can see, Morton has done nothing illegal. Yet we've been monitoring him for thirteen days. And it seems to me, Commander Smyth is pretty close to this GB13 group, as if he's protecting them. Assurances have been given – publicly – that the group has no governmental links or support. I wonder if that is not actually true.'

Hardwick stood up. 'Well, you might be right, but you'll need to be very careful. We might think that, it might even be true, but even if it is, we can't do anything about it.'

There was a long pause as both digested the information. Kirsty stood up and walked over to the window. 'I know you're heading off soon, Colin, but I'll just run this by you, anyway.'

'Okay, fire away.'

'I'm thinking my next step is to make contact with Morton. Perhaps bring him and request – demand – he tell us what's going on. Lean on him a little. What does he know that would make someone want to try to kill him, and in public too? Maybe that could come under the heading of protective custody? After all, we know he has returned to Edinburgh but not to his own house. Maybe he's scared. Why?'

'Kirsty. I wish you luck with it, but please tread carefully. If I'm anywhere near this when I get back to Millbank, I'll ask around and, whatever, I'll be in touch.'

Morton was woken up by Emily. He was confused to discover he was still on the sofa under a blanket. Daylight was emanating through the drawn curtains and screens.

'I thought it best to leave you, Willie. You were right out of it.'

'Oh, Em, so sorry. What time is it?'

'Just after 8 a.m. I'll put the News on.'

He swung himself into a seated position and could feel all the different points of stiffness and the separate aches of his body. His legs, his hips, his thighs, the backs of his wrists hurt, were sore or merely ached. It was like an orchestra of pain and each muscle, each joint, each sinew contributed or soloed. He stood up unsteadily and wandered through to the kitchen.

'Coffee? Here you are.'

'Oh, god, Em, thanks.' He glugged a mouthful and finished the mug and took another half mug. It tasted like the best coffee he'd ever drunk. 'What is this?'

'Eh? The usual. Fairtrade Colombian. I get it from the deli.'

'Oh. It tastes great. Better than usual.'

'Well then, I'm happy.'

It was the third item on *Good Morning Scotland* and Willie was wearily amused to hear himself described as 'a respected Scottish journalist'. The Northumbria Police had so far not released the identity of the dead man but had confirmed that a gun had been found at the scene.

A paperboy had delivered the *Standard* and Emily brought it through to the kitchen. The story was, as Hugh had promised, on the front page, alongside a picture of himself. Good, he thought, things are starting to move.

Emily made him some toast and then cycled off to work. He reread the paper. It was fine but there was mystery, so much still unsaid, unclear. The whole story would come out eventually. He looked out of the window at Lochend Grove. Nothing moving, no-one about. There was a wan sun drifting in and out of cloud but it looked a dull day and he was sure it would be cold. He was starting to feel a little deflated, mildly depressed despite his front page story success. The sense of anticlimax after the nervy excitement and danger of his near-death experience. He didn't like it. It wasn't him. He wished Emily had had the morning off. He always felt better when she was around. He phoned Sean Kermally at the Scottish Parliament.

'It's a good first step,' Sean told him. 'You've done very well and I'll be sure to tell the FM what you have done. We've got some stuff to hit them with now. But we have a lot more to do. We need to keep the story going. Today's objective is to get the police to make the link between this GB13 group at Westminster and what happened, or what nearly happened, on the train. The identity of the man. Was he working for GB13 or even worse, was he some kind of spook? This man Neil – that's what he was called by Edgar Kellett MP – who threatened you in the Trafalgar Room? Who *is* he? Who does he work for? Kellett will know and the police will have to ask him.

Morton tried to concentrate. 'Yes, I suppose they will.'

'Anyway, we have footage of them now thanks to you and that will help to bring out the truth. Are you alright, Willie? You seem a bit…'

'I'm fine,' Morton said. It was what you always said, even though you weren't. 'Just a bit weary still, after all the…'

'Good,' Sean said. 'Thank goodness, eh? And this Lord Craile and all the rest of the motley crew? How far up the food chain does it go, this conspiracy to interfere with the democratic system? Oh, when is your meeting with the police?'

'Ah, soon,' Morton grunted. 'Ten. I'm meeting my solicitor there.'

'Right. Well, you can help to put pressure on, Willie, by asking them when they're going to release the would-be-assassin's identity. And what do they think was his motive? Most of all, Willie, you need to keep safe and sit tight. I think it's likely that we'll have a meeting here to brief the FM, maybe tomorrow, but I'll let you know. I mean, we can't have this kind of thing going on without an official explanation.'

'Okay.'

'The FM gets oversight of MI5 ops in Scotland, you know, Willie. Well, at least she's supposed to. That was something implicit in the devolution settlement, but maybe it's time things were made a little more formal, eh? Maybe we need new legislation to enable Scottish Government officials to have a statutory role in security intelligence oversight. Or maybe we should have a Scottish rep on the Joint Security Committee?'

Willie watched a man on a bicycle dismount across the street and wheel his bike into the shed. He had fresh veg, possibly leeks and potatoes in his pannier. Allotment? 'I hear what you're saying, Sean. But I can't see the UK Government ever agreeing to that. That might make a good think-piece story though.'

'Yes. Yes, absolutely, Willie. That's positive thinking. Anyway, for today you should get the police to check over your flat. Make sure there are no bugging devices in there. We can put that out to the media too, even if they don't find any.'

When Willie put down the phone he realised he would have time to walk to the police meeting. He looked out of the window into the back green. Didn't look like rain. The fresh air and exercise would do him some good.

CHAPTER TWENTY-THREE

As he walked to the meeting, Morton felt comfortable, even relaxed, in the salty raw air of Edinburgh, among his own folk. He was aware of sidelong looks from some passers-by. The cause was not hard to comprehend. His face was on the front page and even now the TV networks were probably scrambling to get their own picture of him for the main evening news. He wondered if he should have suggested that someone, possibly Sean, tip them off about the meeting but no, he concluded, better to play this straight. The police media advisor would be present at the meeting probably, given the potentially huge media interest that would be gathering around the story over the course of the day.

It was nice to see his old friend Archie MacDonald again. The solicitor had been in the same year at George Watson's, and they'd locked together many times in the muddy scrums of the Second XV and later the FPs.

They shook hands in the hall. As the junior partner at Halbron, Finlay & MacDonald, Archie's once full head of hair was a distant memory. Sparse ash-coloured strands now marked the outer margins of a former blond empire.

'More trouble?' MacDonald smiled ironically. 'Still, I'm always glad of the business. But you could have had the decency,' he chortled, 'to get yourself properly arrested. Instead of just *in for questioning*, what?' He shook his head in mock sorrow. 'The exciting life you lead!'

'How is the family, Archie? Or perhaps I should ask, how is the *clan*? Assuming it's not increased since the last time I saw you.'

'Ah, five now, I'm afraid.' He grinned broadly. 'You're behind the times, old man!'

'Good for you. Scotland needs population growth.'

Archie grinned self-consciously. 'Aye, that was uppermost in our minds at the time: it was purely a policy decision.'

'Well, shall we?' Morton indicated the interior.

'Up before the beaks,' MacDonald grinned, adding, 'Seriously old man, you nearly copped it. Very worrying. Let's hope they catch the swine.'

'Eh?' Morton looked at him. 'He's dead! Didn't you hear?'

MacDonald sniffed peremptorily. 'Aye well… Being deid is a strong defence, m'Lud!'

The room was a nondescript classroom-type affair or perhaps a cafeteria for staff with yellow walls and narrow windows high up that emitted a suffused dim light. Morton imagined it was at the rear of the building, north-facing. There was a stack of extra tables and chairs in the corner and four tables had been put together for the meeting. The room smelled of sweat or sour milk, or perhaps insufficient ventilation.

As Morton had expected, a police media officer, Sheila Galbraith, was present at the meeting. She was a severe-looking lady wearing tortoiseshell specs, whose hair, almost torn out at the roots, was pulled into a bun at the back of her head. Next to her sat Chief Superintendent Brian Dunn, in full uniform, gold braid on his cap brim, flanked by a smart younger female Inspector Lorna Scanlon. A middle-aged female note-taker in civilian attire sat at the far end.

'In your own time,' instructed the Chief Superintendent, removing his cap and placing it reverently in front of him. You could tell he was proud of the trappings of his elevated rank. 'If you'd like to make a statement about the incident and anything else…?'

Morton started by describing his attendance at the meeting at Westminster.

Dunn seemed bemused by this and interrupted. 'Where are we going with this? How is this connected to the incident on the train at Berwick?'

'I'm coming to that. The two incidents must be connected, as you'll hear.'

Dunn looked at him sideways, frowning intensely. 'So you misrepresented yourself to get into Westminster, masquerading as someone else? You *lied*?'

Archie interrupted, with his professional manner. 'Chief Superintendent, let's not be naive about the world we live in. Journalists are wont to do such things – not illegal – in pursuit of a story in the public interest.'

'Please continue,' Inspector Scanlon invited him with a flick of her fingertips. He saw cerise nail vanish. She glanced at the Chief Super. 'Perhaps we'll keep our questions or comments till the end?'

'Very well.'

Morton was amused by the deftness of the junior officer in clearing away the objections of the grumpy police chief. There was a twinkle in her eye too, he noted. She would go far. He backtracked to explain about his resemblance to Philip Gallimont and the mysterious GB13 group, and told them he had already had stories published about it. The media officer, Sheila Galbraith nodded.

'Yes. We're aware of that,' she said, adjusting her specs. 'Carry on.'

Finally, he got through his tale but then the questioning started and he had to backtrack, and go off on tangents. As the hour went by, he felt himself becoming a little frustrated. He felt like simply handing them the front page of the *Standard*. 'I feel I've gone over everything I can remember several times now,' he said, 'but I was hoping you might have some answers for *me*.'

Chief Superintendent Dunn regarded him blandly. 'Well, what sort of...?'

Morton shrugged. 'Like the identity of the man who attacked me? What his motives might have been? What his precise connection with the people who threatened me in London? Like who ordered the man to attack me? Who is this man *Neil* and who does *he* work for? And then there is the mysterious Lord Craile.'

Inspector Scanlon tapped her pen on her notepad, then glanced at the Chief Superintendent before answering, who sat glumly, perhaps vacantly, frowning. 'We don't have the answers,' she said, 'at the moment, Morton, but I can tell you we are in contact with Northumbria CID as regards the identity of the man and the gun that was recovered.'

'It's my understanding,' she continued, 'that the identity of the deceased cannot be confirmed because... until his relatives have been informed. That's the reason for the delay.' She looked straight at Morton. 'The *only* reason. The witness statements, however, have all corroborated your version of events.'

'Well, they would,' Morton said.

'Quite,' Archie MacDonald said, nodding.

'And we have asked them, and also The Met, to provide us with information that might or might not connect the incident with the Westminster meeting and its aftermath.'

'Oh good.'

From the far end of the table, Sheila Galbraith scrutinised him through her thick specs. 'We have been contacted by a lot of media organisations so we will be putting out a brief statement from this meeting, outlining what has been discussed. I presume that is okay with you and your representative?'

'Fine,' said Morton, 'I anticipated that.'

Archie sniffed. 'And if you could copy that to me, please.'

'Of course. The statement will be very general: simply that the meeting took place to discuss the incident, that you cooperated fully and that our investigations are ongoing.'

After the meeting, Morton stopped at the Reception desk to sign for his belongings, his jacket and coat. He examined the coat. No bullet hole. He had felt sure there would be. Where had the bullet gone? He had a momentary warm memory of the old raincoat and of Hannah who had given it him and smiled. He imagined her working at the Coffee Place in Berwick. Probably busy with the lunchtime crowd.

As they stood outside on the steps, in the raw wind, Archie turned to him. 'Willie, your reputation for attracting trouble is growing by the day. I'm a little alarmed you might have made enemies in high places. Did you see the Chief Super's face when he heard about the meeting in Westminster?'

Morton laughed. 'He could probably feel his OBE just slip-sliding away!'

'Ha! But to be serious for a minute, Willie. Obviously, you know what I'm about to say. For heaven's sake, man, don't take any further risks! You have your story – I don't suppose there's any point in me saying you should now leave it to others to follow up on this particularly nasty group? I mean, they clearly have the resources, you know, to make life difficult… well, if it was their man on the train. God save us, but Willie, at the very least, if you are determined to get to the bottom of it, keep the police informed. And me, too, of course.'

Morton grinned. 'Archie, the next time I'm hanging off a train door, you'll be the very first person I call, assuming I have a hand free, of course!'

'Don't joke about it, old chap. This is serious.'

'Okay, seriously, I think now the story's out and my fizzer is on the front page, I'm safer than I was. They wouldn't dare come after me now, or all the world will know.'

'There's some security in that, I suppose,' his friend agreed, reflectively. 'Just don't push it, old chap. You never know. The First XV might need you one day. Preferably in one piece.'

He was feeling much happier by the time he met up with Emily at Pizza Hut on North Bridge for a quick lunch. They shared a vegetarian pizza and loaded up on the 'all-you-can-eat' salad bar. Morton had a beer and Emily a cranberry juice. The place was crammed and they had had to wait five minutes for a table. They discussed the media development of the story. Emily's Tweet had been retweeted sixty times with twelve likes and dozens of replies.

'It's not surprising, Em, given you have… how many followers now?'

'Fifteen hundred and sixty-two. Not that I'm obsessed with the numbers.'

'As if!'

'Touch of jealousy there, mister?'

Morton scoffed. 'You couldn't pay me to go on Twitter or Facebook now. I don't miss it. I used to waste so much time on it. It generates a world of its own that only loosely intersects with the world I live in, if you know what I mean.'

'You're only saying that because you can't be bothered keeping up with it.'

He snorted. 'Maybe. I just think it's a big empty hollow place. Everybody talking about themselves, or boasting and nobody listening or paying any attention.'

'Interesting. That's not how I see it. I find it very useful.'

'Anyway, the story is on all the media,' Morton told her, 'although still focusing only on the train incident.' He told her about his police interview and the pompous Chief Superintendent. 'Archie told me to play safe and not to push it.'

'You should listen to him. I've news too,' Emily said and made a face. 'I've been asked onto a panel discussion on *Scotland Tonight*. Sorreee.'

Morton was a bit miffed but he said nothing. It was his story and he felt it already moving away from him.

'It's better if I do it,' Emily said, trying to reassure him. 'Think of it as an escalation. We're building up the importance of the story. Then, when more of the context – GB13 and so on – is in the public domain, they'll all be wanting you on their programmes. At the moment, we're stoking the flames. Upping the ante one bit at a time. But Sean will have told you this. If you jump in to the story now, you'll kill it all in one go. Think story, Willie.'

Morton raised his eyebrows and tried for irony. 'Well, you've certainly changed your tune since last night. You were all for hiding me away from the world.'

'I think you're pretty safe now,' she said.

'No, not entirely, Em. Not until the mystery of this GB13 and its links or connections to the Cameron Government are all out into the light of day. Have you, by any chance, been able to look into this Lord Craile creature?'

She tossed her hair and pulled it back into her white scrunchy. 'I had a busy morning so I didn't have long but I found out a few things. He's a former hereditary peer, right, but not one of the ninety-two who were elected to remain, so he doesn't sit in the Lords. He's Lord Craile of Ardbuithne, on the island of Mull. A decorated war hero from World War II, but crippled. He is very wealthy indeed.'

'Yes,' Morton said, 'I already knew that. And he took Blair to court over the Lords Reform. Well, really over his own failure to be elected to remain in the Upper House.'

Emily exclaimed. 'Oh! Didn't know that. Goodness. He owns a couple of malt distilleries and was Chairman for years of the Independent Scotch Malt Whisky Producers' Association, a trade body representing small brewers that sold out to Diageo in the nineties. He lives in a castle adjacent to one of his distilleries. They say he has a personal piper who plays under his window every morning and evening to get him up and put him to sleep.'

'Bloody hell, only a few things?' Morton said warmly. 'You've done well.'

Emily adjusted her heavy specs and smiled modestly. 'He's quite litigious. Loves to take anyone he doesn't like to court, although I was unaware of the Lords Reform case. I'll have to look that up. Politically of course, as you'd expect, he's very far right. He was one of Sir James Goldsmith's fans a few years ago, and there are rumours he chucked a few quid behind Nigel Farage and even to some nefarious far-right groups. Anyway, Willie, what points do you want me to stress tonight?'

'Oh, well, let's see,' he said. He took out a Post-it pad. On the pink pages he scribbled as he spoke. 'One, the likelihood – certainty – of a connection between my being threatened and the attack on the train. Two, the apparent closeness or links… or at least, the *mystery* of the connection between the group and UK Government and/or spooks various. The basic line is,' he chuckled, 'well-respected Scottish journalist… and I don't mind if you repeat that line *often.*'

Emily laughed. 'I bet you don't. Who said it, by the way?'

'Ah I think it was on Radio Scotland… going about his normal business, blah-di-blah… You could also query the group directly. How can they use the resources of the House? Who are they? What is their function? Three, is the dead man one of their assassins? Build up the outrage, rack up the paranoia. Are they spying on us as we sleep? Are we safe in our beds? Etcetera. Oh, and the seventy-five per cent thing – we're keeping that until later. There's footage of the discussion about it. We can use that, but later,' he paused and smiled. 'According to Sean, we'll bring that out at the best time – when the Government has been forced to denounce this GB13 and its thuggish activities. Then we'll reveal their real aim and that will be the final nail in the coffin of its prospects of ever being introduced as legislation.'

'Rightly so!' Emily snorted. 'I've never heard of anything so anti-democratic. Makes the forty per cent rule in the 1976 Devolution Referendum look positively altruistic.'

'Yes, but,' Morton said, counterfactually, 'isn't it just *so* extreme that it could be the catalyst for UDI? Everyone would see it for what it was, an authoritarian way to prevent Scots' votes from ever counting, not that they actually do at the moment, of course, but you know what I mean. There's the pretence of it now. But with this… I mean, why would

215

we want to bother continuing to send MPs down there, to be completely invisible?'

'I'll have to bite my tongue not to mention it tonight,' she said. 'It fair makes my blood boil!'

'I know, I know, Em, but at least you can speak up tonight on the other aspects and help to move things on. I'll be stuck here watching it all happen.'

'You've done enough. Get some beers in. Relax.'

He grinned. 'Ooh, I can do the couch potato. I've learned how. Hmn, beers and crisps. That doesn't sound too bad, while you do all the work.'

CHAPTER TWENTY-FOUR

Colin Hardwick was back at his desk in the Irish and Domestic Counter-Terrorism section on the second floor of Thames House. Since his return from Edinburgh, things had been moving rapidly behind the scenes. He remembered his promise to keep Kirsty updated and felt a nagging feeling of incompleteness about his Edinburgh assignment. Some of that, he privately admitted, was that he had enjoyed her company and regretted his early reassignment south. But he had a good excuse to speak to her again on a number of matters directly related to the work and went in the lift up to Desmond Thorpe's section. He also hoped to find out about the situation regarding Neil Smyth.

'Hi, Desmond, got a moment.'

'Yup.' Thorpe was reading a file, head in hands and he barely looked round.

Hardwick stood, rolling up his shirtsleeves and tried to make his voice sound casual, even matey. Blokes together. 'All alone, Desmond? Where's Commander Smyth these days?'

Thorpe scrutinised him suspiciously. 'On annual leave. What was it you wanted, exactly, Colin?'

'I need to do a video-call to the team in Edinburgh. Bring them up to speed with events.' He glanced at the Comms Officer. 'Unless you have already?'

'No.' Thorpe stood up and slouched off. 'All yours. Time for my lunch break anyway.'

'Thanks.'

It was a little unusual being at the London end of the video-conferencing point with the Scotland station, instead of the other way round.

He was relieved to see Kirsty on the screen. What he was going to pass on was not for the ears of Crispin Hayes. It was too sensitive a subject for the trainee.

'Colin,' Kirsty smiled warmly, 'good to see you again. How are things down on the farm?'

'Funny. Well, I said I'd keep you updated as and when. Lots happening just now down here. You still doing surveillance ops on your target?'

'Uh, no, Colin. The transmitter in the watch is still working but he's left the watch in his flat, so it's no use to me. However, he has switched his mobile back on, but isn't using it much. But what's the point anyway? It doesn't tell me anything I don't already know. The story is all over the Scottish media.'

'Not much of a stir down here yet, at any rate on the media front. However, Kirsty, other things are moving rapidly. Philip Gallimont has been arrested, on his return from holiday.'

'Right.'

'It seems that the Scottish Government put out a warrant for him. They've been investigating Ardbeag Holdings, going through that list of properties Gallimont had, and a number of associated companies too, for potential property fraud. They're even about to open up inquiries on a number of deaths related to the acquisition of the properties.'

There was a long pause and the screen blanked. 'Still there, Kirsty?'

Kirsty reappeared, frowning at the screen. 'Good grief, Colin! You mean the deaths of the former owners of the properties?'

'That's about the size of it. Relatives of a number of elderly people who owned the properties before they were sold and acquired by Ardbeag are now claiming that their relatives may have been put under undue pressure to sell, and maybe some of them are claiming something worse.'

'You mean, they think their relative was…?'

'Helped on their way? Well, maybe. Would be awfully difficult to prove. Personally, Kirsty, I doubt it. But pressure to sell, possibly, even coercion. There's no doubt they acquired a lot of property in rural areas very quickly and most of the owners were single elderly: widows, widowers and some quite frail by all accounts. Anyway, I wanted to let you know that that is ongoing.'

'Thanks. But inquiries are restricted to the property company? No connection to this GB13 group?'

'Well, yes, it seems there is. Not just funding – and, by the way, the funding paper trail seems pretty clear – but Gallimont and a couple of others in a similar role are the link between the two.'

'What a mess. And the man on the train?'

'Roy Brand. The police are holding off releasing his identity until we can clear up his background. He has been used by Six a few times in the Middle East, Syria, Iraq, long ago, as a support agent. Completely deniable of course. And we're talking decades ago, Kirsty. But more recently he is – was – a member of some far-right groups as well, so that identity will be produced and there'll be no provable link to us. And, Kirsty, it looks like there is a connection with Neil Smyth, who is still on annual leave, apparently.'

'So you're telling me it *was* an authorised hit?'

'God no, of course not! Smyth will have to explain himself in due course. It seems there were some messages from him on Roy Brand's phone, including a photo of Morton, can you believe. So they have had to be laundered. In the meantime, the advice to the PM will undoubtedly be to act fast against GB13 to divert further attention to any other people who might be involved, if you can understand what I'm saying here, Kirsty.'

She nodded. 'I get the idea. From what you've said, it looks like there's a lot of damage limitation going on. Why did no-one spot that this group were getting out of hand?'

'You might well ask. Seems they have a lot of support in Government. At high levels too – a lot of support. Their aims are broadly legal of course – legislation, parliamentary pressure – but maybe someone turned a blind eye to these other activities.'

Kirsty took a sip of coffee and grued. It was cold. 'So, Colin, all in all, do you really think Morton is a target? Given that he's blown everything to the four winds? And of course, done nothing wrong whatsoever.'

Hardwick was taken aback by her tone. He paused. 'Well, you'd have to speak to the Intel Analysts, but my gut feeling is, no, he's too hot at the moment. On the other hand, have you wondered what else he might have got out of attending the meeting? Apart from his media coup of getting himself threatened and then chased and nearly bumped off? He went to a lot of trouble just to hear some boring speeches by politicians.'

'I see what you're saying. There must have been some other motive. Or was he just fishing for random information?' Kirsty mused.

'Well, I passed that concept on to the Intel Analysts and they've looked over everything that was said at the meeting, minute by minute.'

'Right. And…?'

'They concluded Morton has further information that he may intend to use. And one of the things he would have learned is that the main funder and ipso facto leader of GB13 is a man called Lord Craile. I wouldn't be at all surprised if Morton, with his track record of getting involved on the ground, doesn't try to make contact with – get an interview with – Craile. That's quite feasible, fits Morton's pattern of working. He likes to see both sides.'

'Surely that wouldn't happen? I mean, why would Lord Craile agree?'

'I agree, Kirsty. But Morton isn't a man to be easily put off.'

'Where does this Lord Craile live?'

'Not sure exactly, but it's in the Highlands somewhere.'

'Should we warn him?'

'I understand he's almost impossible to contact,' Hardwick told her. 'Pretty reclusive.'

'Well that might help, if the press come a-calling.'

Willie Morton sat in the small living room of his flat, looking out at the Saltire flying from Edinburgh Castle. He'd slept well, his first night in his own bed, having returned from Emily's after watching *Scotland Tonight* together. But he was restless, frustrated. It felt as if the story was leaving him behind. Everybody was getting involved in it, except him. It was as if he was a bystander of his own success. His old rival, Davie Begg of the *Daily Record*, had come up with a new angle, getting wind of Scottish Government investigation of

Ardbeag Holdings and of course everyone had the news that David Cameron had ordered a full-scale investigation into the activities of GB13 in advance of a face-to-face meeting request from Nicola Sturgeon. Radio Scotland's bulletin at 8.30 a.m. had the revelation that Gallimont had been arrested.

The story was out there, all sparked by *his* efforts, his experiences. He should have been pleased, imitation being the sincerest form of flattery. But he felt that there was no investigation of why these people had done, or were doing, what they *were* doing. Whatever that was. What was their reason? Were they simply Jock-bashers? And the more he thought about it, the more he began to see a way to regain the story. He would interview the leader, Lord Craile, and ask him.

He phoned Hugh Leadbetter on his office phone number. He knew it was indiscreet, probably the line was tapped, but he needed to be doing something.

'Willie? What's cooking today?' He could imagine the editor leaning backward in his chair taking the call, the untidy, cramped office, piles of broadsheets on the floor, the desk, everywhere, even the slightly fuggy air of the office.

'I've had an idea, Hugh. I know… *again*! Listen, everybody and their granny is now trying to slay the bogeyman, those nasty people in GB13. But what we need, Hugh, is an interview, to try to put *their* side of the story.'

Leadbetter was incredulous. 'Good grief. Willie! They tried to bump you off! They don't want tae talk to you, they just want to shoot ye!'

Morton cleared his throat. 'Yes, I know, but they claim to be a legal pressure group. So I'm sure I can get someone to speak to me about their aims and motives.'

'They'll just tell you shite, man.'

'We need to hear what drives them. We need to bring it out into the open. And even if it is incoherent nonsense, well, our readers can make up their own minds. We're journalists, not politicians.'

'Aye, of course, Willie, but it's not do-able, not at the moment. Naebody will speak tae ye anyway.'

'I think I'm going to try speaking to this Lord Craile. He's the main funder and the incoming leader. He lives in Scotland too, in Mull, so I can get there quite easily. If he won't speak, well, no harm done.'

'God sake, Willie! Let me send someone else. We'll do it properly. Phone him first and ask him.'

'Warn him we're coming?' Morton expostulated. 'No way, man. Even if he doesn't agree to speak to me, I will try to get a picture of him and his castle or whatever, then I can stand up some kind of story. Admittedly, it'll be mainly based on what I already have from the meeting in the Trafalgar Room and some additional speculating. Are you there?'

'Willie, there's nae point in me trying to stop you, is there? You've made your mind up. And I suppose it's completely pointless me telling you to stay safe?'

'Ach, don't worry, Hugh. Anyway, I'll keep in touch.'

And as soon as Morton put down the phone, he felt better. He had a plan, something to do. Felt less helpless. He texted Emily and ignored her anguished replies. He texted Sean. There was no reply from him. He checked up on buses, bike hire and accommodation in Oban. He hadn't been back there since his desperate crossing of the Firth of Lorn in a small dinghy at night. That was eight years ago.

He packed a small rucksack with notebook, camera, toiletry items, iPad and phone and headed over to Elder Street to catch the National Express Coach to Oban via

223

Glasgow. The coach was full and very warm and he drowsed most of the way, except for the half hour wait at Buchanan Street station in Glasgow when he had to change coaches. He slept again as the coach travelled north and, just five hours after setting off, he was stretching his legs in the Oban afternoon sunshine. It was nice to be in the place without people chasing him.

He resisted the urge to return to the guesthouse he had previously used and instead checked into a comfortable small hotel on the esplanade near the cathedral, overlooking the emerald-green, low-lying, north end of Kerrera Island. It was amazing to him that he had once actually crossed that dark stretch of turbulent water in a tiny rubber dinghy, fleeing from men with guns, helicopters. Amazing what you can do when you have to. He had never got to the bottom of it last time, had been fobbed off, warned off, and had felt the power of the British State to stop his investigations. It had proved to be not quite such a free country as he had thought. He was less naive now of course. He stayed in his room for a while until it began to get dark and then strolled along the breezy esplanade in the swinging light of streetlights, among crowds of tourists.

He went into a hotel bar on the front quite near the railway station and had a pint and a packet of crisps, looking out the window at the harbour and the lights of an incoming red MacBraynes ferry. He didn't feel hungry but bought a poke of chips and ate most of them strolling back to his hotel, listening to the tide whispering on the seawall out in the dark blustery night.

He watched TV, but the story seemed to have petered out. He knew that could not be, but it worried him a little. He had not been able to find any contacts for Lord Craile, other than the address which was simply: Ardbuithne House, Lochbuie, Mull. And anyway, he favoured the surprise arrival. Catch him off guard.

He slept well and breakfasted enormously on a fry-up; eight items, including fried bread, mushrooms, beans and black pudding, as well as the usual sausage, egg, fried tomato and bacon, washed down with a half-litre of strong black coffee.

Sated, even a bit bloated, he strolled along the blustery esplanade towards the red sandstone edifice of the Columba Hotel and found a bike-hire shop, where he hired a mountain bike.

'I'm going over to Mull by ferry,' he told the skinny, bespectacled male assistant in black combat trousers and sweatshirt. 'Will I be able to take the bike on the bus?'

The youth glanced at him. 'Bus, aye? Where are you heading?'

Morton shrugged. 'I was going to get the bus from Craignure partway to Fionnphort, then get out and cycle.'

The assistant assured him it was possible. 'Big buses – double-deckers, run by West Coast Motors. They have a luggage bay underneath, aye? Shove it in there. It's early season yet, shouldnae be nae problem. What about a helmet?'

'Ach no. I'll not bother.'

The assistant grinned. 'Sure? Feeling reckless? Can be dangerous on Mull, ye ken. You might get knocked over by a sheep.'

'I'll pass, thanks,' Morton said, smiling. 'Don't worry.'

He tested the bike along the road to the MacBraynes' Ferry Terminal on the other pier. It had a sturdy red frame, seven gears, front and rear lights powered by a dynamo and thick knobbly tyres. He bought sandwiches, water, chocolate bars and a small pork pie in the supermarket, then went and bought his return ticket on the ferry to Craignure.

He bought a *Standard* and searched for any follow-up on the story. Buried on page eight was a small news piece about the arrest of Gallimont as part of ongoing investigations into Ardbeag Holdings over suspected property fraud. The front page featured the ongoing row between senior Tories over the EU. They were panicked by the success of the amphibious Farage and UKIP.

It was amazing how deftly the big red steamer picked its way through the narrow entrance of Oban Bay avoiding little islands in the wide channel of the Firth, heading straight for Duart Point. Morton strolled on the upper deck, then sat reading the paper in the lee of the wind. He didn't have any problems on boats this size, it was only wee boats that terrified him. He looked back at the stone birthday cake of MacCaig's Folly above the town. He might go up there on the way back, he decided, if he had time. Good view all around from up there.

Ahead, Duart Castle on its rocky headland was a splendid spectacle for the tourists to gawp at. Soon they rounded the point and he saw the miniature railway that ran to the splendid Torosay Castle and gardens. That was a tourist magnet too. The ferry began its reversing manoeuvre, casting up a tide of backwash onto the shore as it backed in alongside the narrow pier at Craignure. The hamlet consisted of a few houses, a large campsite and a pub. He went down to the car deck to collect his bike.

He knew there were three buses to Fionnphort from Craignure each day. He was well in time for the second, at 10.50 a.m. The journey to the western side of the island for embarkation on the Iona Ferry took just over an hour, but he would get off just ten minutes into the trip. He had calculated that it would take too long to cycle the five miles from Craignure, as well as the further five miles on to Ardbuithne House from the road junction. He wasn't here for the cycling. The bike was a means to an end, and he liked the idea of stealth it implied. In a rural area, a cyclist does not cause alarm bells to ring. Cyclists were either residents or tourists intent on sport, not freelance journalists stalking their prey.

CHAPTER TWENTY-FIVE

The bike-hire assistant in Oban had not been kidding when he told Morton the bus would be quite big. It was an enormous red monster and emblazoned across its side was the mantra: Discover Iona, Mull and Staffa. The driver, a cheery local, was an enthusiastic cyclist himself. His face blanched when he heard Morton saying he would need to get out at the Lochbuie crossroads. He winced.

'That's no far, no above five miles. And a braw bike like that?'

'Dicky knee,' Morton invented. 'And it's six miles further on to Ardbuithne, and six back to the bus stop.'

'Ach, away, it's a nice easy road if you were fit.' He frowned and sniffed. 'Ah well, it's your funeral. A return, you want, aye?'

Most of the other passengers were heading all the way to the Iona Ferry. He was the only cyclist. The driver heaved the red bike into the luggage space.

The bus engine came on with a shudder. Air-conditioning blasted out and indeterminate bagpipe music on a CD player emanated through speakers. Tourists outnumbered locals most of the year Morton guessed. They set off on the A849, one of only two 'A' roads on the island. It ran in a long dog-leg around the coast from Salen down to Craignure and then west to Fionnphort. The bus breasted the rise above the sprawling campsite and the narrow-gauge railway and entered the woods, came out into the sunshine with a view east over the Firth of Lorn and the mainland and then dived into more woods and came to a halt at a junction beside an impressive monument. Morton got off sheepishly.

The driver got down and helped him out with his bike, wished him luck with his dicky knee then the bus drove away. Morton looked around. It was the middle of nowhere. A small white board on a post marked a Bus Stop opposite a passing place. No human habitation in sight.

He read the inscription on the monument. Gaelic poet and composer Dugald MacPhail (1818–1887). He could see the top of a mountain in the distance and wondered if it was Ben More, the only Munro on Mull. He began to walk back to the junction, pushing the bike.

The single-track road down to Ardbuithne was narrow, but the tarmac surface looked good. He mounted the bike and was soon racing along past a couple of white-painted houses, chased by a collie for a few yards, over a very narrow stone bridge, into low birch woods. There were a few sheep and he scrutinised them as he passed, but they didn't look particularly dangerous.

As he approached the shore of what he knew was the sea loch, Loch Spelve, he had the sense of the road petering out to nowhere, but knew he wasn't even a third of the way along. It was a remote place to live, and Morton wondered why Lord Craile lived here, when he had been a Member of the House of Lords and involved in affairs of State. Maybe he had tired of London? He saw in the distance, a white van parked at a small house by the roadside. BT Openreach, he noted, as he passed by. No sign of any people. Even here, technology was catching up.

Outside another house a mile further on, he saw a man and boy unloading a car. Looked like they were going fishing. He waved, they waved. At the end of the loch there was a narrow spit of land that separated it from the smaller loch, Loch Uisg, and a house prominently sited there with a clear view down the loch. He stopped to look at a war memorial commemorating local men who had died in World War I.

He rejoined the road as it skirted the shingle shore of Loch Uisg. There were some trees and a few scattered crofts and houses along the mile and a half length of the loch. At the far end, as the road rose up away from the loch, giving him a vantage point, he saw ahead of him in the distance, the imposing silhouette of a castle's battlements rising up above the modest cliffs.

Morton stopped in the pine trees and scanned ahead with the binoculars. He could make out that the ancient castle tower had been incorporated onto the gable of a large ivied mansion. He could see walled gardens, glasshouses and a dark rectangular building, partly shrouded by trees, that must be the Ardbuithne Distillery. So there it was: Ardbuithne House. He was here!

Looking down, he saw that the road skirted wide on the level ground around the buildings and that there were half a dozen houses beyond – the hamlet of Ardbuithne. On the right, the ground rose steeply on the slopes of the mountain of Ben Buithne. If he cycled down by the road, he would be seen long before he arrived at the house. But there was a wood in front of him and he saw faint signs of a track through it, heading almost directly towards the big house.

That was the best idea. He stowed the bike off the road in the bracken and sat down in a good vantage point in the wood to eat his sandwiches and observe. With the binoculars, he could see, through the trees, signs of human activity around the houses. There was a sandy beach too, further along, and just below the big house there was a river outfall to the wide sea loch, Loch Buithne, that was part of the Firth of Lorn.

It was pleasant sitting there with the view before him, the hills and the sunshine flickering like magnesium flares off the water and the smell of pine sap. The air was fresh and salty, mild for the middle of February. It seemed a long way away from the fear and claustrophobia he had felt in the Palace of Westminster, yet here, too, even at this peripheral place, there could be danger.

He could delay no longer. He stood up and began carefully to follow the track through the wood, listening to the gurgling of a busy burn. He got to within 100 yards of the big house before he saw anybody. He crouched down instinctively and watched.

A man in a cap with a green waxed jacket stood in the little field beyond the edge of the wood. He had a shotgun under his arm. He was just standing there, immobile. But he couldn't possibly have seen me, Morton decided. He was looking off to the sea. Morton moved a little closer. It wasn't a shotgun. It was more like a rifle. The man moved off.

Morton watched him till he had turned around the corner of the old stone building and disappeared. As Morton moved to the edge of the forest, he reminded himself that it was only nineteen days since he had been hiding in woods outside another big house, the Hirsel. It seemed longer ago. And here he was again. He studied the building in front of him. There were too many windows for him to approach from the rear. The best thing was to go around the old tower and look to see where the front door was. He had his cover story ready: to pretend to be a hiker interested in the old castle. Was it possible to look inside? To make it seem more authentic, he took out the camera and hung it around his neck.

As he crouched at the base of a tree, deliberating, he saw two more men moving along behind the house, coming towards him. They too had guns. Rifles, not shotguns. He kept low. They passed along the outer wall, talking in low voices. They couldn't all be gamekeepers. Nor did these two look the type. They looked too urban somehow. Morton began to suspect the old man must have been warned. These men looked like security guards. He should have contacted his editor by WhatsApp. Maybe the phones at the *Standard* *were* bugged. But were these men from GB13? It seemed unlikely. He sat in the vegetation, wondering what to do. Should he abort, after coming all this way? Not really.

Ten minutes went by. At least ten minutes, although he had no watch to judge it by. He checked his mobile. No signal but the time was 11.52 a.m. The first man reappeared, walking in the other direction. They were doing circuits, guarding the perimeter of the house. There was no question about it, now. He checked his camera and silenced the beeper, then took a quick picture. When, after a few minutes, the other two men reappeared, he snapped them too. Then he thought, well, if they suspect my cover story is fake, the proof is now in the camera. Should he delete the pictures? The thought went against the grain. No, keep them, he decided.

And then Morton realised there was a better way in. He slipped off the track to his left, crouching low, scrabbling his way down to the shingle beach. As he had suspected, there was a small cliff between the machair and the shingle, barely ten feet below.

He dropped down, his feet landing in the soft cushion of shingle with barely a sound. In most places, less than eight feet high, it was enough to let him pass along under the front of the house and then look up to see the lie of the land. The tide was out and there were lots of big rocks that he could use for cover if required. He simply had to make sure that none of the armed men were anywhere near him, and to ensure he didn't clatter any rocks.

He peeped cautiously up through the machair grasses and observed the imposing front of Ardbuithne House. No signs of life. No armed men, no dogs. He continued along for ten minutes, aware that the cliff was diminishing, soon he'd be out in the open, and visible from every window in the house! He noted the front door, beside a large conservatory, which was empty. No-one around. There were no sounds of human life. It was unnerving. Where were they all? Or was it a trap? Were they, even now, tracking him on some hidden CCTV cameras?

It took him a while to pluck up the courage to leave the relative safety of the beach and pull himself up onto the machair. There was no point now in trying to hide. He had to be bold and simply go up to the front door. Then what? Ring the bell? No. That wouldn't be sensible. He had to get to Lord Craile before any of the armed guards spotted him. They were on the outside. He would be safer inside the house.

He was shocked by the noise his feet made when he moved across the pink gravel path to the front door. He tried to assume a confidence he didn't feel. There was no sign of anyone. No sign of the men. He didn't hear voices. The place was a mausoleum.

The front door was open. Of course it was. This was the Highlands. But armed men and an open door? He pushed inwards and it opened easily. He was in a light airy hallway, thickly carpeted. The black eyes of dozens of long-dead stags seemed to follow his every move under thick eyelashes. Mounted on every wall, each set of the twelve-point antlers marked a season of ritual slaughter.

Stairs led up and around at the far end of the hall and he saw several doors. Instinct told him to start at the top of the house. He made for the stairs, feeling like a burglar but driven by fear. Somewhere a bell began ringing, then it stopped. There were no sounds. It was eerily quiet. The carpet was soft, deadening his tread, and he continued to the second floor where the corridor was narrower.

He heard a strange crackling sound from nearby and a sudden chink of glassware. He listened at the door.

CHAPTER TWENTY-SIX

At first, Morton had thought the room, lit only by the leaping flames of a log fire which cast giant shadows on the walls and gilt frames of oil paintings, was empty. Under his feet was a rich, deep carpet. He saw the windows were narrowed by thick burgundy velvet curtains. The thin reedy voice, weak but still authoritative, came as an awful shock, emanating from the high back of an old-fashioned armchair.

Morton came more fully into the room and there was Lord Craile, thin-faced, faded and elderly, grey hair swept over a raptor's bony beak and crusted white eyebrows.

'I was informed that you would be coming. Have no fear, I am unarmed.'

'Neither am I,' Morton told him blithely, taking in the tartan blanket folded over withered legs and the hairs, white in the firelight, on his thin neck, protruding from his pyjamas and dressing gown.

'What is it that you want?' the old man cried peevishly. 'Have you come here to kill me?'

'Of course not!' Morton snapped. He flung himself down in the armchair opposite. The old man regarded him neutrally; eyes like scuffed marbles in watery milk.

'Well then, if not, you might do me a service by pouring another of these. Over there,' he instructed, pointing to a silver drinks trolley beside the burgundy curtains. 'And have one yourself,' he added as an afterthought. 'If you so wish.'

Morton smiled grimly. This was unexpected. He looked at the bottles. Fine malts, the Ardbuithne 12-year old. Of course, the man had his own distilleries as well as his directorship. He was a whisky magnate with a shares portfolio of nearly eight per cent of the world market in Scotch whisky. He poured out two shots into crystal glasses. 'Water?'

'For me, no.' His voice rose to a sharp edge, impetuous. 'But why have you come here?'

'I want an explanation.' Morton put the glass on the small table near the aged man's skeletal hand.

'Of what? I have no explanations to give. Explanation for what? Of what?'

Morton sat down and took out his black notebook and pen. 'Firstly, I believe you sent a man to kill me, on a train.'

There was a long silence. Finally, the old man tremulously sipped his whisky and put down his glass unsteadily on the wooden shelf beside his armchair. 'I did. There, I admit it. For you are my enemy. A traitor to the State. You deserved to die. I must protect my country.'

'*Your* country? Morton exclaimed. 'You don't own it.'

The cold eyes regarded him. 'I have served my country. I know what my duty is. Have you, young man?' He glared fiercely. 'How do you think I got these?' He tapped at his knee with a wavering skeletal hand. 'I have served my country, and my king – and queen.'

'My father served too,' Morton said. 'But that was seventy years ago. He was a teenager when it started.'

The vulpine eyes stared at him. 'What rank did he hold? Where did he serve?'

Morton sniffed at the malt and swirled it around in the shot glass. 'Sergeant. In the Gordons. El-Alamein and the desert, then Sicily. He was everywhere.'

Lord Craile's head nodded imperceptibly. 'The 51st Highland Division. Oh well, he may have been a brave man, but you… you are a nobody. A wrecker. You seek to tear apart our country, sow the seeds of disaffection. You are, whether you like to hear it or not, a traitor.' He shook his yellow fist, glaring fiercely. His eyes filled with water, either mucus or fluid. He began to cough in a paroxysm of coughing. He waved away Morton's help. At last, he breathed more easily. 'Why,' he asked, 'why do you not see that what you are doing is undermining the fabric of this wonderful country, the best, the most envied in the world?'

Morton stared into the leaping fire of the burning logs. His anger had dissipated, perhaps anaesthetised by the burning fire of the malt he had downed in one. 'There is a democratic process in this country,' he said. '*That* is what is envied. And we all have democratic rights. But you have shown that you are willing to shoot people for exercising those rights. You are not a patriot – you are a fascist!'

'Pah! Words! I fought fascists. You did not. For hundreds of years we have fought as comrades, we have grown together and developed, we Scots and the English… we have become one country.'

Morton interrupted. 'You talk of Scotland as though you own it. You may feel you are a Scot but your Scottish affectations, your rank and honours, Eton, Cambridge, the Guards – no doubt, eh? And your tartan, your whisky millions – it is all a disguise to throw us off the scent. You and your forebears sold us out for wealth and rank.'

The old man gripped his glass but said nothing, glared.

'Yes,' Morton continued, 'what better way to hide than to clad yourself in the garb, owning the very icons of Scotland, using as credentials the malt whisky that you own so much of. I love a single malt, yes, I do, but I hate that every sip I take, I'm contributing to your swollen coffers. But you know, *old boy*, you could own all the tartans, all the whisky, all the bagpipes in the world and it still wouldn't make you a Scot! What kind of patriot denies his country's existence as a nation and its ambitions and aspirations to be a State?'

And Morton smashed his glass into the fireplace, where it flared up in a delicate green and red perfume, then subsided.

Unnoticed by Morton, Craile had pulled a blue cord on his lap. Distantly, a bell rang.

'You sad, hollow old man,' Morton repeated, shaking his head. Some interview, he was thinking. Part of him regretted his outburst, another part even felt some kind of pity for the old man. 'You're living in the past, in a Scotland that has long ceased to be.' His voice had softened, moved by the pointlessness of the argument he was making really only with himself. 'We're changing,' he said, 'moving forward. You're like a ghost of our past.'

The door opened soundlessly and in rushed a burly man in tartan trews and military dress-jacket. There was no doubt of his anger. Morton could tell from the man's expression that he was about to be attacked and jumped to his feet, ready to defend himself.

In a quaking voice, Lord Craile instructed his man first in Gaelic, which Morton did not understand, then in a silky English: 'MacGillicuddy, no more. I want this man gone. Gone. Utterly. Let there be no more of him.' Then he lapsed into Gaelic and finally came only the sound of his rasping breaths.

MacGillicuddy looked from Lord Craile to Morton and a smile spread on his face, the firelight making his face red and demonic. He looked like a sergeant major who had been overdoing it on the regimental sherry. His voice was soothing. 'Rest now, your lordship. All is in hand. I will deal

238

with this intruder the old way. It will be a pleasure.' He drew from a scabbard behind him, a blade, flashing in the light of the flames. It was halfway between being a sword and a *sgian-dubh*.

'No, I don't think so,' Morton told him. 'I'm going to leave.'

'You won't leave without my permission,' the man said, advancing. He was a violent brute, fit, angry and armed. The blade flashed in the firelight. It was no heirloom, Morton realised, backing into the corner, behind the table. His hand found a whisky bottle and closed over its neck.

'A man tried to kill me the other day,' Morton babbled. 'He *died*. And I've had just about enough of you lot. Get out of my way!'

The man lunged with the knife. Morton gasped in pain. He felt a searing cut across his forearm. He threw the bottle at close range but MacGillicuddy waved it off, grinned. 'You will have to do better than that, sir!' He lunged forward again, over the tabletop.

Morton evaded him, grasped the wrist that held the blade but the man was too powerful. Morton stumbled, all his efforts expended trying to force back the hand that held the blade, away from his face. The man was exultant, a devil, snarling, aroused by violence.

They struggled, the table falling away between them, its contents sliding to the carpet. He heard a buzzing noise and there was a flash of lightning in the room. The man toppled onto him with no fight left in him, no strength, his arm fell, still grasping the blade and Morton was holding up a lifeless body that had wires attached. *Wires?*

A young woman in a black wetsuit stood in the door and she held a weapon. He stood, trapped under the body of

MacGillicuddy as if in a frozen dance tableau. There were wires and some kind of a dart sticking into him.

'Are you alright, Morton?'

'Eh, yes,' he said faintly.

MacGillicuddy slumped lower to Morton's knees.

'Is he dead?'

The woman came towards him. 'No. Tasered. He was going to kill you.'

'I think so. He was bloody strong.' He extricated his feet from the fallen body and came around the table. 'Thank you, but who are you? He stared at Lord Craile who seemed to be asleep. 'This man' he said, 'told him to kill me.'

'Yes. I know.' She put her weapon away, clipping it to her black webbing belt and took out some cable ties. 'I'm going to remove the Taser dart and cuff his hands and feet. He'll be alright in a while. Wait here.' She bent over the prostrated figure.

Morton reached over and shook Lord Craile. 'You!' he shouted. 'Wake up. I haven't finished with you yet!' He slapped him lightly across the cheek, then regretted his action when the old man's head swung loosely.

The woman grabbed his hand. 'Come out of the room. I saw that,' she said. 'And I'll have to report it.'

'Report it? Who *are* you?'

'I work for the security services.'

'Really?'

She smiled. 'Kirsty Haldane.'

'Oh, Emily told me about you! You probably just saved my life. For the second time in three days, I was nearly...'

'We know all about that.'

'Who's *we?*' Morton wanted to know.

'All in due course, Morton. First, I have to make some phone calls.'

Morton was trembling and jerky in his limbs as he sat in a thick armchair in the wide oil-painting-lined corridor of Ardbuithne House. He was in aftershock, trying to focus his thoughts, trying to breathe slowly and deeply in and out. His mind jumping all over the place. He thought about the recording he had made at the London meeting. Was it out in the public domaine? Had the media got hold of it? Who was this woman, Kirsty Haldane? Was MI5 protecting him now?

As Morton sat, waiting, he wondered where all the people were. The men with guns. It seemed too quiet. There were no sounds of human activity but he knew that MacGillicuddy would soon be recovering. His idea of an interview had been a disaster. As he pondered whether to make a run for it, Haldane reappeared.

'I cannot be seen to be assisting you, Morton,' she said. 'That would be counter to my remit as a serving officer. However, I could not allow a murder to take place, nor can I prevent you from pursuing your legal activities as a reporter.' She smiled. 'For instance if you were to have taken photos of the man who attacked you, or Lord Craile, during your – shall we say your *interview* – with him, I could not have stopped you,'

Morton sat and thought about it. Then he rose and went back into the living room and snapped several pictures of Lord Craile in his chair. The old man was asleep or unconscious, so he propped his head up to make it look like he was awake, as far as possible – he was so old! Then he took photos of the insensible MacGillicuddy on the floor still holding the big knife. He wanted to take a picture of the woman who had saved him but her threatening look showed that was going too far.

'So, I can write about this and have it published?' he asked, brightening. 'That would be okay?'

Kirsty Haldane smiled and pushed back hair from her forehead. 'Of course, it's a free country. They'll try to stop you, of course, but if you are quick, you can get the story out.'

'Who will try to stop me?'

'Come off it! You *know* who! The same people who have been chasing you all over the place up to now.'

'But I don't know who they are. I couldn't work out if it was GB13 or the security services.'

'Well, that's your job, isn't it?'

'Can I quote you in the story?'

She smiled, hands on hips. 'What do you think?'

'I think probably not.'

'Correct. I only stepped in to prevent a death. In fact, I'm shortly going to disappear. And perhaps it would be best all round if you didn't mention I was ever here. In fact, if you do that, I might be able to help you again. Do you see what I'm saying?'

'I think so.'

'I suggest you look around, see if you can find some material you can use and get out, go back home, write your story and take it from there. Probably it's a story best suited to social media, but you'll know best. You've done pretty well so far.' She scrutinised Morton. 'Are you alright? You're not injured? And, by the way, how did you get here?'

Morton struggled to remember. 'Ah. Bike. I came by bike, on the ferry.'

'Of course. Can you cycle back?'

'I think so.'

She frowned. 'On the other hand, that might be tempting fate. I think I'd better help you get away from here. And it's best if we go now, before…' she nodded at the prostrate figure of MacGillicuddy who was starting to make jerking movements and grunting sounds. 'Where is your bicycle?'

'I left it up by the road at the top of the wood.'

'Right come on then, before anyone else comes. I don't want to have to explain what I'm doing here and I suppose you don't either.'

'Nope.'

'Right, follow me closely and do exactly as I say.'

Morton was only too glad to have a guide. They descended the carpeted stairs to the front hall, where they stood listening. No sounds. They went to the front door, looked out.

'Looks clear,' Haldane said. She pointed to the left, to the ivied old tower that was part of the gable of the house. 'That's where we head for, then we get beyond into the trees.'

'There were men with guns,' Morton told her. 'When I came in, I mean.'

'Right. I saw them too. Can't see them now, though. I had a look earlier. Probably on lunch break. Come on.'

Their luck held. Morton was fascinated by his companion. Twenty years his junior in age probably but so agile and so confident. She sounded Scottish and yet she was with MI5. He could hardly believe it. They made it around the tower and into the woods, where they crouched down, getting their breath back.

'Now, where is your bike?' she asked.

Morton pointed up the track to the road.

'Right. Go get it and bring it down. I'll wait here.'

Morton frowned. 'Eh? Isn't your car up there too?'

243

'Didn't come by car. Hurry up. The men could come back at any time. And keep low down as you go. Make sure and check there's no-one on the road when you get up there.'

'Okay.' Morton did as he was told. It took only five minutes to get up there. He retrieved the rucksack and pushed the bike with care back down the track to where Kirsty Haldane crouched, keeping watch.

'It's all clear,' she told him. 'No sign of the men. Now we've got to get down to the beach just around behind… past those rocks. There's a sandy bit. That's where I've left the boat.'

'Boat?'

'Rigid inflatable.'

'Oh.' Morton's face betrayed his anxiety. 'Um, I assumed we'd be going back via the ferry. I have a return ticket.'

Kirsty smiled. 'No. We need to get away sharpish. Don't tell me you're scared of boats?'

Morton gave her a fearful glance. 'Is an RIB actually a boat?'

She grinned at him. 'Ach, you'll be alright.'

'It's just that I had to cross the Firth of Lorn once before in one. With a paddle. At night. I didn't enjoy it.' He pulled a face.

Kirsty sniffed. 'Ah well, that's the transport we have. Or you could stay and ask Lord Craile and his buddies to put you up for the night?'

'No, probably not.'

'Right. When I say, jump down over the machair onto the shingle. I'll bring the bike.'

'Okay.'

Once they were on the shingle and hidden from view, they made quick time around the rocky headland to the small stretch of sandy beach. The RIB was behind a large rock high up on the dry sand. As Morton had feared, it was small, about eight feet long, but at least it had an outboard motor. He felt trepidation, looking out at the wide Loch Buithne, the steep black cliffs on all sides and the open sea beyond, glistening in the sun.

Haldane heaved the bike into it. 'You lift the bows, I'll get the stern,' she ordered, hoisting the craft upwards.

He grabbed his end. Rapidly, they crab-walked down the sand. Morton got his feet wet.

Once they got it into the water, about two feet deep, she grasped his arm and pushed him into the boat. 'Sit there and lean outwards against the side,' she instructed. Then she deftly propelled the dinghy into deeper water, till she was in waist-high, and sprang into the boat.

It rocked as she sat opposite him and grinned. 'Now we're cooking on gas!' She had green eyes, he noticed. She expertly yanked the starter. It caught powerfully, the engine fracturing the silence, loud near his ear. She caught sight of his face then and laughed.

'I don't believe you really are scared. And I thought you were such an intrepid type.'

Morton gritted his teeth. He couldn't explain his fear of deep water. It had gradually been getting worse since his twenties. He didn't want to look scared in front of a young woman, but... he couldn't help it. Haldane backed the dinghy out and Morton felt the changed motion as its rubber sides caught the brunt of the incoming waves. Then it was settling lower into the water, stern lower than its bows and then they were turning in an arc, then racing out into the middle of Loch Buithne.

'I said... bound to see us now!' Haldane was saying.

He looked back over his shoulder without letting go. The big house was getting smaller and smaller, disappearing into the bowl of low hills that surrounded it. He couldn't see anyone. Where were the men with guns? Was MacGillicuddy on his feet yet? The house diminished and disappeared into the hills, a man-made building extinguished by the vastness of landscape. He was tensed up, holding on tightly. Two billows of white water surged under them as they raced onwards. He looked forward over the raised bows. They were heading for a rocky outcrop and, beyond, a further headland of high cliffs and beyond that, the wide open Firth, practically the ocean. He gritted his teeth, his knuckles white as he clasped the rope. He hated the bumps of the boat as it crashed up and down in the black water but gradually the rhythm or pattern became familiar to him, the white wake behind them regular, mathematically perfect.

'Yes, I had you penned as a fearless investigator,' she said, turning the tiller with one hand as they raced around the point and began heading away from Mull. She had sparkly varnish on her fingernails. 'After all, you put yourself at danger several times. Anyway, you're doing okay. We'll be at the car in about twenty minutes.'

'Twenty minutes?' he said faintly.

'Yes. We're cutting straight across to Seil Island. Total of about twelve miles.'

'Do you do this a lot?' Morton asked nervously.

'Do I ever! I *love* this. Used to do a lot more of it, when I was a kid. I don't get nearly enough exercise with what I'm doing now.'

'I can't believe you're with MI5. You look so young.'

'Hah!'

The wind was blasting into their faces and Morton's eyes were full of grit, salt probably, and watering. He saw a rocky outcrop ahead and looked back at it as they passed by.

'Frank Lockwood's Island,' she told him, pointing. 'We're about a third of the way now. What a gorgeous day. Look at this wonderful sky. This is a great piece of water you know. Great for diving I mean. Ever dived? No? What a shame. It's great fun. Yes, many historical wrecks hereabouts. Stories of Spanish treasure. My dad used to take us holidays all up and down this coast, investigating caves. How are you bearing up? Got your sea legs yet?'

'I'm alright,' Morton said. He was trying to look at the mainland and not at the heaving dark swell on both sides. He felt the moistness on his cheeks and occasional spray flushed over the bows. But the regular movement was reassuring to him. He felt okay. As long as there were to be no surprises, no sudden bigger waves. The speed of the boat and its power helped too. He was counting in his mind; how many minutes so far? How many minutes left? They were making fast progress towards the mainland, her red hair blasted back from her face revealing delicate features, the green eyes. 'So how did you get into your line of work?' Talking might take his mind off it.

She smiled. 'The usual, you know. Recruited at uni. Glasgow. I was in the TA you see and loads of other clubs. I've always been interested in sports. I did a degree in Computer Sciences and one day, I was called to see my tutor and there was this chap with him.'

'You don't fit my image of MI5 officers,' he said.

'They are honestly trying to be more diverse.' She laughed. 'Not easy for them. But the dangers we face are wide-ranging and diverse and we need to meet those challenges.'

247

'Sounds like a line from some press release.'

She smiled. 'Does, doesn't it? That's Seil Island ahead. Ever been there?'

'No.'

'There's a folk museum. Very interesting. Lots of slate mines there at one time. Anyway, we're not all public school twats.'

Morton snorted. 'Hah. That's the stereotype. Tories with automatic pistols.'

'You'd be surprised, Morton. As I told your friend, Prof Emily, not all of us are opposed to Scottish Independence.'

'Yes, Emily mentioned that.'

She turned to him quizzically. 'I had hoped she would. I gave her a hint to pass on to you, in fact. To continue to press on the links between GB13 and Government.'

'Oh yes? Well, that's what I've been trying to find. This man Neil... is clearly a link.'

She made a deprecating gesture with her fingers, the sparkly nail varnish glistened in the sun. 'Can't speak about that matter, sorry, Morton. That's off limits for me.'

'Really? Well, that kind of proves....'

'I haven't said anything. Nor will I.' She smirked at Morton as she moved the tiller with a flick of her wrist. 'I couldn't possibly tell you that he is one of us. Oops!'

'Crikey!'

'Crikey to you too! Now hold on, we're turning.'

Morton didn't enjoy the last few minutes of the landing. It was great to see land up close but there was a lot of swell, a lot of jagged rocks, a lot of weightless bouncing around and they had to work hard to get into a little bay between the village of Ellanbeich and the small island of Easdale, which, Morton saw was joined to the mainland by a narrow metal footbridge. Haldane cut the engine and the boat drifted onto the shingle shore. The hamlet was larger than he had expected. He saw a few shops and tourist buses, people moving about, eating ice cream.

Haldane jumped out and pulled the boat onto the shingle. 'Get out now,' she instructed. 'Your feet are already wet so it's no big deal.'

Between them, they lifted the dinghy up to the gravel carpark which was also a turning area and onto the low loader attached to her vehicle, a black Land Rover. There were a few buses parked there and lots of cars. He had made it to dry land.

CHAPTER TWENTY-SEVEN

They'd shared a milky coffee from a flask and a Tunnock's caramel wafer, leaning against the doors of the Land Rover, enjoying the sunshine flashing on the blue surface of the Firth of Lorn, which, Morton noted with surprise, looked as flat calm as a swimming pool. Then he looked the other way as she went behind the vehicle and stripped off her wetsuit and changed into dry clothes.

'Thanks for the coffee,' he said. 'I usually take it black but beggars can't be choosers.'

'Look, I can't take you any further,' she said from behind the vehicle. 'Work to do, you know how it is, and I'm already compromised enough.' She came back around the front of the Land Rover, in tight jeans, her red hair a bit awry.

'Sorry,' he said. 'But thanks for the lift. I mean getting me over.'

'Yes, you'll be alright here.' She used the front mirror to check her hair and pull stray strands back into a tortoiseshell clasp. 'There's a bus in an hour or so, back to Oban from here.' She pointed to a sign. 'There's the stop.'

'Right. That's great.'

'They're quite frequent because of the Easdale Island Folk Museum, you see, and there's the An Cala Gardens and several B&Bs over on Easdale.'

'Okay.' Morton heaved the red bike down from the dingy, and propped it on its stand.

'Nice bike,' she commented. 'You could always cycle. I mean, it's probably only — what — about twelve miles? That's what I'd do. Anyway, I'll need to work out how to phrase this in my report. It is possible Lord Craile will report the incident to the police as a home invasion, or burglary, or even an assault, but I doubt it. In any case, no-one saw me there.'

Morton looked at her. 'If I write up the story with the pictures I have, well of course, there'll be no mention of you.'

'You intend to do that? You think you have enough?'

'Not sure. Probably. When I get back to Edinburgh. I'll talk it over with my editor,' he paused, '…and others.'

'Like Emily? She's smart that one, although…' She began to chuckle as she tightened the cap on the red flask.

Morton frowned. 'Although what?'

She tossed the flask onto the back seat. 'I'm afraid she's regarded as a bit of a troublemaker – in the service, I mean.'

'That's ridiculous! She's a respected academic, a Professor. How could she be… trouble?'

'It's just the way we see things, I suppose.'

'I'm guessing you don't quite see it like that – like they do?' Morton queried, giving her a quizzical look.

'Oh, we're a team, but sometimes the focus changes. Anyway, Morton, try to keep out of trouble yourself – stay safe!'

Morton was a bit miffed. 'I'm entitled to investigate, it's my job. I don't see it as *trouble-making*.'

She laughed lightly. 'No, of course, you don't. And I'm sure you're not. At least, on a personal level, I am sure. It's just that we – they – have a different view of things. They think Britain, you think Scotland. That sums it up really.' She shook her head and tut-tutted. 'As if you have to choose. There'll always be British and Scottish here – even after Indy. Although it will be different, perhaps better. Hey, listen to me!'

Morton grasped the handlebars and the saddle. 'Things change,' he said, enigmatically. 'Perceptions change. Nations change. Anyway, nice meeting you. And thanks again!'

'No bother. You take care.'

He pushed his bike over to the small bus stop, where he stood it up on its stand and watched as Kirsty drove the Land Rover and low loader onto the street and away, tooting her horn once and giving him a cheery wave as she passed. He was alone, apart from a few visitors strolling around the streets of the small hamlet.

He flicked through the pictures on his camera. The one of the sleeping, or unconscious, Lord Craile stunned him. He looked sallow, vampire-like, as if he had just sated himself on the blood of his victims. It was a powerful picture. MacGillicuddy on the carpet clutching his blade was clearly unconscious, but no matter. The blade said it all. Thuggery. He'd been attacked – entirely unprovoked – but he'd defended himself. And that evil old man had ordered his death, proving entirely the point Morton had been making.

Well, he had a story. Not quite what he had expected. He was, even as he considered the overview, composing the detail of sentences in his head. He pulled out his notebook and began rapidly paraphrasing his 'interview', jotting down the phrases the old man had used. *A nobody... a wrecker... sowing seeds of disaffection... Scotland and England one country... a traitor... undermining the fabric of this country...*. Craile had admitted ordering the man on the train to attack him. Morton regretted that he hadn't got that on tape, hadn't got any of it on tape. Perhaps he should invest in a spy-pen? Maybe he could borrow Sean's? Too late for that, now. Anyway, he had the pictures as proof. He'd use five: Lord Craile, MacGillicuddy and his knife, two pics of the armed men –

rifles not shotguns – and a picture of the front of the mansion from the shore. It was a piece for the Sundays he knew, but he'd have to offer first dibs to Hugh. He looked over beyond Easdale to Mull, a pale green strip of land that now looked benign. Someone had once told him its nickname was 'the Captain's locker', allegedly because of the high numbers of English retirees there. That kind of thing had been happening for decades, long before Gallimont came on the scene.

He could see a bus approaching and watched it turn a full circle slowly at the end of the road and stop in front of him. The driver, a bulky man whose blue uniform tunic was too tight across his belly in several places, stowed the bike in the empty luggage compartment and gave him a ticket. He sounded, to Morton, like he was from County Durham or perhaps Lincolnshire, a bit weary, as if he didn't enjoy the job much, or maybe he was just tired. He didn't say much.

The bus picked up three more passengers who sat at the front, and then set off, passing a Community Hall and a primary school, a Post Office, and soon Morton was bouncing high over open heather moorland. The other passengers on the bus were clearly early-season tourists, sitting in the front seats to get a better view. Morton could ignore them and no longer had worries about Lord Craile's thugs. Reception on his iPhone was surprisingly good. He sent messages on WhatsApp to everybody he knew, starting with Emily, Sean, Hugh, but also Luke, Marco and Alasdair. He wondered about Alasdair. It seemed that the canny old rogue was still living at Celia's. He smiled. He was like her big puppy dog, wagging his tail and accompanying her on shopping trips, doing all kinds of tasks for her. They were so different and it seemed odd but true that they had found something in each other that they needed. He wished them luck, although he had a twinge of regret about Celia. He was with Emily though and he needed to work out what the future was with her. He must spend a lot more time with her. Seal the deal, whatever that was to be. Go on holiday together, when this was over, somewhere hot.

The bus slowed to climb up the humped bridge 'over the Atlantic'. What a conceit! The water was only six feet wide. As they passed the Tigh-An-Truish Inn, he remembered that was where Highlanders in post-Jacobite times had exchanged their woollen trews for the kilts that had been proscribed when they were coming and returning from the south. It was funny to think that for most of its history, half of the Scottish population had been Gaelic-speaking. And the other fifty per cent spoke Scots. Also funny to think, Morton mused, as the bus ran along the shore of Loch Seil, then through woods, that the notion of the Highlands as a picturesque wilderness was a modern one. It had been home to half of the population for hundreds of years. Productive, busy, enterprising. Yes, before bastards like Lord Craile had got their hands on it!

His mobile pinged. Message from Emily. *Get trains Oban Glasgow Edinb. Quicker. C u soon, Luv, E xx.* The bus had reached the junction with the A816 at a wide inlet of the sea and was heading north along the shore to Oban. He couldn't have cycled all this. Emily would have. She would have too, no doubt. Kirsty Haldane. She was beyond fit. He smiled. It was hard to think that she was in MI5. She didn't feel like an enemy. They probably weren't all like her. Good Lord, that was a thought!

He stretched out on the seat and let the bright flashing seascape on his left, the vivid moors and distant blue-grey hills on his right undulate past his eyeballs. He was debating the likelihood of Lord Craile contacting the police, but mostly he was thinking about what he was going to eat when he got to Oban – before he got on the Glasgow train.

A long message from Sean informed him that the Scottish Government had instructed Police Scotland to issue a warrant for the arrest of Philip Gallimont, alias Philip Gray, alias Robin Mayberry, and he had been arrested, with help from Northumbria Police, at Newcastle airport on his return from Tenerife. They had established that Ardbeag Holdings was a subsidiary of a property portfolio held by Ardbuithne Estates and so they had started to make a link, as yet tenuous, with Lord Craile. Morton was pleased to hear it. That would help to make his story stand up, tie it all together.

Philip Gallimont was summonsed to appear at Edinburgh Sheriff Court and had refused to make a statement there and was remanded to HMP Saughton after a five-minute appearance. He had insisted on contacting his own solicitor but as one could not be provided at short notice, he was represented by a duty solicitor, whom he refused to talk to. When it was suggested that he posed a high risk of absconding, bail was refused by the Sheriff.

Gallimont found himself being signed in at HMP Saughton, to his disgust. He did not endear himself to the staff there by his attitude and was put into a cell overnight on his own. He believed that he would be free to go, all charges dropped, in the morning. He had been through this before, in Edinburgh just a month before.

Unfortunately for Gallimont, 400 miles to the south, a swift and merciless blitzkrieg had been conducted by the authority of no less than Number Ten itself, a purge of all who had been involved in, or were aware of, or implicated in

GB13. Commander Smyth had been summarily dismissed, although in the service it was known that had previously occurred twice and each time he had re-emerged. There was no information on what he had been promised, or indeed, who had given him the news. He simply became absent. Dardon, Menzies, Spadeworth, Wilkins had all been contacted and made to feel the wrath of the PM. In HMP Saughton, Philip Gallimont could not have known that his support mechanism had already been swept away and that he had been thrown to the wolves. He would start to have an inkling of this in the morning when he saw that he had the same duty solicitor he had had the day before and learned that no special interventions had occurred from the Home Office or anywhere else. Three days later, he would appear again and be further remanded as inquiries continued into property fraud and other potential crimes.

Prime Minister Cameron was cleaning up in advance of a face-to-face meeting with Scotland's First Minister, which had already received considerable advance publicity. Unwanted publicity on his side. It had been billed as a battle of wills. Commentators had spun it as a meeting where he would have to apologise, confess to dirty tricks, abase himself before a nationalist, a sworn enemy, his nemesis; five feet six inches in her two-and-a-half-inch red heels, Nicola Sturgeon. The shoals of spin-doctors in Downing Street toiled night and day to no avail to spin the meeting as one where Cameron would deflate the nationalist hyperbole and emerge with a verbal promise of no more Scottish Referendums 'for a generation'. He wanted to appear as the benefactor, waving his magic wand of further stronger powers for devolved Scotland in the forthcoming legislation. That was his game plan. He knew that attack was the best form of defence. The legislation promised more powers and he would talk these up till it seemed like the Referendum losers were actually the winners. And the reporters and commentators and correspondents sharpened their pencils and licked their lips. It was all good copy.

Sean Kermally and a small team of IT specialists had finished editing the footage Morton had supplied them into a four-minute video of mixed quality and uploaded it to YouTube, although as yet not available to the public. Edited down from over an hour, it showed MPs and Peers of the Realm and a serving senior officer of MI5 discussing the introduction of binding legislation to prevent consultative referendums ever being held unless seventy-five per cent of the House agreed and then frogmarching a reporter out of the room for no apparent reason. It seemed a powerful and vivid statement of what Westminster would do to the Scots now that the threat of the Referendum was over. The losers must be punished, prevented, nailed down in their coffin for ever more. Many English people were sick of hearing about the Scots and Scotland.

A London cab driver expressed the view of many when he told a Scottish MP who had had the misfortune to get into his cab: 'You've had your bleedin say, Jock, and we're bleedin sick of it, so get back in your bleedin box!'

To some MPs the plan seemed a sensible, practical measure to ensure constitutional stability. They didn't think about unintended consequences. But to Scotland's MPs who were nine per cent of the House of Commons membership, the idea obliterated all notions of partnership, of willing participation, showed the naked fist of authority at last.

Where there had been leeway for Scottish representatives

to act on purely Scottish mandates and obtain Westminster's agreement, via a Section 30 Order to hold a referendum, as in September 2014, this would now be legally impossible. Future Prime Minister's hands would be tied. For most of the members of the Commons, this seventy-five per cent rule was an excellent idea. The House was, after all, a legislative body and Scotland a tiny constituent part, whose whining complaints must be endured from time to time. The Parliament spoke with one voice and heard with one ear and most of the time, that ear was listening to its own echo.

Willie Morton typed up the story on his iPad on the train journeys from Oban to Glasgow and on to Edinburgh and emailed it to Hugh. He downloaded the pictures from his camera and sent them. Hugh was ecstatic. That was the word in his final text: *Am ecstatic, u r quids in, my fav scribe. H.*

Morton had reiterated to him how important it was to legal the story, before putting it to the subs. He didn't want to incriminate himself and be arrested for trespass, burglary, assault... or worse. It was conceivable that Lord Craile might be too ill for the police to interview. Imagine, Morton closed his eyes in horror, imagine if the old stoat croaked and it was put down to him? Better not to think about it. But it was a worry. Putting out the story was a way of confirming he'd been there, uninvited, and he could hardly call Kirsty Haldane as a witness to his claim that he'd been the victim of an unprovoked attack by an armed man. Again.

CHAPTER TWENTY-EIGHT

Kirsty Haldane had received a message during the night reassigning her to Thames House. Her op was complete and her attendance was required at a wrap-up meeting the next day. She had been warned there were some loose ends but given no further information about what they might be. She wasn't unduly worried. She was a little disappointed and surprised by the suddenness of the decision but no more than that. She showered, breakfasted on coffee, a croissant and jam and some fruit then packed and checked out of the Holyrood Aparthotel, pushing her suitcase out onto the Royal Mile. She decided to call in to Scotland station and say cheerio to Crispin. She just had time before catching the shuttle bus to the airport from Waverley.

Crispin wasn't in the office but she could see two men in the ops room through the open door. There was an awkward silence then one of the men stood up and came to the doorway, the taller and thinner of the two.

'You must be Kirsty Haldane?' He was lean and thin-faced, with a prominent scar from his right eye into his hairline. He was in his early thirties, she guessed. Not handsome, she thought irrelevantly, his ears were too big for such a bony face.

She shook his hand. 'That's me,' she said, raising an eyebrow.

He saw the direction of her glance. 'I'm Saul Dunan,' he said, rather reluctantly, 'and this is Richard Blenkinsop.' He indicated his seated colleague in the ops room.

'Right,' Kirsty said, frowning. 'I've been reassigned today. I've been up here for nearly four weeks but the op is completed.'

Blenkinsop appeared in the doorway. A solid young man, ruddy face, of boyish bulk, younger but he was the leader, Kirsty felt sure. He spoke with the minimum of words necessary. 'We heard. But we're not covering the same ground, exactly. Similar.'

'Oh really?' Kirsty said, filled with sudden anger and also a measure of dread at what this might mean for her. Loose ends? Had she made an error? Lord Craile, of course. They knew about that. There was another pause.

Dunan indicated the coffee machine. 'Have you time for…?'

She could tell from the cold tone of his voice that it was an empty courtesy. They wanted her gone. 'No, I'm heading for the airport. Thank you anyway. I just wanted to say good bye to Crispin.'

'He's not here,' Blenkinsop said. Statement of fact with no bells on it. She felt he was no charmer.

'I noticed. Well, I'll just have to leave him a note.'

'Okay,' Dunan said, forcing a smile. 'Nice to have met you.'

'And you.' She turned and spoke over her shoulder. 'Similar, you said. You're covering similar ground to my op?'

Blenkinsop smiled faintly. It was barely a smile, more a grim stretch of his lips. 'Sorry. We can't discuss that.'

'Of course not. Well, bye, see you around.'

'Yeah. Stay safe,' Dunan said. Blenkinsop had already gone back into the ops room.

Kirsty stood in the outer office scribbling a personal note on the pad on Crispin's desk. She felt humiliated. It was clear

260

there was overlap between her op and what they were doing and she'd been kept out of the loop. She sighed and looked at her watch. Nothing she could do. She clutched the handle of her suitcase and propelled it out of the office into the hallway and towards the lift. She was going to miss Scotland, but onwards and upwards.

Inside the ops room, Saul Dunan went over to the window. 'That was a little awkward, I felt.'

'Me too,' Blenkinsop said. It was just the kind of thing to say at such moments. 'But we were right not to get into it with her.'

'Think she suspected anything?'

'No, how could she?'

'You're right, Richard.'

'She'll find out soon enough when she's in the hot seat. She'll have to answer for anomalies and incomplete reports she made. Forget it. Let's run these FR scans. Starting from about 8 p.m. last night, when we know where he was.'

Blenkinsop and Dunan had been working in Edinburgh for nearly twenty-four hours, based in a room at West End Police Station, liaising with Special Branch. It was not uncommon for Five to run two operations simultaneously over the same terrain although their brief was very specific. The Intel Analysts had studied all of the information provided by Hardwick's team and had created a new Scotland station op tasked with building a file on the group known as EH4i, or Ethical Hackers For Independence, although it was understood the name was not an official one. It was a loose group but one name stood out: Luke Sangster. He seemed to be the key to unlocking the mystery of Cerberus, a codename that had cropped up at the time of the media revelations about the allegedly illegal bank-rolling of the No side in the referendum campaign.

Dunan keyed up the stored CCTV footage of the Marchmont locale where they suspected that the suspect lived. It was a high density housing area of tenements, split into student flats and CCTV was patchy but shops and other premises and buses moving up and down Marchmont Road gave coverage at the limits of the search zone.

'Okay,' Blenkinsop instructed. 'Use the last-known location, which was the pub. We know he was there for nearly two hours. Start from his arrival there and work backwards.'

'Got him.'

'Scroll back. Okay, there, he's clearly walking across the Meadows. We'll pick him up on Melville Drive. Assume four, maybe five minutes to walk across.' The blurry pictures showed a man walking quickly backwards, other people walking backwards, cars and a bus, driving backwards.

'Come on! Where are you?' Dunan muttered. 'Maybe he came out of the Meadows in another direction?'

'No, keep on. I don't think he's particularly aware of surveillance. We can check these other exits later, but let's assume he walked over quicker. Try two minutes earlier.'

'Bingo!' Dunan exclaimed. 'There's our boy. Marchmont Street, walking on the pavement, heading south. Oh, he's turning off left.'

'Sciennes Road,' Blenkinsop said. 'We're going to lose him. No cameras there.'

'Wait! Now he's turning right.'

'Marchmont Crescent, which leads back to the main road. That must be it, Saul. Go further up the main street. Any cameras looking across that junction back into Marchmont Crescent?'

'I'll see. Yes. Just at the next junction. There he is!' Dunan's voice rose a semi-tone. 'North side, I mean east side, second tenement along from the junction. We have him!'

'Not so fast, Saul. Cross-reference that with the time-dated FR scans, using all available cameras in all networks. Then, if that checks out, we're on the road. Another coffee, while we wait?'

While the coffee perked, Dunan went out into the outer office and glanced at the note Kirsty had left on Crispin Hayes' desk. 'Think we should have told her Hayes is off to Geneva?'

Blenkinsop said: 'Coffee's ready. What have you found?' He came over and read the note. 'Aw, that's sweet. Perhaps we should. But we didn't have to, so we didn't.'

It took the FR scanner less than ten minutes to decide that there had been so sightings of Luke Sangster in the Marchmont vicinity for the past eight hours.

Blenkinsop put down his mug. 'Okay, that's it then. He's there, so we're on. Showtime.'

Dunan reached for his jacket. 'Let's do our thing,' he said. 'Earn our daily bread.'

The front page story of the *Scottish Standard* supplied by Willie Morton had been very cleverly rewritten on legal advice with some of the strongest statements following 'allegedly' or 'it is alleged that…' It was a powerful denunciation of the power of one man to subvert democracy. And the picture of Lord Craile's vampire-frail features amongst the pictures of his hired armed thugs conveyed the corruption of the old order. The face of GB13 was presented as a man steeped in unquestioning authority, autocracy, oligarchy, a millionaire who believed he had the right to have anyone who questioned him killed. Referendums and parliamentary majorities meant nothing to him. He would suppress the voters if they did not agree with his view of the world.

The piece questioned the level of support he had received from the UK Government, referred to collusion with MI5 officers, and attempted to link the group and its thuggish elements with mainstream opinion in England. This, the piece, argued, was what Westminster would do to keep Scotland from expressing its democratic views, if they differed from those of the London Establishment.

Hugh Leadbetter had heard as early as 10.30 a.m. that sales of the paper were going through the roof. Online subscriptions too had rocketed and by midday, he issued instructions to print a second edition to resupply the major newsagents in Edinburgh and Glasgow – something he had never previously encountered in his eighteen years at the *Standard*. The front cover and links to the article were being widely shared on social media and it featured in Twitter's top five trending stories of the day. He picked up the phone.

'Willie?' he growled. 'You're a star! The story has gone gold.'

'Good to hear. I suppose it'll be on *Reporting Scotland* tonight?'

Leadbetter grunted. 'I wouldnae go that far. The BBC? But it'll be all over the place, STV, Channel 4, RTE, RT... you name it, but maybe no BBC Scotland. It's a bit too anti-establishment for them, I'd say. But well done, lad. If you wanted to talk about a full-time contract...?'

'Morton laughed. 'Ha! Not the first time you've asked me. But the answer's still the same.'

'A shame. But I understand. Where are you?'

'My place.'

'Have you had any media inquiries yourself?'

'Actually, I'll be on STV *News at Six*, apparently and also *Scotland Tonight*.'

'Nice one, I'll tell the news team to look out for it and do follow ups. Have a nice day!'

'Hah!'

Their approach was stealthy and efficient. They parked the Mondeo a street away and walked to the tenement entrance. It was one entrance among dozens of similar in a small warren of streets of four-and five-storey tenements. They looked, to any passer-by, like police officers and were barely given a second glance. Probably attending a break-in report or following inquiries about a half-ounce of marijuana. Dark-haired men in black coats, suits, black shoes.

The door entry system had a service button for postal delivery and they noted that there were sixteen flats in the tenement. Dunan pushed the service button and they entered the hallway. It was moderately clean and had no obnoxious smells, also completely silent as if everybody was at work, or at lectures or sleeping late. The tenants' mail boxes were numbered but with few obvious signs of names.

Blenkinsop methodically scanned the mail but it was pointless. Most were circulars. 'Sixteen flats,' he said quietly, 'but I'd put my money on it being top-right. That way he has the maximum chance to get out if he heard someone coming up the stairs.'

Dunan looked at him. 'You don't think he'll have a spy-cam here?'

Blenkinsop sniffed. 'Unlikely. I can't see one. Come on, let's start at the top.'

They stepped quietly up the concrete stairs, checking the names on the doors. They used sign language, as they worked up to the top floor. They were listening for noises inside the flats. Light shining through scummy skylight windows illuminated the stairwell. On one doormat was a worker's muddy boots, on another, a folded-down child buggy. On the top floor, there were only two flats and the left one had the name Costello, the right one was blank. Blenkinsop pointed to it.

Dunan got down onto one knee and gently prised up the aluminium letterbox. It occurred to him that postmen were no longer using them, in favour of the boxes in the hall on the ground level. His view was obscured by a thick dark fabric. He tried with a ballpoint pen to move it, but after a moment, he stood up, shaking his head. They conferred in whispers.

'Has to be this one,' Dunan said.

'Blenkinsop nodded. 'The letterbox baffle, the lack of a name. I'd say this is it.'

'Right, we're on,' Dunan whispered and knocked on the door. They waited, listening hard. Nothing. No sounds in the flat, or on the stairwell. 'He must be here. We'd know if he'd gone out.' He knocked again and they waited a little longer.

'Okay, let's do it,' Blenkinsop said. He produced a small cold steel jemmy bar from an inside pocket in his coat and placed it between the door jamb and the lock and hit it with the heel of his hand a couple of times.

Dunan smiled. 'Not as good as you thought you were.'

Blenkinsop grimaced. 'The mortice is on too and the snib. That can only mean one thing. He *is* inside.'

'Right, stand back, let me.' Dunan ran at it from the other side of the landing and booted it with his sole. It splintered but held. He tried it twice more before the door swung open. 'We're in,' he said, grinning. 'I rather enjoyed that.'

The flat was empty in both senses of the word; nobody and barely any furniture, no carpeting, bare wooden floors. But in the smaller of the two bedrooms was a pile of flattened cardboard boxes and a rolled-up sleeping bag.

'We can get forensics on that,' Blenkinsop said. The living room was empty, except for torn paper blinds which failed to keep out the sunshine. In the galley kitchen a kettle had recently boiled and a damp, warm teabag had soaked through a square of kitchen towel. 'He was here, very recently.'

The door to the room at the far end seemed to be locked. There was a key still in the lock on the *inside*.

Blenkinsop took out his jemmy but Dunan booted the door in with one kick. They rushed in... no-one! The room was warm with electronics, a digital cave, a hacker's office, several desktop PCs and a laptop were connected together and thick cables wired to a satellite dish on the wall outside and a broadband hub.

'It's his hacker's set-up,' Blenkinsop said. 'We'll need to get the techie squad to go over this, tooth and nail.'

'Funny we missed him,' said Dunan, 'there's still warm tea in the mug and these computers are hot. Are you sure it *was* locked – or maybe just a bit stiff?'

'If we've missed him it's only by minutes,' Blenkinsop said. 'All the stuff is here. But my guess is the forensic and techie squads won't find much. It'll all be on a portable hard-drive – anything of interest, that is, and he'll be away with it.'

'Wait! Seen this?' Dunan said, 'look here. Footprints on the shelves going up to... Bingo! An attic hatch.'

'Aw.'

They looked up. The aluminium framework held wooden shelves and on the middle one was a clear footprint. It wasn't a shelving unit, it was a ladder. And directly above, was a hatch into the attic. Blenkinsop looked at Dunan.

'Your turn.'

Helped by Blenkinsop, Dunan stepped up onto the flimsy shelves and reached up to the hatch and pushed it upwards. Then he grasped the rafters inside and pulled himself up. His muffled voice came down to his colleague. 'Right little hidey-hole. He's gone out the skylight here.'

Blenkinsop waited.

A few minutes later, Dunan peered out through the empty hatch. 'He went out the skylight and, I think, over the roofs. I've checked the attic – nothing.'

'Right. We'd better get some help here,' Blenkinsop said, taking out his mobile phone. 'He clearly has an escape routine. I'd bet he was here when we arrived outside. Maybe he does have a spy-cam in the hall or on the stairs.'

'Pretty nifty,' Dunan said grudgingly. 'I wouldn't like to go over the roofs that's for sure.'

Blenkinsop sniffed. 'Agile, I'll give him that. But maybe he wasn't going very far. We'll find out, eventually.'

Dunan grinned. 'He can run, but he can't hide.'

CHAPTER TWENTY-NINE

In his early days as a freelance, Willie Morton had been overjoyed to be asked to appear on TV and radio programmes to talk about his work or his stories. Now, he only appeared if an appearance fee had been agreed. Some programme-makers deplored it, used as they were to getting authors willing to appear for free, in order to plug their books, and politicians just keen to get their greasy mugs before the voters. Once, he had refused to appear on a well-known programme because they told him it was not usual for them to pay contributors. News bulletins didn't pay, that was the convention, but news magazine programmes and talk shows did, or should.

'Look, this is work for me,' he wearily told the household name who was the presenter, 'I'm a journalist. I make my living from my work. There's a standard fee as agreed by the NUJ. Fair enough if I was plugging a book, but I'm not. My time is money. You want me on your show, you pay me a fee!' As a result, he was rarely invited to contribute on TV. He didn't care, but this was different, this helped move along his story and anyway, they'd indicated there was a fee before he even asked.

Inevitably the news programme concentrated on the more sensational aspects: whether there would be a police investigation into Lord Craile and the GB13 group and into the level of involvement of the British security and intelligence services in colluding with the group. There was also the question of the attacks on Morton and whether he would be pressing charges.

'I'll be taking advice from my solicitor on that,' he said. 'But you'll be aware that I have been attacked three times in pursuit of this story.'

'Three times?' The camera cut away to Simon Fane's ruddy face and sandy bird's-nest hair.

Morton nodded, looking serious. 'Firstly, I attended a meeting of the group in the House of Commons and was frogmarched out and subjected to assault, as you saw on the video clip. Luckily, I escaped. Then, I was nearly killed by a man with a gun on a train, following on from the first incident and linked to it,' he said.

A cutaway shot to Fane's concerned features. 'You believe the two incidents are linked?'

'Clearly. The police are investigating but it is a fact that the man who tried to kill me…'

'Roy Brand?'

'Yes. He had a photograph of me and what he said to me at that time clearly showed he had been tipped off, or instructed. And the third time was during my interview with Lord Craile on the Island of Mull. Craile admitted to me, and admittedly I have no recorded proof of it, that he had ordered the attempt on the train. He certainly ordered his man, Mr MacGillicuddy, to attack me with a knife or sword, to kill me, actually. That was what he wanted.'

'And somehow you overpowered him,' Fane concluded. 'Despite the fact he was armed with a big knife?'

Morton's expression wavered. 'I had help, but I'm not at liberty to say any more.'

Fane's eyebrows and face expressed astonishment. 'This is news,' he said. 'I don't think this was in the newspaper story this morning.'

Morton winced. 'It wasn't. I left it out because I'm under an obligation of secrecy.'

'Good grief!' Fane expostulated. 'This is most mysterious.'

'Not at all. It's perfectly straightforward. There is a witness whose identity I agreed not to reveal. And I really am not going to, no matter how much you push me.'

'I wouldn't dream of it,' Simon quipped. 'You are the victim here.' He smiled wickedly. 'Any other little snippets that you've left out that you might like to share with our viewers?'

Morton flushed. 'No.'

'Very well then, Mr Morton. What is your next move?'

'We still have not got to the bottom of the links between this group and the UK Government. Despite Mr Cameron's protestations that there is no link, it is obvious...'

Later, Morton and Emily went for a drink in Rose Street and settled into the sofas in the Victorian interior of The Kenilworth. He had a pint of Belhaven 80 Shilling and Emily had a sweet cider. He liked the mirrored interior, the gleaming glassware. It reminded him of the Café Royal.

'Fancy going on to the Café Royal?' he said. 'I've not been in ages. I love that bar. Used to go a lot.'

'We should book a table and go and eat there.'

'Yes, but I like the bar bit too.'

'It's really a food place. The bar is tiny.'

'But there's always something going on. Famous faces.'

'You're a famous face. Well, you are now.'

'I'm not on TV as often as you.'

'Speaking of which, you shouldn't have mentioned Kirsty being with you in the... that was rather a hostage to fortune. The media hate secrets. They'll keep pushing.'

'How on earth was I going to say I'd overpowered that big strong ape all by myself? It wasn't credible.' He frowned at his pint. 'Sooner I see Archie the better. He's out this evening. Some event involving one of his clan.'

'His clan?' Emily queried. 'What clan?'

'His family, I mean. He has five kids.'

'Five?'

'So you think it went well though, apart from that?'

'Very well. It'll be big tomorrow too. Are you planning to raise a court action?'

'No, no, of course not,' Morton said. 'God, the costs. Me up against the brewery millionaire? No way! I just have to hope the police come up with something. Or Sean.'

'That would certainly keep the story going.'

'And what about you? You can get in on it.'

'Maybe. What I was hoping was, I could, or we… a small group of like-minded people, I've mentioned them before…'

'Oh, yes, your hackers group, Luke's lot. What was it? Ethical Hackers for Indy…?'

Emily pulled a face. 'Never liked that name and it's not the name anyway, too flippant. Anyway, we should be coordinating an investigation into the financial side of things with this GB13, Lord Craile… but Luke seems to have disappeared.'

'Disappeared?'

'Well, he's always been elusive. None of us knows where he lives, what his circumstances are, whether he's married or works. He's very secretive. Extremely good hacker though. The best of them, by far. And he takes it very seriously.'

'So how do you know he's disappeared, if he's so secretive anyway?'

'He turned up for last night's meeting but left early and hasn't been seen since and he had promised to do something today which has not happened. I'm worried about him. You know that he's a link between our group and Cerberus?'

Morton smiled. 'Ah yes, this mysterious Cerberus. Who is he, or she? Have you ever met?'

'No. No-one meets Cerberus. That's the point.' Emily frowned. 'Though I sometimes wonder if *he* is Cerberus. I mean Luke. Unlikely, I suppose. Well, I worry about him. I really do. We need him.'

The media was full of the story the next morning though thankfully not one reporter had picked up on the slight slip he had made on STV's *Scotland Tonight*. As he scanned the papers in the General Reference section of the Edinburgh Central Library on George IV Bridge, he saw a news story in the Glasgow *Evening Times*:

Peer admitted to Hospital

A former hereditary peer, and decorated WWII veteran, Lord Ronald Eustace Craile, former Member of the House of Lords has been admitted to BMI Ross Hall Hospital in Glasgow, suffering from chest pains. Lord Craile (97), who served in various theatres of war during World War II, lives at Ardbuithne House on the Isle of Mull. It is understood that the peer who had been under recent strains due to newspaper stories linking him to parliamentary pro-Union pressure group, GB13, suffers from a number of complex medical issues…

Morton wondered about that. At least it proved that he was still alive. He wondered who would pick up the mantle now of behalf of the group. One thing he knew: it wasn't going to stop. The Unionists never give up, he mused, they simply change the names of their groups and move their funds around to avoid scrutiny. Or pretend to be ill. He wouldn't put it past him. Try for the sympathy vote. Hadn't he, himself, had a moment of pity for the man despite knowing – despite having been told by him – that he had ordered his death on two separate occasions? Sympathy for the devil!

CHAPTER THIRTY

There's nothing like a hill walk to get rid of the cobwebs, Willie Morton thought as he and Emily toiled up Radical Road alongside the rugged slope of Salisbury Craigs. There was the early presentiment of spring in the air. Crocuses, snowdrops and aconites had begun to appear in the grass at the side of the path. It had drawn many out to see the wan wintry sun and gain some perspective upon the city. Below was the winding road – Queen's Drive. That was appropriate, Morton thought, radicals looking down on monarchs.

They made frequent stops to get their breath back and to take in the view.

'Right,' he said, 'Cat's Nick. Halfway. Once we're round the bend it's downhill for a bit, before the main slog up to the top.'

'You'd think we'd be fitter,' Emily said. 'I mean, I do a lot of cycling but I suppose those are different sets of muscles.'

'Hmn,' Morton said. 'We should do more of this though. Maybe fix up a walking holiday somewhere? Santiago de Compostela perhaps?'

'I remember walking in the Austrian Alps,' Emily said. 'That was great. Lots of mountains and lakes.'

Morton nodded. He wondered who she had been with then. They didn't much talk about their pasts, previous partners. There was a lack of engagement altogether, as if each was scared to get too involved. There was something unsatisfactory about it. He thought about how quickly Alasdair and Celia had got together. 'There's the French Alps or the Dolomites,' he mused. 'I've always wanted to do some real Alpine terrain. Make at least ten days of it, preferably a fortnight, get really fit. We should fix up something, if you want?'

He wasn't sure if she'd heard him. She was up ahead. But she stopped and waited for him and said: 'Well, we could set something up for late spring, early summer, Willie. Fit in with the spring teaching vacation in early April. Or wait till the end of May.'

'Ideal. Let's do that.' Morton said. He took a deep breath. 'That'd be great, Emily.' He stretched his neck and massaged it, turning his head till he could hear the crunching vertebrae.

'Neck a bit stiff?' Emily asked.

Morton grunted. 'A bit. It'll wear off.' He inhaled deeply. 'You know what, Emily, this last couple of weeks has shown me the vulnerability of our institutions. Eh? Parliament, the devo settlement, could be swept away by Westminster at any moment. Yes, there's these new powers, which will probably turn out to be a lot less impressive than we expect.'

Emily nodded. 'Oh, yes, that's for sure.'

'But they can mostly ignore Scottish public opinion. And the apparatus of the State does their bidding. We are *troublemakers*. That was the word she used.'

'She? Oh, you mean the spook, Kirsty?'

He nodded. 'Amazing woman, almost frightening.' Ten days after his encounter on the Isle of Mull, she was already merging into myth for him. He wondered what she had said about him in her report. 'Apparently, Em,' he said, 'MI5 sees you as a big troublemaker. In fact, come to think of it, she didn't specifically call *me* a troublemaker, at all.'

Emily laughed. 'Maybe she fancied you.'

Morton scoffed. 'Naw. I'm way too old and decrepit for her! She knew I was feart in that boat. That kind of lass would need a real he-man, the full Bond.' He grinned and laughed out loud. 'Not just the Man from Milktray!'

'Hah. I apologise for ever calling you that!'

'Don't. It was funny. Unless she prefers girls of course. Anyway, as I was saying, because the Scottish Parliament does not have the powers of a State we are just one legislative act away from oblivion, you know. We have no powers of our own to ensure our continued existence. Well, that's devolution: power retained so the powers we do have can be revoked at any time.'

'Welcome to my world,' Emily chuckled. 'This is what I teach. And you're right. They have the entire apparatus of State, but, you know, they still feel insecure about *us*.'

Morton frowned and rubbed his hairline where the material of the beanie hat had been rubbing his forehead. 'Insecure? About *us*? I don't see that.'

She looked closely at him. 'Hasn't it dawned on you, Willie? That's what this seventy-five per cent rule was all about. They don't just want to save the Union or strengthen it. They want to nail us down in it forever.'

'That's never going to work, is it?'

'Well, here's an analogy for you, mister clever journalist. They are like the husband who isn't satisfied with his wife's assurances that their love-making is the best she's had. He wants her to publicly deny the existence of any previous lovers, all of her history, all of her memories. To take possession of her completely in the past, present and future.'

Morton laughed. 'That's some analogy, Em! You'd have to hire a psychiatrist to explain it to me.'

Emily tutted. 'Come on, you know this! The British Establishment don't just want us – of our own democratic volition – to be *in* the Union, they want to know for absolutely certain that we can never *escape* the Union. And they're scared of the risks of democracy. They remain terrified that we might be unfaithful when they're not looking, or even ask for divorce at some time in the distant unforeseeable future!'

Morton grinned. 'So, like – they think the Referendum was just some kind of dirty weekend?'

They shared an incredulous laugh standing there on the Cat's Nick bend in the bright breezy sunshine in Holyrood Park and a great sweeping mood of joy came over Morton. It felt like the beginning of something. His worries, anxieties and fears had dissipated in the breeze, temporarily at least. He took out his water bottle. The plastic bottle caught the sun as he raised it. He sipped a mouthful. It was cold and refreshing. 'Want some?'

'Go on then, thanks.'

'This is the best vantage point in the city,' he declared. 'You can see everything from here, the whole city, the Pentlands.'

'You're right,' Emily agreed. 'I never tire of it. Yes, we came pretty close last year so it's not a surprise that their first instinct is to stop us ever trying again.'

'The surprising thing to me,' Morton mused, 'is just how much support they had. I mean GB13. You wouldn't believe it: high-ranking grandees, senior echelons of the SIS, financiers, business leaders and organisations with international connections. How on earth did they think it was a good idea? Maybe it was just an overreaction to the Referendum, I mean, that they came so close to losing.'

'Could be. Maybe they felt their access to the grouse moors and the salmon fishing might be impaired.' Emily laughed ironically.

'Well, anyway, Cameron has publicly condemned the idea, I mean the seventy-five per cent concept.'

'He only agreed to do that, Willie, because he's a pragmatist. He saw how counterproductive it would be.'

'Well, that's true. I mean. Look at the polls. The exposure of the plot and the relocation scheme, and the thuggery, has given Nicola a big boost. Support for Indy is up too.'

'Yes. There's a historic inevitability about it now, don't you feel, even though we lost last year.'

'Maybe,' Morton said. And he thought about it. Was the 300 year experiment coming to its end, losing its allure? It certainly looked like it. 'You might be right. The GB13 group has been forced to pull in its horns a bit, but it still has a lot of support, both covert and overt, down there. Because, I suppose, it expresses a universal trait of the English: they simply can't compute that we might decide to leave. And they don't understand what it would mean.'

Emily nodded, handing him back his bottle. 'Talking of insecurity… well, we were, remember… on our part, we'll never know what they are up to behind the scenes. The spooks I mean. They are part of a system that is fundamentally opposed to our democratic aspirations.

Morton closed his eyes and shivered. 'That's a really gloomy thought, Emily. Ah well. Come on, let's get up the hill.'

'Well, if your neck's up to it.' She smiled.

'I think so.'

They reached the turn-off from the path which climbs steeply up the area known as the Gutted Haddie, which twists and turns through gorse bushes and winds through bare rocky outcrops ever upwards. They were in single file now, unable to talk. Soon, they came out onto the upper plateau of the hill. It never ceased to amaze Morton how a small hill like Arthur's Seat could be such hard work to climb, like a mountain, yet it was only 823 feet high. The path took them over to the pinkish-grey shiny rock of the upper slope – like a real mountain peak. And it had a proper cairn, always mobbed by tourists taking selfies. And beneath, on all sides, hazy vistas of Edinburgh to north, east, west and south.

'Lovely,' Emily gasped. 'Ooh, let's take a selfie!'

'We did that last time,' Morton murmured. 'And that was only a couple of weeks ago!'

'Don't be a party-pooper! Smile!'

They found a place to sit and eat the sandwiches Emily had prepared and the mini pork pies Morton had brought. And crisps, grapes, flapjacks. It was good to stretch the legs out and enjoy the sun on their faces. They looked down on Dunsapie Loch and out to the coastline at Portobello and Joppa.

'There's a heron, look,' Emily pointed out, 'on the far shore of the loch.'

'I think I see it. Where's the flask of tea?'

Emily pointed to his daysack. 'Isn't it in the side pocket? No, on the other side. Oh,' she tutted, 'I don't think I remembered the milk, you know.'

'You'll just have to take it black like me,' Morton grinned. 'Man up!'

'Stupid phrase!' Emily complained. 'Discriminatory.'

'Allegedly. At least tea sales are not boosting their coffers. As far as I know.'

'Whose coffers?'

'Well, people like Lord Craile. The Scotch.'

'The Scotch,' Emily sniffed, unwrapping the sandwiches. 'That's an interesting dialectic point, Willie. During the early nineteenth century some people – Sir Walter Scott, for example; even Rabbie Burns at his most sarcastic or insincere – talked about the *Scotch*, kind of mixing us up with the drink. It was meant to be a compliment, I think, but it certainly had patronising overtones.'

'Yes, I think so.'

'And it also connotes meanness too, of course. The term figures a lot in the decolonising narratives, on our undergraduate course, Political Power and National Identity in Britain, some of which I wrote.'

Morton took a sandwich and studied its contents. 'Good on you, Em. Yes. Scotch is still the top marker for Scottish identity, bigger that its rivals – tartan, kilts, haggis. Would you agree?'

'Oh, yes, no doubt.'

'Well, what better place for a Unionist to hide. Funny isn't it? They look more Scottish than the rest of us. Like they will out-Scottify us, somehow. Even the ones with posh accents that went to Eton and Cambridge or Oxford. Look at our colourful kilts and tweeds and plaids, they say, and our obsessive attention to detail about whisky and the clans – and they do so love to be here in Brigadoon, lording it over us, shooting animals and ordering ordinary folk about. But they don't realise that being a Scot is not about ownership, icons, gey-gaws, even the heritage such as it is.'

'Such as it is,' Emily echoed. 'Of picturesque wilderness, annihilation of the Gaelic, removal of the people, the extinction of what they think denotes Scottish identity.'

'Absolutely! But Scotland is the people who choose to live here. From wherever they come, those who believe in the nation's potential for self-expression. These creeping Lords and their toadying minions spend their whisky millions trying to scotch us.'

'You do know that less than twenty per cent of the whisky industry is controlled in Scotland,' Emily pointed out, offering him a second sandwich.

Morton smiled at her. 'Really?' He chomped into the sandwich, egg mayo and cress. 'Less than twenty?'

'It's true, Willie. More than eighty per cent of the vast global whisky industry's profit is siphoned off by wealthy shareholders who live elsewhere, who don't even pay tax here. And as for jobs – the numbers employed in whisky in Scotland is less than the number employed cleaning toilets.'

'Is that so?' Morton began to laugh. 'Well, isn't it about time the whisky mega millions benefitted people in Scotland? After all it's made from our water, it's our national drink. Has our name on it.'

'You can but hope,' Emily said. 'Scotch in name only and, my goodness, when talk turns to Scotland getting independence they're pretty damn quick to scotch that idea. Might affect their worldwide profits and the share price on the Shanghai Exchange!'

Morton laughed. 'It's all fucked up. But, you know what, Em, our real national spirit… We will always be here.'

Emily pretended to look startled. 'What? On Arthur's Seat?'

He chuckled. 'Don't be facetious, Em! You know what I mean. Here we are…Auld Reekie, the home of inspiring patriots and mendacious traitors, statesmen and honest folk.' He glanced around, pointing to the north, to Calton Hill and the old Royal High School. 'Hundreds, perhaps a thousand years on, here we are, in all our glory and all of our ignorance.'

'Amen,' said Emily. 'Where is that flask of tea? All this blethering. I've never heard you talk politics like this before, Willie.' She looked at him sidelong. 'You're on the turn, I think.'

'Ach, their starry talk's a wheen o' blethers. Who said that?' Morton asked.

Emily grinned maliciously. 'Was it Groundskeeper Willie?'

'Naw, you *know*!'

Acknowledgements

I would like to thank Lesley Riddoch and Jean Lee for their support and for being inspirational to me and Paul McDaid for his invaluable advice on London matters. I would also like to thank several individuals who wish to remain anonymous.

Author's Note

All the characters in this book are fictitious although their activities may bear a very close resemblance to reality. Where real persons and places are mentioned in the passing this is not intended to infer anything other than respectful acknowledgement of their existence. The roof space of the Palace of Westminster is, of course, out of bounds to the public.

The New Waverley Centre is not yet completed at the time of writing, but due to the much lower costs of fictional construction, I have been able to open it four years early. Activities within it, in MI5's Scotland Station, are a figment of my imagination.

Coming soon, from Twa Corbies Publishing

Book three of the Willie Morton conspiracy thriller series

Oblivion's Ghost

Willie Morton is tasked to find Luke Sangster, brilliant former student and leading member of Ethical Hackers for Independence, who is missing after MI5 raided his Marchmont flat.

To them he is the known troublemaker who uncovered financial irregularities and offshore money-laundering of leading backers of the No Campaign in the 2014 Referendum.

In a digital Scotland, under surveillance like never before by shadowy forces using all the authority of the Investigative Powers Act, Morton must find out if Sangster is alive and living off-grid somewhere – or dead.

But first he must find out who Sangster is – or was.

Publication Date: Spring 2020.
Pre-order by title.

Lightning Source UK Ltd.
Milton Keynes UK
UKHW010802291020
372446UK00004B/555

9 780993 384059